Cowboys.

Every boy's hero...every woman's fantasy.
They can rope, they can ride...

But can they change a diaper?

In Vicki Lewis Thompson's bestselling miniseries,

THREE COWBOYS AND A BABY

we discovered what happened when three intrepid cowpokes bravely
ventured where none of them had ever gone before—the nursery!

But now that they're there—and discover they like it!—
they're in for an even bigger surprise!
Because a fourth strapping cowboy has just stepped forward
and announced...

D1359975

Dear Reader,

It's time to pop the cork on the bubbly and break out the fireworks! I'm celebrating the grand finale of my THREE COWBOYS & A BABY miniseries and my first-ever single title release!

I hope you've stayed with me through the series. If not, I'll wait while you catch up. In Harlequin Temptation #780, *The Colorado Kid*, rancher Sebastian Daniels was sure baby Elizabeth belonged to him. Wrangler Travis Evans had a different idea and laid claim to the little girl he called Lizzie in *Two in the Saddle* (#784). While these two cowboys were busy sorting out their paternity issues, Boone Connor showed up in *Boone's Bounty* (#788), and insisted the child belonged to him.

All three of these books were published in the Harlequin Temptation series, but the rip-roaring conclusion needed more room. More specifically, my hero, Nat Grady, needed more room—especially considering the shock he's in for. Raised by an abusive father, wary of emotional entanglements, he has no intention of ever becoming a daddy. But Mother Nature has other ideas....

Writing this single title has made me as excited as a cowpoke headed into town after his first trail drive. So here's *That's My Baby!* If I were a smoker, I'd be passing out cigars!

Warmly,

Vicki Lewis Thompson

THAT'S MY BABY!

Vicki Lewis Thompson

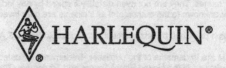

HARLEQUIN®

TORONTO • NEW YORK • LONDON
AMSTERDAM • PARIS • SYDNEY • HAMBURG
STOCKHOLM • ATHENS • TOKYO • MILAN • MADRID
PRAGUE • WARSAW • BUDAPEST • AUCKLAND

With love to my husband Larry,
whose faith in me has never dimmed.

ISBN 0-373-83438-1

THAT'S MY BABY!

Copyright © 2000 by Vicki Lewis Thompson.

Visit us at www.eHarlequin.com

Printed in U.S.A.

CHAPTER ONE

JESSICA FRANKLIN'S STOMACH gurgled with anxiety as she waited at JFK for the 5:45 flight from London. After seventeen months apart, she had to meet Nat Grady, the man she'd loved—still loved, damn it—disguised as a bag lady. Then she had to tell him about Elizabeth, the baby he had no idea they'd conceived, the baby she'd left in Colorado to keep her safe.

The embarrassing truth was, Jessica had picked up a stalker. She thought of it like that, as if she'd contracted a deadly disease and was no longer fit to be a mother. Growing up, she'd felt stifled by her wealthy father's attempts to protect her from kidnappers. She'd left home, spurning a life of bulletproof cars and bodyguards, insisting she could live quietly and anonymously without all that. It infuriated her to be wrong.

About ten feet away, a woman clucked and cooed at the baby in her arms. Jessica ached every time she saw a mother and child. For her own good she shouldn't watch them, but she couldn't seem to stop torturing herself. Babies drew her like magnets. When she spotted one, she'd stare shamelessly as she tried to guess the child's age and wondered whether Elizabeth would look anything like that, act anything like that.

This one looked to be around eight months old, Elizabeth's age, and he was a boy, judging from the outfit. Jessica couldn't imagine her baby this size. When she'd left her at the Rocking D Ranch, Elizabeth had been so tiny, just barely two months old. Jessica had never imagined that their separation would be this long. But now that Nat was home, she would see her baby again. Soon.

The little boy laughed and Jessica counted four teeth. Elizabeth would have teeth by now. She would be crawling, getting into everything, learning to make noises that were the beginnings of speech.

Like ma-ma.

Jessica endured the pain. At least Elizabeth was safe. She'd known she could count on her friends Sebastian, Travis and Boone to keep her baby that way until Nat came home and they could all decide what to do.

Weary passengers trudged into the gate area from customs and Jessica's pulse raced as she anticipated the meeting to come. She still hadn't decided on her approach. The thought of Nat Grady brought up so many emotions she had to ask them to stand in line and take turns being heard.

Usually the first feeling to shoulder its way to the front was anger. She'd fallen head over heels in love with the guy, but for the year they'd been involved, he'd insisted they keep their relationship secret from everyone but his secretary, Bonnie, a woman who had invented the word *discreet.* Even his best friends, the three men she'd left in charge of Elizabeth, didn't know she and Nat had been seeing each other.

She should have recognized the secrecy thing as a warning signal, but love was blind, and she'd accepted Nat's explanation that his friends were a nosy bunch and he didn't want outside interference in their relationship until he and Jessica knew where it was going. All the while he had jolly well known where it was going, she thought bitterly. On a train bound for nowhere.

If only she could hate him for that. God, how she'd tried. Instead, she kept thinking of what he'd said the night they'd broken up. *I shouldn't have let you waste your time on me. I'm not worth it.*

Then he'd left her, his real estate business and his friends to head for a tiny, war-torn country where he'd worked as a volunteer in the refugee camps. Along with her other emotions connected to Nat, Jessica battled guilt. If she hadn't pushed him to end the secrecy and marry her, he wouldn't have left the country. She was sure of it. He'd have stayed in Colorado, making love to her, the sweetest love she'd ever known.

Instead, to get away from her and the demons she'd demanded that he face, he'd plunged into a violent place where the lines of battle blurred and changed every day. As a civilian he had no weapons and no military training to protect him. He'd spent seventeen months in danger on account of her, and if he'd been killed or hurt, she would have blamed herself.

She was also to blame for the baby, after he'd told her flat out he never wanted kids. A woman her age should have known antibiotics canceled the effect of birth control pills. But she had some gaps in her sexual education, thanks to growing up shadowed by her own personal bodyguard. She hadn't known.

She needed to tell him it was her responsibility. Still, she thought he should know about the baby, in case the stalker got lucky. But before she told him anything, she'd have to convince him who she was. The dark wig, the baggy clothes and the thick glasses wouldn't look familiar to him. But once he'd figured out it was her, what would she say first?

Nat, we have a baby girl named Elizabeth. Too abrupt. A man who'd said he never wanted children might need to be eased into that kind of discussion. *Nat, I'm disguised like this because I have a stalker on my trail.* Too much, too soon. He'd just returned from dodging bullets. He deserved a little peace and quiet before she gave him that bad news, coupled with the information that if anything happened to her he'd need to watch out for Elizabeth, whether he cared to or not.

Her stomach felt as if she'd swallowed a bagful of hot marbles.

A man in a business suit came toward the woman with the baby, and the baby bounced happily, reaching out for the man. When the father lifted the baby into his arms and showered him with kisses, Jessica had to look away.

She took off the glasses she was wearing as part of her disguise and brushed the tears from her eyes. She had to pay attention. Nat could be coming along any minute, and she didn't want to miss him.

A tall man with a full beard and hair past his collar appeared in the stream of passengers. He wore a battered-looking leather jacket, jeans and boots. A scuffed backpack hung from one broad shoulder, a backpack not too different from the one she carried. Her gaze swept past him, then returned. He moved through the crowd with a familiar, fluid walk, as if he were striding along to a country tune. Nat walked that way.

She looked closer, past the rich brown of his beard, and her heart hammered. The mouth. She'd spent hours gazing at that chiseled mouth, classic as the mouth on one of her father's prized Rodin sculptures. She'd spent even more hours kissing and being kissed by that mouth, and her tongue slid over her lips in remembrance. Nat. In spite of the anger and guilt, pure joy bloomed within her at the sight of him. Nat. He was here. He was okay.

Suddenly whatever she decided to say seemed unimportant. She just had to get to him, wrap her arms around him and give thanks that he'd returned in one piece. Her nightmares had begun the day she'd learned where he was, and CNN had been her lifeline ever since.

No matter how furiously she'd counseled herself to remain calm when she saw him, she was miles beyond calm. She was weepy with gratitude for his safe return. He was an oasis in the desert her life had become without him.

Drinking in the sight of him moving through the crowd, she sighed with happiness. Thank God he looked healthy, his skin tanned and his hair still lustrous, reflecting the terminal's overhead lights. But she'd give him the herbal supplements she'd brought, anyway, and insist that he take them. He didn't eat right under the best of circumstances, and no telling what he'd existed on over there.

He was so appealing that she couldn't help wondering if he'd become involved with anyone while he was gone. A beautiful waif of a woman, perhaps, who spoke little English, but who had awakened his protective instincts. A woman who'd fallen deeply in love with the big, handsome American cowboy who'd come to help. Jessica knew how easily such a thing could happen, and her heart hurt.

But if he had found another to love, that wasn't her business. He was free to do as he chose.

Seventeen months. That was a long time for a single man of thirty-three to go without sex. He might not have fallen in love, but he might have taken a woman to bed....

She wouldn't ask. No, she definitely wouldn't ask. But the thought made her want to cry.

Moving closer, she focused on his face, trying to meet his gaze. They'd had a magic connection between them, and maybe if she caught his eye, he'd see beyond her disguise and recognize her, heart to heart. He'd be startled, of course, and might wonder if she'd gone crazy while he was out of the country.

In a way she had. Crazy with worry...and love. Still love. But she wouldn't let him know that she still loved him. She would be very careful about that, unless...unless he had gone a little crazy, too. Although she'd lectured herself to squash that hope like a bug, she'd let it live.

At last Nat glanced her way, and she opened her mouth to call to him. But instead of saying his name, she drew back in uncertainty. His gaze was so hard and uncompromising that it intimidated her. He'd changed.

For a minute she wondered if she'd been wrong in thinking this bearded man was Nat. No, she hadn't been wrong. It was him. But his blue eyes, once so full of good humor, looked like chipped ice. She wondered what he'd seen in those camps that had put that grim look on his face.

He gave no sign of recognizing her as he turned and headed down the terminal. Her courage failed and she closed her mouth. But she had to catch him, had to let him know about the baby before he called anyone at the Rocking D in Colorado. Sure as the world someone at the ranch would tell him immediately that she'd left Elizabeth there, although she hadn't named the father. But Nat would know, once he was told the baby's age. She couldn't let him find out that way.

She had to hurry to keep up with him. Dodging luggage, people and motorized carts, she kept him in sight as he followed the signs directing him toward ground transportation. She knew he planned to stay in the city for a few nights and take care of some business before flying back to Colorado. His secretary, the only person Nat had contacted before coming home, had said so.

Bonnie didn't know about the baby or the stalker. She just thought she was helping Jessica create a romantic homecoming surprise for Nat. During the year Nat and Jessica had been secretly involved, Bonnie had set up many of their rendezvous locations, and she'd seemed to relish the role of matchmaker.

When Nat and Jessica had separated, Bonnie had called Jessica, urging her to try to patch things up. Jessica had refused, convinced that Nat had meant for the affair to end from the beginning, which was why he'd kept it such a secret. But when her pregnancy was confirmed, she'd called Bonnie and learned that Nat was out of the country and unreachable. Since then, Jessica had made use of her friendship with the secretary to find out exactly when Nat was due back.

The escalator foiled Jessica's plans to catch up with him. People and wheeled carry-ons bunched onto the grooved metal steps between them and made it impossible for her to get close. But she didn't really want to confront him here, anyway, she finally realized. Her news was upsetting enough without being delivered under harsh overhead lights with the din of people and the clatter of baggage to interfere with an emotional conversation.

He'd undoubtedly take a taxi from the airport to his hotel. She'd follow in another taxi and catch him in the lobby. Much better. Maybe they could go for a drink to discuss their options.

The chill of an October night cooled her overheated system as she bustled outside and followed him toward the taxi stand. She gained some valuable time as he convinced the cabdriver to let him ride in front. How like Nat to hate the idea of being chauffeured. She'd been drawn to his democratic instincts from the beginning.

She hated being chauffeured, too, but she didn't have time to discuss that with the driver of the next taxi in line. With a quick no thanks, she brushed aside his offer to help with her backpack. ''I'm in a big hurry,'' she said as she hopped in the back seat.

''Right.'' The driver hustled himself behind the wheel. ''Where to?''

''Follow that cab,'' she said, pointing to the one Nat had entered.

He swiveled in the seat to stare at her. "You're kidding, right?"

"No, I am not kidding!" She panicked as the other cab pulled away from the curb. "That one! And don't lose it!"

"You better have money," the cabbie muttered as he started after Nat's cab. "You better not be some nutcase who's watched one too many James Bond movies, or I'll drive you straight to the nearest precinct station and turn you over to the cops."

"I have money." Jessica watched Nat's cab gain a little distance and clenched her jaw. "Just keep up with them. That cab has a vee-shaped scratch on the trunk. Did you notice that? That's how you'll know which one to follow."

"I see the cab. I just wanna know what's with the cops-and-robbers routine. I don't wanna be a whatchamacallit—accomplice."

"I'm not breaking the law." Jessica was losing patience with the cabbie. She was pretty much out of patience, anyway, and being back in New York put her even more on edge. The closer they came to the jeweled city on the horizon, the more she felt the tug of her father's influence.

"I don't wanna get mixed up in anything," the driver said. "I just wanna do my job, y'know?"

"In the movies, the cabdriver never complains about having to follow another taxi," Jessica pointed out. "He just does it."

"See? What did I tell you? You think you're in a damn movie or somethin'! I'll bet they just let you out of the nuthouse. Gave you a pack of meds and told you to have a nice life. And it's my bad luck that you picked my cab to act out your delusions."

"I'm perfectly sane." Jessica might not like being chauf-feured, but she was used to it, and she'd never had a driver question her the way this one was doing. Of course, she was used to limos. And this guy didn't know who she was.

He didn't know the paper beside him on the front seat was the product of her father's news empire. "Quick, he just changed lanes!"

The driver sounded highly insulted. "I can see that he changed lanes, lady. I didn't start driving yesterday. Do you even know who's in that cab?"

"Yes."

"Yeah, right. You probably think it's Elvis."

"I know who's in the cab. I need to talk to him."

"Why? Who is it?"

Many times as a child Jessica had watched her mother deal with questions she didn't want to answer. Her mother would stiffen her spine and speak in what Jessica thought of as her to-the-manner-born voice. Jessica had never tried the technique, but she decided to give it a whirl.

Straightening in her seat, she lifted her chin and said, "I don't believe that's any of your business."

Her effort seemed lost on the cabbie. "It sure as hell is my business! I'm transportin' you in my cab! And I'd appreciate it if you'd lay off the high-and-mighty tone, unless you're about to tell me you're kissing cousins to the Rockefellers, which I sincerely doubt."

Close, Jessica thought. But apparently she didn't have the presence to carry it off. Then again, she did look like a bag lady. Maybe her mother's success in turning aside impertinent questions had as much to do with her elegant clothes and her position in society as her tone of voice. Yet in her heart of hearts, Jessica believed that even dressed in rags with no fortune to command, her mother would make people do her bidding. She'd certainly kept her husband and daughter in line for years.

Jessica sighed. Barring a personality transplant, she'd need to give the cabbie some explanation for why they were tailing another cab into the city, or she was liable to be dumped by the side of the road. "The man in the other cab is an old boyfriend," she said. "I've changed since we last met, and he didn't recognize me, but I really need to talk to him."

"Maybe he doesn't want to talk to you."

"Maybe not," she acknowledged, "but I have some information he needs to hear."

"Aw, jeez, I know where this is goin'. We're talkin' about the patter of little feet, right?"

Jessica couldn't think of anything but the truth. "You might say that."

"Poor bastard. But them that plays, pays. I learned that one the hard way. Do you have any idea where he's goin'?"

"To a hotel in the city, I imagine."

The cabbie heaved a sigh. "All right, then. I'll catch him for ya."

"Thank you." Jessica settled back against the seat as the sparkling skyscrapers of Manhattan hovered ever nearer. Habit caused her to pick out the Franklin Publishing Tower dangling between sky and earth like one of her mother's diamond chokers.

She spoke only briefly with her parents these days, stopping long enough in her flight to put in a quick call every couple of weeks. They thought she was "seeing the country." None of her conversations with them in the past few years had been significant, anyway, and she hadn't seen them since she'd left home.

They didn't approve of her decision to abandon their world and try to create her own life, and their attitude toward her had been curt ever since she'd moved to Colorado. Her current predicament, having a child out of wedlock and a stalker on her trail, would only confirm what they'd always assumed—that on her own she'd make a mess of things. She didn't want to give them a chance to say we told you so.

"How far along are you?" the cabbie asked.

Jessica blinked and tried to figure out what he meant.

"When's the baby due?" he asked, clarifying his question.

"I, um, already had her," she said. "I left her with friends."

"Wait a doggone minute! You already had the kid, and you're just now nailing the father? Are you sure he's the father and this isn't some kind of shakedown?"

"I'm sure. He's been out of the country. I couldn't contact him before."

The cabbie's gaze flicked into the rearview mirror. "Okay, I'm gonna believe you. The reason is that your voice sounded strong when you said that. After all these years of drivin' cab, I can tell when a passenger's blowin' smoke. You can hear it in their voice. So what did you name her?"

"Elizabeth." Speaking the name brought a lump to Jessica's throat and she wondered if she'd cry when she talked to Nat about the baby. She hoped she wouldn't cry. She didn't want his pity, only his support.

"Pretty name. I got two kids. Both boys. Rory and Jonathan. I had to marry my wife on account of Rory, but it's worked out okay."

Worked out okay. The lukewarm comment made Jessica shiver. She'd never in a million years want a marriage that *worked out okay.* Even if Nat had a burst of responsibility and proposed marriage to give Elizabeth two parents, Jessica wouldn't agree. But Nat wouldn't propose. Marriage scared him to death. The only thing that scared him worse was fatherhood.

"Your guy doesn't seem to be goin' into Midtown, like you thought," the cabbie said. "Looks like we're headed for the Hudson Parkway. Still want me to follow him?"

"Absolutely." The route made her nervous, though. She

knew it only too well. But it was only a coincidence that the first time she set foot back in New York since leaving her parents' estate, Nat would lead her back in the direction of the Hudson Valley, straight toward Franklin Hall.

"Like I said, I hope you got money," the driver said. "For all we know, the guy's headed for Vermont to see the leaves."

"I doubt it."

"You ever seen the leaves?"

"Yes." She'd taken a trip through Vermont in the limo with her parents the October she turned nine. The long black car had seemed to take up far too much space on the narrow back roads, and it had looked ridiculous sitting parked on the village square in one of the hamlets where'd they'd stopped for hot cider.

She'd been aware of people staring, but she'd grown used to that. She'd ignored them and gazed longingly at three children playing in a yard full of red, yellow and orange leaves. They'd rake them into piles and then dive into them, scattering the leaves in an explosion of color before raking them up and starting all over. Their laughter had made her feel so completely alone.

Her memory clicked over to a crisp fall day in Aspen. Nat hadn't really understood why she'd begged him to help her gather leaves into piles and jump with her right into the middle of them. But he'd helped her do it, anyway. The lonely child within her had loved every minute, and she'd loved Nat for being such a good sport about it.

"My wife's after me to take her and the kids up there next weekend," the cabdriver said, breaking into her reverie, "but I told her I do enough driving during the week. Besides that, it's bumper to bumper on those little back roads. The word's out about those leaves."

"You should take her, anyway," Jessica said, suddenly feeling sorry for the woman who had no passion in her life.

"Get a sitter for the boys. There are some nice bed-and-breakfast places up there. It's a good spot for couples."

"You mean couples with bucks. Those cozy little inns aren't cheap. My wife would probably rather have a new couch."

"Ask her. I'll bet she'd rather have the weekend."

"I'll bet she'd rather have the couch. You're gonna have that for a good ten years or more. The weekend's over and done, and you've got nothin'."

"You have memories!" Jessica protested, battling now for this unknown woman's right to be romanced, at least once in her life. "They're worth more than anything."

"I don't know. You can't sit on memories. Listen, we're headed out of the city entirely. You sure you want to keep going? This is turning into an expensive ride."

"That's okay. Keep going." As they left Manhattan behind, she could hardly believe the direction they were taking. They'd left the Hudson Parkway to follow the familiar route that wound along beside the river. If they kept going like this, they'd drive right past her parents' estate.

"High-priced real estate up here," the driver said. "But what I always think about, especially this time of year, is that story about the Headless Horseman. Sleepy Hollow, and all that. That story scared the daylights out of me when I was a kid."

"Me, too." She hadn't thought about it before, but now she realized that when she allowed herself to think about the person stalking her, she felt sort of like Ichabod Crane trying to escape the Headless Horseman.

"My boys love that story, but kids today don't scare so easy, I guess."

"I guess." Jessica wondered if Elizabeth would grow up braver than she was. Her self-image of strong independence grew shakier the closer they came to Franklin Hall.

Less than a mile from her parents' gate she told the

driver to slow down. At last she'd allowed her instincts to take over, and they had told her exactly where Nat was going. By the time the left-turn signal on the cab ahead of them flashed in the darkness, she was prepared for it. For reasons she couldn't begin to imagine, Nat was going to Franklin Hall.

"Pull over under that tree," she told the cabbie. "I'll get out here."

"What are you gonna do?" He pulled off the road as she'd asked, but gone was the camaraderie they'd established. He sounded nervous and suspicious again. "I can't let you get out here, in the dark. And you sure as hell can't follow him into that place. They got one of those automatic gates, and there are probably Dobermans running around or something. I should never have agreed to this. You're some psycho or something, aren't you?"

Jessica's teeth chattered from the adrenaline rush of being so close to Franklin Hall again, but she tried to stay calm. "I *can* follow him into that place," she said. "I used to live there. I know the gate code."

"No way!"

"Look, I'll prove it to you. First let me pay you what I owe." She glanced at the meter and handed him some bills, along with a generous tip.

He looked a little happier upon seeing the money. "Just let me take you back to Manhattan, okay? I won't even charge you. But I can't leave a woman on a lonely country road like this. If I was to read about you in the papers, I'd never forgive myself."

Jessica watched the taillights of the other cab disappear down the winding lane leading to the main house, which was obscured by trees. "Okay, you can pull over to the gate now. I'll show you I can open it."

"I'll pull over there." He guided the car across the road and stopped, his headlights shining on the ten-foot-tall gates with the scrolled letters *FH* worked into the intricate design. "But you're not opening that gate. I know the kind of people who would live here, and you're not that kind."

"Appearances can be deceiving." She opened the car door. "You can stay here until I open the gate, and then go on back. That way you'll know I'm inside the protection of the fence."

"What if you're attacked by dogs?"

"There aren't any dogs. At least not the last I heard." She opened the door and got out, hefting her backpack onto her shoulder. "Thanks for bringing me out here," she said. "And do ask your wife about taking that weekend trip to a bed-and-breakfast." She closed the door.

He rolled down the window and stuck his head out. "You just show me you can open that gate. When you can't, I'll take you back to town, no questions asked. You can stay at the Y."

She turned to smile at him. "Thanks. You're a nice man. But I won't need to do that." She still wasn't sure what she would do once she was inside the gate, but that was her first step. The code came back to her the minute she stepped up to the keypad, and she punched it in without hesitation. The gates swung slowly open.

"I'll be damned," the cabbie said. "Who are you, anyway?"

"Doesn't matter." She gave him another smile. "Good-bye."

"This'll be one to tell the guys."

A chill passed over her. "Please don't. Don't tell anybody about this." She had no idea how close her stalker might be.

"Look, if the police question me, because somethin' bad happens, then—"

"They won't. I'm just asking you not to gossip to the other cabdrivers. Can you promise that?"

"Yeah, I can promise that. Better get in there. The gates are closing again."

"Right. Bye."

"Take care of yourself."

She turned and ran through the gates before they clanked together with a sound that brought back that familiar feeling of claustrophobia. Once again she was a prisoner of Franklin Hall.

CHAPTER TWO

NAT HAD PREPARED himself for wealth, yet he was still blown away as the cab pulled up in front of the floodlit colonial mansion. In bandbox condition, the exterior was the color of ripe wheat, and the ivory trim looked as if it had been freshly painted that morning.

Jess had once lived here. The knowledge sent adrenaline rushing through his system, sweeping aside the fatigue of a transatlantic flight. Surely her parents would be able to tell him where he could find her.

The circular driveway had taken them up to an elegant entry, but the big draw of the house was obviously the view from the back, which sloped steeply down to the Hudson. On the way in, he'd caught glimpses of the majestic river through the trees, and the driver pointed with excitement when a barge, lit up like a Christmas tree, glided past, its engines thrumming in the night air.

Nat's real estate training kicked in. He quickly calculated what the house alone must be worth, not even considering the grounds. Even in the dark they appeared extensive and manicured. The newspaper business had been good to Russell P. Franklin.

"Nice place." The cabdriver switched off the engine.

"Not bad," Nat agreed. But impressive as the house was, he wouldn't want to live in it, and he couldn't picture free-spirited Jess here, forced to spend her childhood behind locked gates. He was beginning to understand how lonely she'd been as the only child at Franklin Hall.

Opening the car door, he was greeted by the friendly scent of a fireplace in use. That heartened him, although he doubted the setting was as cozy as the living room at the Rocking D in Colorado. But he didn't need cozy right now. He needed information. He hoped to God her parents had some.

He turned toward the driver. "Listen, I don't know how long I'll be, so I'm sure you could wait in the house, where it's warmer."

"Nah. Thanks, anyway, but I'd rather stretch my legs and have a smoke, if it's all the same to you. I'll be here whenever you're ready to go."

"Okay." Nat was too impatient to argue the point. "Knock on the door if you change your mind." Leaving his backpack in the cab, he exited the car and mounted the steps to the front door, which looked as proper as a starched shirtfront. He lifted the brass knocker and rapped twice.

Almost immediately a uniformed butler opened the door.

Nat introduced himself. He was ushered quietly inside and relieved of his leather jacket. The butler had a strong British accent, and Nat remembered Jessica mentioning him. Barclay. Her father had hired him away from the Savoy.

The foyer lived up to the promise of the outside. A crystal chandelier sprinkled light over antiques that had been waxed and buffed until they shone. A table against one wall held a small bronze that Nat thought might be famous. He wasn't up on art, but it looked familiar.

On a larger table in the center of the large entry, a bouquet of fall flowers filled a blue-and-white urn taller than a two-year-old child. Nat would bet the flowers were replaced every day. Their scent mingled with the tang of paste wax, and something else—maybe the smell of money, Nat thought. The contrast with the poverty he'd recently left made the elegant setting seem almost obscene.

"Mr. and Mrs. Franklin are in the library," the butler said. "If you'll follow me."

As Nat walked down the hallway, an Oriental carpet that looked old and priceless cushioned his steps. He glanced at the gleaming railing on the stairway spiraling up to the second floor, and a vivid image of Jess sailing down the banister tugged at his heart. She'd only gotten away with it once, she'd said, but she'd never forgotten the joy of risking the forbidden.

He'd been having trouble finding evidence of her in this formal setting, but the banister looked as if it had been made for sliding down. Still, she'd probably never swung on a tire in the backyard or played hopscotch on the front walk. He was glad he'd seen this place, if only to understand Jess better.

His last picture of her tortured him—her long red curls tousled from lovemaking, her brown eyes filled with angry tears. *Don't you love me enough?* she'd cried.

He'd left without answering the question, which effectively gave her an answer. He'd heard some object hit the door and shatter after he'd closed it behind him.

For Jess, love meant marriage and children. He hadn't been willing to give her either one, because he'd thought he'd be lousy at it. He still thought so, but she'd haunted him the entire time he'd been gone. Another worker in the refugee camps, a sweet and willing woman, had offered herself. He'd gladly accepted, but to his chagrin he discovered that he couldn't make love to anyone but Jess.

Finally he'd faced the truth. Sometime during the year he'd been seeing Jess, while he'd thought he was guarding his heart, she'd crept past the gates and set herself up as a permanent resident. He could either live the rest of his life alone, or he could try to overcome his fears and give Jess what she wanted.

Bad risk though he was, she'd been eager to take a

chance on him once. He wondered if she still would. In the refugee camps he'd dealt with people who'd been ripped away from loved ones by force and had to scratch for every bit of human connection. After witnessing that, tearing himself from Jess seemed like ego run amok. He'd been offered so much, and he'd foolishly rejected it.

The thought of having kids still scared him to death, but maybe, in time, he could get used to that, too. If he expected to create an adoption program for war orphans, he'd be a real hypocrite if he didn't at least consider that option for himself.

But first he had to find Jess. And he had no clue where she was. For seventeen months he'd pictured her in her little Aspen apartment. When he hadn't been able to locate her there, he'd gone slightly crazy.

The butler paused in the doorway of the library to announce him, and Nat was so lost in thought, he nearly ran into the guy.

"Mr. Nat Grady to see you, sir," the butler said.

"Show him in, Barclay," boomed a voice from the interior of the room.

The butler stepped aside and Nat tried to control his eagerness as he walked forward. These people could lead him to Jess.

Russell P. Franklin, a robust, silver-haired man, rose from a leather wingback in front of the fireplace and came toward him, hand outstretched. Mrs. Russell P. remained seated in her wingback. She strongly resembled Jess, but Nat assumed the red hair was a beauty-salon copy of the color she'd been born with. Still, he couldn't help thinking that this might be how Jess would look in twenty-five or thirty years. He wanted to be around to see that.

Adele Franklin smiled a greeting, but at the same time she surveyed him carefully. Under her scrutiny Nat remembered how grungy he was in comparison to his hosts. No doubt their sweaters and slacks were everyday casual wear, and they probably cost three times what Nat would spend on his hotel room tonight. Good thing neither Adele nor Russell knew yet that he had designs on their only daughter, or he'd probably be thrown out on his ear.

"Glad to have you stop by, Grady," Russell said. His handshake was warm and firm. "Come over by the fire. What will you have? A drink, something to eat?"

"Scotch would be great." Nat didn't plan to drink much of it, but he'd been a real estate broker long enough to know the value of accepting someone's hospitality if you wanted to make the sale. This might turn out to be the most important sales call of his life. He would have preferred a beer, but this didn't look like a beer-drinking household.

"Good." Russell looked pleased as he signaled to Barclay. "And have the cook rustle up a few sandwiches," he added. "This man's been existing on airplane food."

Airplane food was gourmet fare compared to what the refugees had to eat, Nat thought. But this wasn't the time to tell them that. "I hope you'll excuse the way I look." He stroked his beard. "I came straight from the airport."

"No excuse necessary," Russell said. "A man involves himself in a cause such as you have, he doesn't have time to worry about appearance."

"It does rearrange your priorities." Nat sat on a love seat positioned between the two wingbacks and directly in front of the marble fireplace. The stout logs crackled smartly, as if aware of the honor of adding heat and ambience to Franklin Hall.

Windows on either side of the fireplace looked out on the inky flow of the river and the dark shore beyond, where only an occasional light showed signs of civilization. Books, mostly leather-bound, lined the other three walls of the room. There was even a rolling ladder to reach the top shelves.

Adele and Russell each had a book resting on a table beside them, a bookmark inserted in the pages. Then he realized there was no television in the room. Apparently the Franklins still believed in reading as a way to pass an evening.

Nat's career in real estate had centered primarily on land, but he'd handled a few homes, and some had been real showplaces. None of them equaled this house. The cost of running Franklin Hall for a day would probably feed a refugee family for months.

Adele leaned forward. "You are quite a humanitarian, Mr. Grady. The rest of us may have sent a little money over to help those poor people, but you invested something far more precious—yourself. I commend you."

Her voice startled him. Jess's voice. He wanted to close his eyes and savor it. "I don't really think of it that way, Mrs. Franklin," he said. "I just had to go." And not only to escape his demons concerning Jess. That was another thing he needed to settle with his ladylove. If she'd found out about his work in the refugee camps, she probably thought he'd only run away from her. But his decision to help the war-torn country was far more complicated than that.

"Call me Adele," Jess's mother said with a warm smile.

Her eyes were gray, not brown like Jess's. But otherwise she reminded him so strongly of her daughter that he couldn't stop looking at her. She wove her fingers together in her lap the way Jess did, and when she spoke she wrinkled her forehead slightly, as if putting real thought into what she was about to say. He remembered loving that about Jess.

"By all means," Russell said. "Let's not stand on formality."

At that moment Barclay arrived with Nat's scotch, a tray

of sandwiches, and what looked like mineral water for Adele and Russell.

"Here's to your dedicated efforts on the part of the refugees," Russell said, raising his glass toward Nat. He took a swallow and sat back. "Now, why don't you tell us what you have in mind?"

"I'll be glad to." He was passionate and absolutely sincere in his dedication to the war orphans foundation, but he'd used it without remorse as his ticket into Franklin Hall. Once he'd discussed the foundation, he planned to casually mention Jess. He forced his attention away from Adele and concentrated on Jess's father.

Russell had brown eyes the color of Jess's. But where her gaze had reminded him of a wild fawn's, Russell's could have belonged to George Washington when he led his troops across the Potomac. The man was a fighter and an empire builder. No one who looked carefully into those eyes would underestimate Russell P. Franklin.

Nat thought briefly of his own father. Nobody underestimated Hank Grady, either, least of all his son. Nat especially didn't underestimate his father's ability to be cruel. Yet Nat had been fed and clothed. Now he appreciated the luxury of that.

Shutting out the image of his father, Nat carefully outlined his plan for a foundation that would oversee the welfare and possible adoption of the orphaned children he had recently left. He had several potential backers in mind for the project. If Jess had still been living in her apartment, as he'd expected when he'd called from London, he wouldn't have put Franklin on the list and risked causing Jess problems. But she hadn't been in her apartment. The phone had been disconnected.

Both Russell and Adele seemed eager to hear the details of his plan, and he realized that getting their support for the foundation was a done deal. He was happy about that, but it wasn't the most critical part of the interview.

"We'd be honored to have the Franklin Publishing Group be part of that effort," Russell said when Nat finished. "I'll talk to my accountants in the morning and see how much of your budget we can cover. Your ideas are well thought out."

"Thank you." Nat smiled. "I've had a lot of thinking time."

"Some people could think for years and not come up with a practical scheme," Russell said. "I appreciate dealing with someone who has a head for business. Philanthropy is a fine thing, but some of these confounded do-gooders quiver at the very idea of fiscal responsibility, and that makes me nervous. It's too easy to pour money down a rat hole if you don't have some checks and balances in place."

"That's why it was important for me to be over there so long," Nat said. "I've lined up some excellent people who are ready to help run the program."

Russell nodded and sat back in his chair. "Are you planning to approach other backers about this while you're in town?"

"Yes, I am. But I wanted to see you first."

The older man regarded him like a benevolent uncle. "I'm sure you'll get the backing you need. But I should probably warn you that not everyone is as liberal as I am. You might want to shave."

"I probably will." Growing a beard had been practical when hot water and shaving gear had been scarce and cold wind had chapped his bare skin. He'd also blended in better with the refugees, and after a few months, the beard had seemed natural to him. Now that he was back in this country, seeing it in the mirror every day would serve to remind him of his mission. Still, Russell had a point. And then there was the matter of Jess. She had very tender skin....

"I rather like your beard," Adele said.

"Yes, but you're not a conservative businessman, Adele," Russell said. "Some of these fellows get suspicious if they see a lot of facial hair. A mustache, now that's no big deal, but a full beard conjures up the idea of radicals and hippies, y'know. It could affect whether Nat can get them to turn loose of their money."

"I understand," Nat said. "Besides, I might give my secretary a heart attack if I walked into the office looking like this."

"You sell mostly unimproved land out there in Colorado, don't you?" Russell said.

"That's right." Nat spied an opening. "Have you ever visited the state?"

"No, I never have. Flown over it many times, but never did stop. Pretty country, I understand."

"It is that." Nat thought he saw a flicker of emotion in those brown eyes. Adele gazed down at the fingers she'd laced tightly in her lap. Nat waited to see if either of them would mention that they had a daughter living in Colorado. Neither of them did. He'd have to plow this furrow on his own.

His pulse rate spiked. This was undoubtedly a touchy subject, but he didn't intend to leave without getting into it. "Unless I'm mistaken, your daughter, Jessica, lived in Aspen for a while."

The atmosphere in the room changed immediately. The camaraderie disappeared as Adele and Russell tensed and looked uneasily at each other. Finally Adele gave an almost imperceptible nod, as if to let her husband handle the comment.

"And how would you happen to have come by that information?'' Russell asked. His question was quietly phrased, but the tone was one of command.

''I met her.''

They regarded him in stony silence.

Nat forged on. ''But I've lost touch with her. I tried calling her from London and found out the number I had for her isn't good anymore. I thought you might be able to tell me where she is,'' he finished, matching his tone to Franklin's as he met his gaze.

Russell had not changed position in his chair, but somehow he seemed bigger, more formidable. The publishing tycoon had replaced the affable philanthropist. ''What is she to you?'' he demanded.

''She saved my life.''

Adele gasped.

''And exactly how did she do that?'' Russell asked. A muscle twitched in his jaw.

Nat had wondered if she'd ever mentioned the incident to her parents. ''She might have told you about helping four clueless cowboys who'd decided to go skiing,'' he ventured.

''No, she did not.'' Russell continued to drill Nat with his gaze.

''We...she's a very independent person.'' Adele laced and unlaced her fingers. ''She doesn't fill us in on all her doings.''

''That's an understatement,'' Russell barked. ''So, what happened out there in Colorado?''

''Well, some friends and I went skiing and stayed at the lodge where she worked at the desk. I guess she figured out we were beginners who might get in trouble, so she offered to go along and watch out for us. Unfortunately we didn't give enough credit to her warnings. We blundered into an avalanche, and I was completely buried. She figured out where I was and told my friends how to dig me out. If she hadn't been there, I might not have made it."

Adele sagged back against her chair, her face pale. "An avalanche." She glanced over at Russell. "She could have ended up in it, too, Russ."

"Of course she could have!" Russell's jaw worked. "But she thinks she knows best, so what the hell are we supposed to do?" His voice trembled with obvious pain and frustration.

Nat had only heard Jess's version of the difficult relationship she had with her parents, and of course he'd sided with her in her bid for independence. But seeing the strain they were under because of her leaving, Nat couldn't help sympathizing with them. She was their only child, and they were frantic with worry because they could no longer watch out for her. Nat could relate.

"Is she still up in Aspen?" he asked.

Russell lost his tenuous hold on his composure. "We don't know where the hell she is! We—"

"Russell." Adele's quiet authority stopped his tirade immediately. "Jessica calls," she continued, sitting up straighter and sending another warning glance at her husband. "She updates us every couple of weeks. About six months ago she decided to see a bit of the country, so she's traveling around."

A cold chill zipped up Nat's spine. Something about this scenario didn't sound like the Jess he knew. She was a nest-builder, not a vagabond. She'd loved her setup in Aspen, and she'd told him it was the perfect place to begin her study of herbs. "Traveling where?" he asked, trying to keep the panic out of his voice.

"God knows. She's behaving like a damn gypsy!" Russell shot a belligerent glance at his wife.

Her voice remained low and well-modulated. "Russell,

we don't know this young man that well. I think perhaps you should—''

"I think I should reconsider supporting this foundation, is what I think!" Russell turned back to Nat. "Tell me, Grady, how did you know that Jessica is our daughter? As I recall, she wanted to 'fade into the woodwork' as she put it, so she could—and I quote—'live a normal life.' She didn't intend to tell anyone she was related to me. How did you find out?"

"She told me," Nat said. Concern for Jess tightened his chest. "After the avalanche we became friends." It was all he dared admit in this charged atmosphere. "I don't think she ever told anyone else, but she told me. Now that I'm back in the country, I wanted to…say hello." Yeah, right. Say hello. And then kiss her until neither of them could stand. And make love to her for about three days straight.

Adele leaned forward, her gray eyes intent. "Did you have a close relationship with our daughter, Mr. Grady?"

He'd been demoted from that first-name basis pretty quick, Nat thought as he wondered how to answer her.

"What the hell kind of question is that, Adele?" Russell asked. "The man said they were friends. Don't go making something more of it."

Adele ignored her husband and continued to study Nat. "She never mentioned being involved with someone," she said, "but I knew it had to happen, sooner or later. She's a beautiful girl."

Nat's throat went dry. "Yes."

"She didn't trust many people," Adele continued, her gaze steady. "If she trusted you enough to let you know who she is, then I suspect you're more than a friend to her."

He'd hoped to avoid getting this specific, but he wasn't going to lie to her parents. "We're more than friends," he said.

"Oh, that's terrific!" Russell said. "Are you telling me you left my daughter high and dry while you went running all over God's creation helping strangers in that little piss-ant country over there?"

"I..." Nat cleared his throat and faced Russell. He'd come into this room thinking of himself as a world-weary champion of the underprivileged. But he was beginning to feel more like an irresponsible teenager. "Yes, sir, I'm afraid that's exactly what I did. And I'd like to make it up to her."

"You'll have to catch her first."

Nat damn well intended to do that. At least it didn't sound as if she'd found herself another guy. "Do you happen to remember where she was the last time she called?"

Adele's poise cracked a little. "She won't tell us," she said, a quiver in her voice.

The tightness in his chest grew. "What do you mean?"

Adele's knuckles showed white under her delicate skin as she clenched her hands in her lap. "She only says she's on a grand adventure and she'll fill us in later."

"What?" Nat set down his drink and stared at her, incredulous.

"She apparently uses a pay phone," Adele said, "and she gets off the line before we can—"

"This is unbelievable!" In his agitation, Nat got to his feet. "I know she wants to live her own life, but refusing to tell you her whereabouts is ridiculous!"

"I wanted to hire somebody to track her down," Russell said, sounding defeated. "Adele won't let me. She says if we do that, we're liable to lose her forever."

"At least now she calls!" Adele stood, as well. "If you get heavy-handed, she'll stop doing that!"

"Then I guess I'll have to find her," Nat said. And she'd better have a damn good explanation for her behavior when he did. Maybe her mother and father were overprotective, but it was obvious to him that they loved her. They deserved better treatment than this. Either something was terribly wrong, or his darling Jess had turned into a brat.

"Don't tell her you came to see us," Adele said. "Please. She might think we asked you to find her for us."

"Don't worry, I won't involve you."

Russell levered himself from his chair. "But if you want that foundation money, you'll tell us where she is when you locate her," he said.

Nat gazed at him. As fair as that sounded, he couldn't agree to it. First he had to talk to Jess and find out what had caused her to take off like this. "I can't make that promise. I will try to convince her to come out of hiding so you don't have to worry so much about her, but under the circumstances, maybe I should withdraw my request for foundation money."

"No, no, you shouldn't." Russell's mouth twitched in a ghost of a grin. "But you can't blame me for trying to use some leverage."

Nat smiled at him. "No, I can't."

"My accountants will contact your Colorado office in a few days."

"What if Jessica finds out that you're helping with this foundation? Won't she make the connection?"

Nat had had enough. He'd learned that life could be short and brutal, and he didn't have time for games. "Look, the welfare of those orphans is too important to let Jess interfere with the fund-raising. Unless she's a different person from the one I knew, she wouldn't want to interfere, no matter what her personal situation is. And I intend to find out exactly what that is."

"You sound so sure you will," Adele said.

"That's because I am sure I will." He refused to consider any other possibility.

"You called her Jess," Adele said. "Does she go by that now?"

Nat looked at her. "No. I just...I call her that." He realized how familiar that sounded. Her parents didn't shorten her name when they spoke of her.

"I see," Adele said. Obviously she saw everything.

Russell cleared his throat. "I don't know your exact relationship to my daughter, and I don't think I want to know," he said. "Maybe you left her high and dry and maybe you didn't. But if you find her and can let us know, this number will get you straight through to me." He handed Nat an embossed card.

"I'll find her."

Russell extended his hand, and there was an unspoken plea in his gaze. He was obviously too proud to voice it, but it was there, nevertheless. "Good luck to you, son."

CHAPTER THREE

JESSICA DIDN'T BOTHER to follow the road around to the house. She moved through the trees, greeting each one as an old friend while she tried to decide what to do once she arrived at the mansion. She couldn't imagine what Nat was doing there. She was afraid to hope he was looking for her.

Her first glimpse of the house brought a rush of homesickness. Glancing up to the second floor, she picked out the darkened windows of her bedroom. Her parents wouldn't have changed it. She and her mother had flown to Paris to choose the golden toile de Jouy fabric that draped the windows and the antique canopy bed. The bed probably had sheets on it, just in case she returned.

Most of the time she'd felt trapped in this house, but she'd also felt incredibly safe. Safety sounded good right now.

But if she walked into the house and accepted the protection her parents would love to give her, she'd lose all the independent ground she'd gained. And the fight wasn't only about her now. Elizabeth deserved to grow up like a normal child instead of being followed by bodyguards wherever she went.

Oh, but the tug of home was strong, even after all this time. They were burning oak in the fireplace. The familiar smell of the smoke made her throat ache. She could picture her mother and father, each in their favorite wingback chair, reading glasses perched on their noses as they settled down with a favorite book. The love seat had been designated as hers, positioning her right between them.

When she'd been small, before she'd begun feeling stifled, the love seat sandwiched between her parents' chairs had been a good place to be. She hadn't exactly been allowed to sprawl on that seat while she read, but they'd let her tuck her feet under her as long as she took off her shoes first.

In those early days, at precisely nine o'clock, Barclay would arrive with refreshments—lemonade in the summer and steaming cocoa in the winter. And gingersnaps. Jessica could almost feel the crunch between her teeth.

She wondered if Nat was sitting on the love seat at this very minute. What on earth was he saying to her parents? A horrible thought came to her. If she told Nat about Elizabeth and the stalker, he might insist that she come back here and inform her parents. If he wanted to tell them himself, she wouldn't be able to stop him.

With Elizabeth's freedom at stake, maybe she'd better not tell Nat too much until she was sure he wouldn't go running to her parents with the information. She didn't think he'd sell her out, but she couldn't be sure. After all, he'd come here tonight.

But she needed a plan.

The cab Nat had arrived in sat empty in the driveway as the driver strolled around smoking a cigarette. He returned to the cab to stub it out in the ashtray, which was a good thing, she thought. Herb, the gardener, would have a fit if he found a cigarette butt lying on his velvet lawn. He had enough trouble contending with the autumn leaves, which he snatched up the minute they dropped from the trees.

Still, she missed Herb and his persnickety ways. She missed all of the staff, even stuffy Barclay. She hadn't realized how much until she stood in the shadows looking at the house that had sheltered her for so many years. But then, she supposed zoo animals would miss their keepers if they were suddenly turned loose. You had to give up something to get something, as her father was so fond of saying.

The cabdriver walked away from the car again and headed for the slope leading down to the river. About that time, the lights of a barge appeared from upriver, and the rumble of the boat's engines drifted toward her on the night air. The driver stood with his back to her, his hands in his pockets as he gazed at the approaching boat.

Jessica's pulse leaped as she recognized her opportunity. Nat had ridden in the front seat on the way out here. No doubt he'd do the same on the way back. While the cabbie watched the barge sail past, she could hide on the floor of the back seat. The boat's engines would muffle the sound of her opening and closing the car door.

Unless Nat happened to come out at the exact moment when she was sneaking into the cab, she'd be able to hitch a ride without being noticed. When they arrived at Nat's hotel, she'd reveal herself and hope that the cabdriver didn't have a weak heart.

As for Nat, maybe he deserved the jolt she'd give him. For all she knew, he was telling her parents about her involvement with him, which she definitely didn't appreciate having him do without checking with her first. To be fair, he would have had some trouble checking with her first, but still, in coming here he'd overstepped his bounds.

The rumble of the boat's engine grew louder. Good thing *she* didn't have a weak heart. It was skittering around like crazy while she waited for the noise to reach its loudest point. Okay. Now. She hurried toward the cab. The back door was locked.

She lost precious time opening the front door and reaching around to lift the button on the back door. Fortunately the barge's engines drowned out the sounds she made. Or at least she hoped they did. The rhythmic rush of blood against her eardrums made it difficult to gauge how much noise she was making.

Luck seemed to be favoring her. The cabdriver didn't turn around and the front door remained closed. She climbed into the back seat and shut the car door as quietly as possible. The driver stood watching the barge edge down the river. He probably didn't think he needed to watch over his cab when he was inside the gated confines of Franklin Hall.

Putting her backpack on the floor, she lay on her side across the hump and put her head on the backpack. Not so good. And she'd thought she was roughing it when she'd had to give up first-class for coach.

She shifted position several times trying for some level of comfort. Finally she gave up. Comfort wasn't in the cards for this ride. She'd have to hope, when the cab reached the city, that she wouldn't be too crippled to walk.

Now if she could only stop gasping for breath, she might actually be able to pull this off. She forced herself to inhale slowly and deeply. She almost choked on the stale cigarette smell wafting up from the carpeting.

I'm doing this for Elizabeth, she told herself. She turned to face the back seat instead of the front, which gave her a little more breathing room. Gradually she became more accustomed to the obnoxious odor.

Nat's backpack was within reach on the back seat. She stroked the frayed canvas, as if that would somehow start the process of connecting to him. He was not the same man who'd left her in Aspen, that was for sure. But then she wasn't the same woman, either. Maybe they'd find no common ground other than the most obvious—their child. But Elizabeth's welfare was worth any amount of sacrifice she had to make.

Despite her awkward position on the floor of the car, she

began to relax. Then she heard the front door of the house open and close. Suddenly she couldn't breathe. Nat was coming.

"All set?" the cabdriver called.

"Let's go," Nat replied.

His voice splashed over her, drenching her with longing. She wanted him. No matter how she'd tried to stamp out her feelings, the sound of his voice brought back a flood of memories—tender, lusty, explosive memories. And of all the times they'd made love, the most electrifying had been the night they'd conceived Elizabeth. He'd become such a part of her that night that she'd thought for sure he'd agree to break the code of silence.

Instead, he'd smashed their love to smithereens.

Her heart beat wildly as the front doors of the cab opened and the dome light flicked on. If either of them decided to look in the back seat during that brief time, they'd see her.

They didn't.

The engine started, and she discovered one other unpleasant fact. She could smell car exhaust down here. Wonderful. Now she could worry about asphyxiating herself.

As the cab began to move down the driveway, Jessica was sure she could feel every rock and pebble in the road, especially when the tires threw them up under the car. But she didn't dare move, at least not until they were well on their way back to the city.

"Did you get your business settled?" the cabdriver asked.

"Not exactly," Nat said. "But it was a start."

Please let this be a nosy cabdriver, Jessica prayed. She just might find out something that would partially make up for being crammed in here like a doomed mobster.

Unfortunately for her, the cabbie wasn't all that interested in Nat's business at Franklin Hall and started talking about the World Series instead. Jessica clenched her teeth as Nat happily traded opinions on the relative merits of each team in the playoffs. Guys and their sports.

Yet even though the conversation bored her to tears, she loved listening to Nat's voice, and his low chuckle was enough to trip the switch on her libido. She didn't focus on his words, but absorbed only his tone.

Maybe because she was lying in the dark, she began to think of how it had been lying with Nat in the dark. Gradually her mind replaced his talk about baseball with other words, polished gems from her treasure-house of memories. *I could spend forever looking at you, Jess. And kissing you. Your skin tastes like milk and honey. Come here, woman. Come let me make love to you. For the rest of the night. Who cares about sleep when we can do this?*

She hadn't forgotten a minute of the time they'd been together. She wondered if he'd forgotten it all. But if he didn't want anything more to do with her, why had he traveled to Franklin Hall the minute he set foot on U.S. soil?

Cautiously she wiggled over so she could see out the window. It wasn't a great view, and the hump on the floor forced her to arch her back to an uncomfortable degree, but she'd be able to tell when they reached the city. She was more than ready to get there. The exhaust fumes were making her woozy.

"There's the Franklin Tower," the cabbie said. "They say Franklin's office takes up the entire top floor. A huge office, they say, with a three-hundred-sixty-degree view of Manhattan."

She knew that office. Jessica brought her attention back to the conversation in the front seat. Maybe the driver would finally try to get some gossip out of Nat.

"I've heard about his office," Nat said.

He'd heard it from her. Nat had been the only person who knew about her background, and when he'd abandoned her, she'd lost more than a lover. She'd lost the one person she could talk to without constantly guarding her speech.

When she'd left New York, she'd severed all ties with friends because she couldn't be sure they wouldn't somehow give her away and leave her open to the kidnappers her father spoke about endlessly, the ones waiting to snatch a rich man's child. She'd heard his warnings for so long that she believed him. She'd just wanted to find a different way to avoid that fate.

She'd made new friends in Aspen, but none of them knew she had a famous father. Only Nat. Keeping the secret had been more of a burden than she'd planned on, and confiding in Nat had been a welcome relief.

"That Franklin, I guess he's a real wheeler-dealer," said the cabbie, obviously fishing for information. "I've also heard he's tough to get along with."

No joke, Jessica thought. *Try having a different opinion from his and see what happens to you.* The lights of the city were all around her now, with horns blaring and even more fumes coming up through the floor of the cab. Her head started to pound, and she closed her eyes to see if that might help.

"Someone did tell me that Franklin was hard to get along with," Nat said. "But he seemed like a reasonable guy to me."

Jessica's eyes snapped open. Nat thought her father was *reasonable?* What sort of a turncoat was he, anyway? Her headache grew worse.

"So you two got along pretty well, then?" the driver asked.

"I think so," Nat replied. "Anybody with that much power is bound to rub people the wrong way once in a while, and he makes for an easy target, but he struck me as a decent man who tries to do the right thing."

Jessica couldn't decide which was worse, the fumes or Nat's praise of her father. Both of them were making her sick.

"And I also think the person who told me he was hard to get along with probably has some authority issues to work out," Nat added.

Authority issues? What the hell did he know about it? Jessica's automatic yelp of protest was halfway out before she remembered that nobody was supposed to know she was hiding in the back seat. She clapped her hand to her mouth, but it was too late.

"Jesus!" the driver cried. "Somebody's in the—"

"You watch the road! I'll handle it!" Nat climbed into the back seat and grabbed Jessica by the front of her jacket.

She was too stunned to speak.

Gasping for breath, he hauled her up to a sitting position, which knocked her glasses askew. She pushed them back into place and tried to keep from throwing up. The exhaust fumes had really made her nauseated.

"My God, it's a woman," Nat said in amazement.

"What's a woman doing in my cab?" the driver babbled hysterically. "Is she armed?"

"I don't know," Nat said, breathing hard. "Are you armed?"

She shook her head, still trying to keep from tossing her cookies.

"She's not armed," Nat said to the driver. As his breathing slowed, he peered intently at her. Multicolored lights streamed in through the cab windows and slid across his face, making it difficult to read his expression. But he seemed to be studying her, as if trying to solve a riddle.

"I'm heading for the nearest cop shop," the cabbie said.

"Don't do that yet," Nat told the driver quietly. "Let me see if I can find out what's going on here." He looked down at Jessica. "Where did you come from?"

She didn't trust herself to open her mouth without losing her lunch, so instead she took off her glasses and gazed up at him.

He stared at her, stared at her hard. Then, while he kept his gaze locked on hers, he reached up with his free hand and hit the switch on the dome light.

She blinked in the glare of the overhead, but when she could once again meet his gaze, she saw the dawning recognition there.

"Jess?" he whispered.

She nodded. Then she scrambled for the window, rolled it down and threw up.

ENDLESS HUMILIATING moments later, Jessica was finally ensconced in the bathroom of Nat's hotel room with the door locked. Swearing under her breath, she stripped down, pulled off her wig and stepped under the shower. In all the scenarios she'd played in her head about this meeting, none of them had included barfing.

Fortunately she'd only baptized the side of the cab and the sleeve of her coat. In the hullabaloo following her hurling incident, she'd been too embarrassed to be able to gauge whether or not Nat was happy to see her. It would have been difficult to factor out the vomit in that calculation, anyway. Not many men would be happy to see a woman whose first move was to spew all over the place.

Once in the shower, she gave in to the urge to wash her hair with the luxurious hotel shampoo. Much as it pained her to admit it, she missed the five-star treatment. In the years since she'd left Franklin Hall, she'd tried not to dip into her trust fund at all, but once she quit her job and went on the lam, so to speak, she'd had to draw some money out. She begrudged every penny she spent, because it was her father's money.

Consequently, she could hardly describe her accommodations in the past few months as first-class. Maybe fifth-or sixth-class.

Knowing Nat and his lack of pretense, she'd expected him to opt for a low-to-medium-priced hotel while he was in New York, but for reasons she couldn't fathom, he'd directed the cabdriver to the Waldorf. From the reaction of the clerk at check-in, she'd figured out Nat hadn't made an advance reservation, so it was a spur-of-the-moment decision.

Maybe he'd done it for her, although she'd died a million deaths standing there in the glittering lobby in her bag-lady clothes decorated with barf. Now, however, as she rinsed her hair under the most excellent showerhead she'd enjoyed in months, she blessed him for his choice.

Ah, the thick towels. Oh, the rich scent of the body lotion. She wanted to be a good girl and not care about such superficial things, but she'd been raised with them, and the sense of deprivation had been more acute than she'd planned on.

She smoothed at least half the tiny bottle of lotion over herself, both because it felt so good and because, once she was finished, she had to face putting on something wrinkled and musty from her backpack. She was sick to death of wrinkled and musty.

From years of experience with luxurious accommodations, she knew that in the room's closet a thick terry robe would be hanging ready for just this moment. Technically it was there for the use of the person who'd rented the room. That person would be Nat.

She pictured herself coming out to talk to him in the wrinkled and baggy jumper and turtleneck she had stuffed in her backpack. Then she pictured herself having the same conversation wearing that thick white robe. The discussion would be difficult enough without looking bad while she had it.

Wrapping a towel around her, she went to the door and opened it a crack. "Nat?"

"Yes?" Instantly footsteps hurried in her direction. "Are you feeling okay? Should I call a doctor?"

"I'm feeling better than I have in ages," she said. "But I have a big favor to ask. Would you mind if I put on the hotel bathrobe that's hanging in the closet? My clothes are...well, they don't look very...the thing is, I—"

"Here." A wad of white terry poked through the crack in the door. "Enjoy."

"Thanks." She opened the door enough to pull the robe through. Oh, yes. Egyptian cotton. It felt like heaven as she pulled it on and belted it around her waist. In the steamy mirror she fluffed her still-damp hair. For the first time in months, she looked and felt like herself.

And now she had to face Nat.

She fluffed her hair again. Then she ran a quick comb through it. She wasn't happy with the last cut, which she'd got done at a beauty school to save money. It took an exceptional stylist to deal with her thick, naturally curly hair. This one had left it too bulky around her shoulders. She tried to tame it with her fingers, but it was no use.

Maybe a little lipstick.

While she'd been on the run, she'd pared down her cosmetics needs to lipstick, mascara and blush. She had the tube of lipstick halfway to her mouth when she stopped to stare at herself in the mirror. What was she doing? Trying to come on to him?

She rolled the lipstick back down, capped it and tucked it into her backpack. She'd take him the herbal supplements she'd brought, though. Fishing them out, she started toward the door. On the way she happened to look down at her feet.

Now, *there* was a sorry sight. She paused to consider her unpainted toes, clipped with a toenail clipper. Not buffed, not filed, not pampered. Her last pedicure had been before she'd had Elizabeth. Nat had always loved her feet.

Stop it, she lectured herself. He probably didn't love any part of her anymore. What she looked like didn't matter. Elizabeth was the only person who mattered in this whole mess.

"Jess?" Nat rapped on the door. "Are you sure you're okay in there?"

"I'm okay."

"Then what's taking so long?"

"I was, um, thinking."

"Well, could you do that out here? We need to talk."

"Yes, we do. We most certainly do." Drawing in a bracing lungful of air, she opened the bathroom door. She found herself staring at his shirtfront. He stood right outside the door, crowding her, invading her space. She would have to walk around him to move any farther into the room.

His masculine scent surrounded her, making her quicken in all sorts of strategic places. She gathered her courage and looked up into his eyes. Her heart stuttered at the fire burning there. "Nat?"

"What's that?" He glanced down at the two bottles of supplements.

"Herbal stuff for you."

His gaze lifted. "Why?"

"Because..." *Because I love you and worry about you.* She didn't dare say it.

He made an impatient noise deep in his throat. "Jess, I have to ask you something."

"Okay." Her heart hammered.

His words were as intense as his gaze. "Is there anyone else?"

Joy rushed through her. *Hallelujah. He still wanted her.* "No. No one else."

With a gusty sigh he took the vitamin bottles and tossed

them on the floor. Then he pulled her into his arms. "Excuse the beard," he murmured. Then his lips crushed hers.

Overjoyed as she was to know that he still cared, she was distracted at first by the beard. Kissing him was like smooching a stuffed animal. But then...then he coaxed her mouth open. She forgot all about the beard as she rediscovered why kissing Nat had been one of her all-time thrills. He could pack more sensuality into a kiss than other men could manage in an hour of whole-body sex.

A few moments of kissing Nat beat a day at the spa for making her tingle all over. One kiss from him and she was so awake, from the tips of her curling toes to the tiny hairs at the nape of her neck. His fingers stroked there, and she turned to melted butter in his arms.

Boiling butter might be more like it. She wriggled against him, trying to get closer.

He shifted the angle of his mouth and tugged at the bathrobe's sash while he muttered something that sounded like *have to.*

Oh, so did she. Had to. She started on the buttons of his shirt. But wait. She hadn't planned on this.

"Need you so," he breathed, backing her toward the bed as he continued to kiss her senseless.

"Wait," she said, gasping.

"Can't." He pushed open the terry cloth and closed his hand over her breast with a groan.

"Nat—" She tried to tell him she wasn't on the Pill. He kept coming, thrusting his tongue in her mouth, making her crazy with wanting him. The back of her knees hit the edge of the bed. She fell against the quilted spread and he came right with her.

Panting, she tried again. "I'm not—"

His mouth silenced her once more.

Oh, God. How many times had she fantasized about his weight pressing her into the mattress, his hand between her thighs, his mouth at her breast? Both of them going wild. If this was a dream, she'd kill whoever or whatever woke her up.

Even his beard was wonderful, brushing her skin like the pelt of some exotic animal. She'd never realized kissing a bearded man could be so erotic. She pulled him closer, arched into his caress, moaned his name.

"God, I need you," he groaned.

"I need you, too." But one unplanned baby was enough. She forced herself to choke out the words. "But I'm not on the Pill anymore. We can't—"

"Yes, we can." He nuzzled his way back to her mouth.

At first she thought he meant that he wouldn't care if she got pregnant. "We can?"

"Yes." He covered her face with a million kisses. "We can. I want to be inside you, Jess."

Could he really be telling her that he'd changed his mind about children? Her heart expanded with the possibility. "Why can we?" she asked breathlessly.

"I had room service bring up condoms. Don't worry." He kissed her cheeks, her eyelids, her nose. "I won't get you pregnant."

She went still. "Would that be so terrible?"

He paused and lifted his head to gaze into her eyes. Although it seemed to take some effort, he gained control of his runaway desire. Then he took a deep breath. "I don't want to start out with a fight, Jess."

A pulse hammered in her throat. "Neither do I. But I need to know. Would it be so terrible if you got me pregnant?"

"You mean right now, at this very moment?" Without giving her a chance to answer, he barreled on. "Yeah, it would. We have a lot of talking to do, and that's one of the things we need to talk about, but I wouldn't want to make a move like that without taking all kinds of things into consideration. I am willing to give it some thought, much more so than when I left. Maybe…I'm not saying positively, but maybe…someday. But not right now.''

The hope swelling in her heart died. Damn, but he was a pain in the butt. She'd meant to find a gentle way to tell him, but suddenly she didn't want to be gentle with this incredibly sexy but frustratingly stubborn man. She wanted to hit him between the eyes.

''It's too late to talk about it, Nat,'' she said. ''Eight months ago I gave birth to our daughter.''

CHAPTER FOUR

NAT STARED down at her as a sick feeling worked its way through his gut. "No," he whispered.

"Yes. I'm sorry to spring it on you like this. I hadn't planned on that, but I've carried this secret for so long that I—"

"No!" He scrambled from the bed, as if eliminating all contact with her would change the message she was trying to deliver. He jabbed an accusing finger at her. "You were on the Pill!"

Jess sat up, drew her robe around her with great dignity and retied the sash. Sometimes, at moments like this when she adopted an almost royal air, he realized that some of her upbringing had stuck with her, whether she wanted it to or not.

"Yes, I was, but—"

"You stopped?" The fear boiling in his stomach erupted into accusations. "You stopped without telling me, didn't you? You thought if you couldn't hook me one way, you'd try something else!"

"How dare you!" She leaped from the bed, rigid with anger.

"What else am I supposed to think?" Oh, God, he remembered how she'd pleaded with him to commit. Her pleas could have come from the desperate knowledge that she might be carrying his baby.

Clenching her fists, she faced him, her eyes dark with betrayal. "You could try thinking that it was an accident."

Her voice quivered. "I had a cold that weekend, remember?"

"Yeah, I remember." She'd suggested their not seeing each other because she hadn't wanted to infect him. But he'd talked her into it by saying he had a great immune system. He'd told her they'd spend the weekend in bed. Which they had. Her cold had made their final argument that much more miserable, because she'd been crying and coughing and sneezing through it all. He'd felt like the worst kind of heel, but she'd been the one pressing the point, not him. And he'd run.

Her tone grew bitter. "I was so worried about you catching whatever I had that I decided to get a prescription for antibiotics, hoping then I'd be less contagious."

"I remember that, too. What does that have to do with—"

"See? You don't know, either! Antibiotics can make birth control pills useless!"

So it was true. The realization washed over him in an icy wave. A child. He had a child. His baby wasn't a refugee, yet still the images of those sad-eyed orphans rose up to taunt him. Life had let them down, and sure as the world, he would let down any child that called him father.

When panic threatened to overwhelm him, he looked for someone to blame. "If that's true about antibiotics, it should be common knowledge! The doctor should have told you!"

"How could he think to? I ran over to one of those all-night clinics, and they were busy as hell. The guy who prescribed the antibiotics didn't know me or my situation, and let's not forget that I was supposed to keep it so damn secret that I was involved in a sexual relationship."

He looked away from the accusation in her eyes. Guilty. He was so guilty. Loving a woman like Jess had been a mistake from the beginning. After only a couple of days of knowing her, he'd realized she was a white-lace-and-promises kind of gal. Pursuing her had been pure selfishness on his part.

But he'd wanted her in a way that reason and fairness couldn't touch. He still did. One glance in her direction and the urge to take her came roaring back, especially now, when he was vulnerable and afraid. He'd discovered making love to Jess was magic. Holding her, pushing deep inside her, his fears always went away.

He could still taste her kisses. Her mouth was red from them, her skin rosy from the brush of his beard. The scattering of freckles across the bridge of her nose had been something he'd missed more than he realized. He loved her more now than ever before, as she stood there defiantly challenging him, her wild mane of red curls a riot of color around her tight, angry expression.

Then it finally struck him that she'd announced that they had a child, but she was here alone. "Where is the baby now?"

The defiance whooshed out of her in no time, and her expression became heartbreakingly sad. "In Colorado," she said quietly. "At the Rocking D."

"With *Sebastian?*" Alarm zinged through him. "Sebastian doesn't know a damn thing about babies! How long—"

"Maybe we'd better go over there and sit down." She gestured to a polished cherry table and two side chairs positioned by the window. "We have several things to talk about."

He couldn't come up with a better plan. It was as good a spot as any for him to be while she flung one hand grenade of information after another. Walking over to the window, he opened the drapes. He'd closed them while she was in the shower as part of his preparation for seducing her. Now he needed a feeling of space.

Below them the city still bustled even though it was nearly midnight. Which meant it was early morning in London. If his body ever stopped pumping with adrenaline, he'd probably keel over from lack of sleep. As it was, he felt as if he'd never be able to sleep again.

"Are you going to sit down?" she asked.

He turned. She was seated primly in one of the Queen Anne chairs, her elbows resting on the arms, her fingers laced together and her feet crossed at the ankles. He thought again how well she fit into this environment. She looked like a younger version of her mother.

He also had the ignoble thought of going over to that chair and trapping her within its arms while he ravished her. There was something very provocative about that bulky terry robe covering her naked body, and the untidy mass of her just-washed hair made her look like a woman in need of ravishing. She had freckles across the top of her breasts, too, and he'd been too busy to take proper notice of them the first time he'd opened her robe. Those freckles called to him.

She'd given birth to his child. He couldn't take it in. His mind kept trying to reject the whole concept.

"I guess you're not going to sit down," she said. "I can understand you being agitated. I really had hoped to break this to you more gradually. But before I say anything more, I need to know if we can keep this between us, or if you will feel some obligation to contact my parents."

He thought of the worry etched into Adele's forehead, and the desperate gleam in Russell's eyes. "They're worried sick about you. They said you've been traveling…" He paused to stare at her. "Have you been hauling that kid around all over the place?"

"Her name is Elizabeth, and no, I haven't. Like I told you, she's been at the Rocking D."

Elizabeth. Her name made her more real, which was not a good thing. "Since when?"

"Since March."

"Holy shit! Is she okay? Is Sebastian—"

"She's fine. I keep checking by phone." Her knuckles whitened as she clenched her hands in her lap. "I had to do it like this, Nat. But first I have to know. Are you going to call my parents and tell them everything?"

"Don't you think they deserve to know? My God, it's their grandchild, Jess!"

"I know." She swallowed. "But they'd want to swoop back in and protect me, and this time they'd include Elizabeth in their net. She'd become a little prisoner, just like I did. Once they knew the whole story, they might even get a court order giving them the right to do that."

Gradually he began to piece things together. Her disguise, her separation from the baby, her traveling around. He walked over to stand directly in front of her. "What's the problem, Jess?"

"I need your word that you won't call my parents."

"You're not getting it. That might be the thing to do."

She looked frantic. "No, it's not! I won't have my daughter grow up that way." Her eyes begged for his understanding. "Please, Nat. Promise you won't bring them into this."

He shook his head. "No promises. I understand what you're afraid of. I've seen Franklin Hall and I'm sure you were very lonely there. But there are worse things than being lonely." And he was the guy who could testify to that. "You'll have to trust me. I wouldn't contact them unless I thought it was absolutely necessary, but if they're your best alternative, and you're being too pigheaded to see that, then—"

"You never lived there." She pushed out of the chair and brushed past him, headed for the bathroom. "Tell you what. My main objective was to tell you about Elizabeth, and I've done that. All I ask is that if anything should happen to me, you'll see about our baby." She went into the bathroom.

He was across the room with one hand bracing the door before she could close it. "Stop right there." His heart hammered in his ears. "What the hell do you mean, if something should happen to you?"

She looked at him. "There are no guarantees in life, are there? Now, if you'll excuse me, I'll get dressed and out of your way."

"The hell you will." Seventeen months ago he wouldn't have thrown his weight around. That was before he'd lived in the middle of a war zone, where life could be snuffed out in an instant. He grabbed her wrist and pulled her back into the room. "You're obviously in some kind of danger, and you are, by God, going to tell me about it."

She resisted, trying to struggle out of his grip. Her color was high, and she was breathing hard. "This macho routine isn't like you."

"I've changed. Now tell me."

"Why should I?"

Both fury and passion put the same bloom in her cheeks and the same hitch in her breathing, he noticed. He might not recognize the difference, except for the look in her eyes. "Well, for one thing—" he grabbed her other wrist "—you're the mother of my child." Saying it made him shudder, but the fact gave him some rights.

Her eyes spit fire. "I have always put Elizabeth first, and I always will. I'll make sure she's safe, no matter what happens to me."

"She needs you." He tightened his grip on her wrists. "And damn it, so do I."

"No, you don't!" Tears of frustration filled her eyes. "You just need me for sex!"

His throat ached with remorse. Of course she'd think that. He forced the words past the lump in his throat. "Oh, I need you for sex, all right. Like you wouldn't believe. But that's only the tip of the iceberg, sweetheart."

Her response was low and choked with tears. "I don't believe you. Now let me go."

"No. Tell me what danger you're in. I have a right to know."

She gazed up at him and he could tell from the turmoil in her eyes how hard she was trying to be tough, how desperately she wanted to handle whatever she was dealing with by herself.

He couldn't let her do it. "Tell me. For Elizabeth's sake." Saying the baby's name, acknowledging her personhood, took another major effort on his part, but he figured it might turn the trick with Jess.

It did. Her shoulders slumped. "Someone's trying to kidnap me," she murmured.

"Oh, God." He didn't remember letting go of her wrists to wrap his arms around her, but all at once there she was in his arms, and he was holding on for dear life as he rocked her back and forth. He buried his face in her hair. "Oh, God, Jess." He knew about kidnapping. In the political upheaval he'd just witnessed, people had been kidnapped all the time. They never came back.

"It's just like my dad predicted!" she wailed, hugging him tightly. "In Aspen I thought someone might be following me. Then a car tried to force me off the road one night. Thank God Elizabeth wasn't with me. I got away, but I saw the same car following me another time, and I knew for sure then. Somebody has found out who I am. They've decided to snatch the Franklin heir."

With growing horror he listened as the story came tumbling out. She'd traded in her car for a different one, packed up the baby and taken her to the Rocking D for safekeeping. For the past six months she'd been on the run. But it had been a creative run.

Using different disguises and modes of transportation, she'd tried to elude the kidnapper. But just when she thought she had, a man would follow her along a crowded street, far enough away that she couldn't positively identify him, but close enough for her to suspect he was the same man. By keeping her wits about her, she'd stayed out of his clutches.

When she was finished, Nat held her tight for a long moment. Then he sighed. "We're calling the police."

"No!" She backed away from him. "The minute you do that, my parents will be all over this situation, and then my life as we know it will be over."

"Your life as you know it is totally screwed up!"

"No, it isn't." She tucked her wayward hair behind her ears, which made her look like a schoolgirl. A sexy schoolgirl.

He was determined not to be distracted. "The hell it isn't. You have a kidnapper on your trail and you can't even risk being close to your baby as a result."

"I can risk it now that you're home."

"Now, wait a minute. Flattering as that sounds, I can't have you thinking I'm an adequate bodyguard."

"You just said you'd changed. And I can see it. You're more aggressive than you were seventeen months ago."

"I'm not a trained bodyguard, and your parents are exactly the people who could—"

"Oh, gee, look at the time." She glanced at her bare wrist and started back toward the bathroom. "Gotta run."

"Oh, hell." He clamped a hand on her shoulder to keep her from disappearing behind the closed door. Holding her firmly by the shoulder, he heaved a gusty sigh. "Are you telling me that if I call your parents, you'll take off and leave me to deal with them?" He didn't relish the thought of facing Russell P. Franklin alone and announcing he'd gotten the Franklin heir with child.

She glanced over her shoulder. Jess was the sort of woman who could be provocative without even trying. "I guess that's about the size of it, Nathaniel Andrew."

"That's blackmail, Jessica Louise."

She smiled a vixen's smile. "I know."

He couldn't decide which he'd rather do, strangle her or kiss that saucy mouth until she moaned. He did neither. "You're blackmailing your parents, too, you know. Your dad wants to put a private detective on your trail so bad he can taste it, but your mother won't let him because she thinks you'll go away for good if he does."

"She's right."

Turning her to face him, he grasped her other shoulder and barely stopped himself from giving her a shake. "Jess, what if this kidnapper gets ahold of you? What if he decides, after getting the ransom money, to just kill you? Have you thought of that?"

She nodded. "That's why I needed to talk to you and tell you about Elizabeth," she said in a matter-of-fact tone. "So everything would be okay for the baby."

The thought of something happening to Jess had the power to paralyze his mind, so he didn't think about it for long. "Setting aside the issue of how the rest of us would fare in that event, let me emphasize that if you got yourself killed, it would *not* be okay for the baby." Panic nibbled at him some more. "I'm a lousy candidate for a parent, and you know it."

"I don't know it, but if you call my parents, we'll never get a chance to find out. They'll have Elizabeth behind the gates of Franklin Hall before you can say boo."

"Sounds like a plan to me." Then he wouldn't have to worry about the baby. He had a business in Colorado, after all. He could pay support, although the Franklins would probably scoff at the pittance the courts would ask of him.

"And I'd have to go with her," Jess said softly.

Ah, there was the rub. The woman he loved would be safe but unhappy. And he would be…lost. Lost without hope of redemption.

"You see, it has to be this way if you and I are to have any chance. If Elizabeth is to have any chance."

As he gazed into her eyes and saw the glimmer of hope there, his feelings of inadequacy threatened to swamp him. "I would botch the job of being Elizabeth's father, Jess. We've been through all that, and you know how I feel about having kids of my own. I'll admit that on the flight over I began thinking that maybe someday I could consider adopting an orphan from one of the refugee camps. But see, that would be different. The kid wouldn't have that many options, and even having me as a parent would be better than nothing."

"Oh, Nat." She moved in close and combed her fingers through his beard so she could cup his face in both hands.

He loved her touch, and decided at that very moment that he wanted to shave so nothing interfered with the feel of her soft hands on his face.

"I've never met your father," she said, "but I know you're nothing like him. You would never beat a child the way you were beaten, or belittle them until they felt worthless, the way your father did."

"You don't know that. It's the pattern I saw for eighteen years. Some of that behavior has to be lurking in me, waiting for the time when I have a kid, and that automatic conditioning kicks in."

Her gaze searched his. "Don't you at least want to see her?" she asked gently.

His stomach churned at the thought, but yes, he'd admit to a flicker of curiosity. "Maybe, from a distance."

Jess smiled. "How far a distance?"

"One of those videophones would be about right."

She held his gaze. "I think she has your eyes."

That rocked him. All along he'd pictured her with woeful brown eyes, like the children he'd left in the camps. "Blue?"

"They probably are by now. The color was still a little indistinct when I...when I left her at the ranch." Her breath caught and her eyes began to glow with longing. "Oh, Nat, please. Let's call the ranch and tell them we're on our way. It's been an eternity. Please. It's still only ten there. They won't be in bed. Let's call them now."

One thing had become obvious—he wouldn't in good conscience be able to shift this new and unwanted responsibility to Jess's parents. Neither could he expect Sebastian to keep on taking the burden, although Nat wasn't wild about heading out there to face this massive change in his life. He'd ten times rather hold up in the Waldorf for a few days and calm his fears by making endless love to Jess.

But it looked as if he needed to take Jess to Colorado. "Okay. Yeah. We'll do that."

"Oh, thank you!" She wrapped her arms around his neck and planted a kiss right on his mouth.

She might have meant it as a friendly gesture instead of an invitation, but it didn't matter how she'd meant it. His body flipped to automatic pilot as he grabbed her and pulled her in tight. He couldn't have kept his tongue out of her mouth for all the gold in Fort Knox.

With a little whimper of delight, she molded herself against him the way only Jess could do. Her body dovetailed with his as no other woman's body had ever done. It was as if they'd been carved from the same block of stone so that when they came together, the seam of separation disappeared.

But she wasn't stone—she was warm and pliant. When

he pushed his hand into the invisible gap between them, she magically made way for him. He tugged at the sash of her bathrobe and the thick material loosened instantly, gaping open over the smooth curve of her breast.

He was there in an instant, cupping the weight, almost out of his mind with the joy of caressing her silken breast again. He brushed the erect nipple with the pad of his thumb and she gasped against his mouth. She'd always been so sensitive to his slightest touch, which had made him feel like a god when he made love to her.

Tonight her reaction seemed even more sensitive, and subtly different. Or maybe it was all in his mind. Once upon a time, he'd thought he knew every intimate detail about her. But in his absence she'd given birth to a child—his child. The knowledge made her body mysterious and exotic. He needed to reconnect with her, if only to convince himself that she was still knowable, still within his reach.

He lifted his mouth a fraction from hers as he rubbed her nipple with his thumb. "Did you nurse her?" he murmured.

Her breath blew warm on his lips. "Yes."

He traced her open mouth with his tongue. "Tell me how it was."

"Sweet." Her breath quickened.

He looked down at her upturned face, her auburn lashes lying against her freckled cheeks, her lips parted, her breathing uneven as he stroked her taut nipple. "So you liked it." He was hard, so hard.

Her eyes fluttered open, and her glance scorched his. "I loved it."

"I wish I'd been there."

"So do I."

Holding her gaze, he deliberately pushed aside the lapel of her robe. Lifting her breast in his hand, he leaned down, heart racing, and slowly drew her nipple into his mouth. She tasted like heaven. He closed his eyes in ecstasy.

She sighed his name and tunneled her fingers through his hair to hold him against her breast.

When he thought he might come apart from the pressure of wanting her, he lifted his head and gazed into her passion-dark eyes. "I'm taking you to bed."

"What about...the phone...call," she whispered weakly.

He scooped her into his arms and the robe fell away as he carried her to the bed and laid her on the quilted spread. His throat went dry at her beauty, and his vocal cords felt like the rusty hinge on an old screen door. His hand went to his belt buckle. "In the morning," he said.

CHAPTER FIVE

WITH A SENSE of inevitability, Jessica abandoned control of the situation and allowed her desire to take her where it would. Making the phone call tonight wouldn't get her to her baby any faster, anyway. Nat needed sleep before he went anywhere.

But sleep didn't seem to be on his mind. She watched him shuck his clothes and remembered all the lonely nights she'd dreamed of his virile body moving in rhythm with hers. She wanted that as much as he did. Needed that, to give her a taste of what she was fighting for.

Her gaze swept hungrily over him. She'd always loved looking at him naked. Maybe it was the long absence, but he seemed even more beautiful now, leaner, stronger-looking, his chest and shoulder muscles more defined. With his thick beard, she couldn't help thinking of some Norse god with thunderbolts in each clenched fist.

When he put his knee on the mattress and braced his hands on either side of her, she reached up to stroke his chest. The muscles under her hand were rock-hard.

She glanced into his intense blue eyes. "You must have worked like a field hand over there."

"I dug a lot of ditches." He leaned closer and nibbled on her lower lip. "I worked until I was so tired, I couldn't stand. And still I couldn't sleep for needing you."

His beard tickled her skin. She longed to give herself to the sensuous delight of his kiss, but first she had to know.

"And did you...find someone to help you with that problem?"

When he stilled, her heart twisted. Cupping his face in both hands, she drew back and looked into his eyes. She saw remorse there, and a crack started to form in her heart. "You did, didn't you?"

"No," he said quietly.

"No? Then why are you looking so guilty?"

"Because it just hit me how she must have felt when I turned her down."

"A refugee?"

"God, no. I would never take advantage of those vulnerable women. Another camp volunteer, from England. She wanted me, or at least she wanted someone like me. I thought I could go through with it. I tried to go through with it." His gaze bored into hers and he sounded irritated. Whether with himself or her, she wasn't sure. "I wanted to forget you," he said. "I wanted in the worst way to be able to make love to her."

The thought of him even considering getting naked with another woman drove her crazy. "So, did you kiss her?"

"Yes."

She couldn't leave it alone. "French-kiss?"

"Yes."

"You had your tongue in another woman's mouth? How could you do that?"

A faint smile touched his lips. "Forget it, Jess. Nothing happened. Not that I wasn't hoping it would. I just... couldn't."

Jessica was pretty happy about that. "Did you take her clothes off?"

"Yes, and now I'm going to take off the rest of yours." His mouth came down, cutting off her next question as he worked her arm out of the bathrobe sleeve.

She shoved him away and gasped for breath. "Not so

fast, buster. I want to get this straight. Were your clothes off, too?"

"Mostly." In one smooth movement he pulled the robe off her other arm and tossed it on the floor.

"And even after all that, you didn't make love to her?"

"No." He pushed her flat on the mattress and followed her down, pinning her there with his chest.

Oh, yes. She loved the satisfying weight of him, the slight abrasion of his chest hair against her breasts. And he needed her. Only her. She gazed up at him, overjoyed with the news that he'd had a chance to make love to someone and hadn't been able to.

Yet she still could hardly believe it. "Is that normal?"

"I doubt it. I think you've ruined me." He framed her face in both hands, and his eyes searched hers for many long moments.

"What is it?" she questioned softly.

"I can't believe I'm really here with you. I'm afraid I'm going to wake up."

"Me, too." She reached up and touched his cheek. "Make love to me, Nat, before we both wake up."

With a groan he lowered his head and kissed her. His kiss was deep and sensuous, as it always was in her dreams, and she arched against him, praying that he wasn't an illusion. Deepening the kiss, he slid his hand between her legs and caressed her inner thigh, but that had been a part of her dreams, too. Even when he slipped his fingers into her moist channel and stroked her until she whimpered, she couldn't be sure he wasn't a figment of her imagination.

But in all the nights she'd fantasized about loving him again, she'd never dreamed of the soft whisper of his beard against her skin. As if that alone could convince her that he wouldn't disappear in a puff of smoke, she combed her fingers through it.

He lifted his mouth from hers. "I should have shaved," he murmured.

"No." Oh, his fingers could work magic, winding her tighter and tighter. "I...like it."

"It must be like making love to a furry animal." As if to make his point, he nibbled his way down her throat, his beard tickling her all the way.

"Uh-huh."

He stroked his beard deliberately over the tip of her breast. "Or some caveman."

She closed her eyes in ecstasy. "Uh-huh."

"And you like this?" he asked in a husky voice as he swept his beard back and forth across her tingling nipples.

She struggled for breath. "Uh-huh."

His low chuckle was laced with excitement. "You're kinky, woman."

"And you love it."

His voice roughened. "Damned if I don't." He moistened each nipple with his tongue and then brushed them dry with his beard. He repeated the process, all the while coaxing her higher with the persistent rhythm of his fingers.

The effect was incredible. She climaxed with a wild cry, arching away from the mattress as he buried his bearded face between her breasts. And he'd only begun. As she lay helplessly gasping from his first assault, he kissed a path down her quivering body until he'd nestled himself between her thighs.

"Oh, Nat." This was no dream. In a million nights of fantasizing she couldn't have imagined the delicious sensation of his mustache right *there,* while his beard feathered her inner thighs, and his tongue...there were no words for it, only sounds. And she filled the room with her moans of delight.

He gifted her with another shattering climax before making his way back to her mouth, revisiting his sites of conquest along the way. By the time he kissed her again, she would have done anything for him, if only she had a smidgen of strength left with which to do it.

"And I thought this beard was only good for keeping my face warm in a cold wind," he whispered.

She could barely move, let alone talk. But she wanted him to feel this euphoria, too. It was only fair. She liked her dry lips. "What about...you?"

He lifted his head and gazed down at her, his eyes alight. "I'm getting to that." He kissed the tip of her nose and his voice was gruff with emotion. "But you know how guys are when they've been frustrated for this long. It'll be fast and furious the first time. You needed a head start."

"Mmm." She figured she'd already finished the race. Twice.

"Don't go away." He leaned over and opened the bedside-table drawer.

She turned her head and watched him put on the condom. Observing him rolling the latex over his stiff penis turned out to be an arousing activity. After the way he'd thoroughly loved her, she was amazed she was still capable of being aroused.

He hadn't worn a condom any of the other times they'd made love, and she wondered if she'd feel the difference. They'd both trusted in her birth control pills, which had ultimately failed them. But she couldn't be sorry about getting pregnant. Even if Elizabeth ended up tearing them apart, she couldn't be sorry.

He slid back into bed beside her and turned on his side. His gaze locked with hers. She grew restless, wanting him again, but the ache was deeper this time. She no longer had that frantic craving for release. This time she wanted connection.

Still looking into her eyes, he took her chin in his hand. Then slowly he stroked down the curve of her throat, and his gaze followed the path of his hand as it swept past her collarbone and over the slope of her breast. His touch seemed to define the shape of her body as his palm glided past her hip and down her thigh. His penis twitched impatiently, yet he took his time, propping himself up on one arm so he could reach all the way to her ankles.

She'd never seen such intensity in his eyes. Under his scrutiny, she became self-conscious. She hadn't lost every ounce she'd gained with Elizabeth, and most days the few extra pounds felt good, womanly. Now she wasn't so sure. "I...guess I'm not quite the same as I—"

His voice trembled slightly. "You're perfect." He met her gaze and there was a sheen of moisture in his eyes. "And after how I treated you seventeen months ago, and even just now, accusing you of trying to trap me into marriage, you should have forbidden me ever to touch you again."

Her throat closed. He was so hard on himself, more judgmental than she could ever be. "Nat, don't—"

"But you let me touch you, let me love you, because you have a good and generous heart." He moved over her, his gaze holding hers. "And for that, I'm eternally grateful."

"I could never turn you away," she whispered.

"You should." He eased the tip of his penis inside her and closed his eyes. "God knows you should."

"I can't." She cupped his buttocks in her hands. "I want this as much as you."

He opened his eyes. "Then, besides being too generous, you're a fool, a bigger fool than I am. And I'm going to take advantage of that, Jess. One more time." He thrust forward and closed his eyes with a groan. "So sweet. Oh, Jess."

She dug her fingers into his buttocks and held him tight inside her. Yes, the condom made a difference, separating them in a way that seemed unfair. She wanted him flesh to flesh, as close as they'd been before. But she couldn't have that, and what she could have was very good indeed. He filled the emptiness that had tortured her ever since he left.

He opened his eyes, and they were blazing with passion. His voice was thick with restrained desire. "When I'm inside you like this, I own the world."

She stroked her hands up the knotted muscles of his back and slipped them around to cradle his beloved, bearded face. "So do I." Her smile quivered as she gazed up at him. "I thought this was going to be fast and furious."

"It will be, the minute I move. I just want to savor this part, the first time I push deep, and I'm leaning over you like this, looking into your eyes, watching them get all dark and soft, seeing your cheeks flush. And your freckles stand out."

"They do?"

"Yeah, and I've missed that so much. I've missed every crazy thing about you, Jess. Your herbal teas, your bossiness—"

"I'm not bossy."

He chuckled. "Yes, you are."

"I've missed your laugh." She felt his penis stir within her and knew he'd begin to move soon.

"I've missed your happy little moans." He eased down onto his elbows, so that his chest brushed her nipples. "Lace your fingers through mine," he murmured. "Like we used to do."

She knew exactly what he meant. It had been their favorite way of making love. She slipped her hands under his so they were palm to palm, fingers intertwined.

Looking deep into her eyes, he gripped her hands tightly in his. "I've missed the way your mouth opens, just a little, when I start stroking." He eased back and came forward again. "Like you want to be open...everywhere." He picked up the rhythm.

"I missed the look in your eyes when you're close to coming," she whispered breathlessly. "You look like a fierce warrior."

He pumped more vigorously, and his voice was hoarse. "Then I must look pretty fierce right now."

"Yes. Magnificent." The grip of his hands was almost painful, but she didn't care. His frantic desire drove her straight to the edge of the precipice with him.

"Oh, Jess." He gasped for breath as he plunged into her again and again. "Can you?"

"I'm there, Nat. Love me. Love me hard."

He groaned. "Oh, *Jess.*"

They came apart together, clutching each other wildly as their control shattered.

As they lay panting and spent, she caressed his sweat-soaked back. "Welcome home," she murmured.

ALL HIS LIFE people had accused Steven Pruitt of being an egghead. By now he was damn proud of the label. In fact, he figured that his eggheadedness was the key to making him enormously rich. Someday he'd be the one staying at the Waldorf. Right under Russell P. Franklin's nose.

In the meantime, he had to be patient. When he thought of the money he would wring out of Russell P. when this thing came down, he could be patient. Trailing Jessica wasn't so different from some of the investigative-reporting assignments he'd had. He'd never needed much sleep, and catnapping on a bench where he could keep tabs on the entrance to the hotel was uncomfortable but bearable.

Some people might think six months of trailing someone in order to kidnap them was too long. But they didn't understand the thrill of the chase. He hadn't understood it, either, until he'd begun following Jessica. Once he'd found out what a rush this cat-and-mouse game could give him, he'd decided to enjoy it for as long as his money lasted. He'd probably never get to feel this much like James Bond again in his life.

He ought to be good for another month or two. What a feeling of power he felt whenever he made her run. By now he knew her well, probably better than the guy she was shacked up with in the Waldorf.

The guy was an unexpected turn of events, but Steven didn't consider him a major obstacle. He might even be of some help. He and Jessica obviously had something going between them, and there was nothing like a little hanky-panky to make people careless. That was all Steven needed to make his dreams come true when he was finally ready to make the snatch—one careless moment.

A KNOCK AT THE HOTEL DOOR woke Nat from a dreamless sleep caused by pure exhaustion. He staggered out of bed, not quite sure where he was.

"Maid service," called a woman through the closed door.

Everything came back to him, and he glanced over at the bed to see if Jess was still in it. The bed was empty. He panicked. She'd left him after all. She didn't trust him not to call her parents and give her location away.

"Come back later!" he called to the maid. Then he heard water running and dashed into the bathroom to find Jess calmly brushing her teeth. Naked.

"What's wrong?" she asked around a mouthful of tooth-paste foam.

"I thought you'd taken off." He grabbed her and kissed her, foam and all. And just like that, once they were skin against skin once more, he was in the same condition he'd been ever since he and Jess had arrived in this hotel room. Apparently he'd stored up a lot of sexual tension in the past seventeen months, and he'd become very particular about who could relieve it. He'd narrowed the candidates down to one, as a matter of fact.

He filled both hands with her breasts. "Come back to bed," he coaxed between kisses.

"We need to call the ranch," she said.

"We will. But I need fortification first." A true statement. And despite her protest, she was responding, heating up like the blast furnace he knew she could be.

Her words came out breathy and excited. "We'll call right after?"

"We'll call right after. I promise. Please, Jess." He was begging and he didn't much care. Besides, it looked as if he could win this one, and making love to her one more time would give him courage for that phone call. He started backing his way out of the bathroom, bringing her with him. "Come in where the condoms are."

She tugged on him, and she'd found a very effective handle. "I have a better idea."

"There *is* no better idea." God, he loved it when she wrapped her fingers around his erection like that. He wondered if he should try some caveman tactics and throw her over his shoulder, except he hated to interfere with all that terrific fondling she was doing.

"Toothpaste," she whispered against his mouth.

"Yeah, I know." In his gusto to kiss her he'd smeared both of them with the foam. It was all over his beard and her chin. "I probably have it everywhere."

"Not quite." Leaning back, she grabbed her toothbrush from the counter where she'd tossed it, stuck it in her mouth and worked up another head of foam.

"What in hell are you—"

"Tell me if you like this."

Before he understood her intentions, she'd dropped to her knees and taken his penis in her toothpaste-filled mouth.

He gasped as cool tingling foam met hot pulsing flesh. Then he groaned in delight as she added embellishments with her tongue. Gripping the counter, he closed his eyes. Oh, this was good. This was very good. Heaven. He wanted it to last forever. His grip on the counter tightened as he trembled and fought for control.

Then he made the mistake of opening his eyes. The mirror running the full length of the counter reflected Jess, totally involved in her task. He came in a rush. The sensation was so intense that if he hadn't been holding on to the counter, he would have toppled over.

He stood there gasping and quivering as she licked him clean and slowly rose to kiss him gently on the mouth.

"How was it?" she murmured.

He sucked in a shaky breath. "Okay, I guess."

"Liar." She kissed him again. "I wasted you."

"You did." He managed to focus long enough to look into her laughing eyes. Then a really unpleasant thought occurred to him. "Where did you learn that?"

She chuckled. "I'm so glad you can be jealous, too."

The wonderful languor that had settled over him disappeared. He'd asked her last night if there *was* anyone else, but he didn't ask if there had *been* anybody else. He slid his hand behind her head and held it gently but firmly so she couldn't look away. "Where, Jess?"

Her expression wasn't the least bit evasive. Instead, she seemed extremely proud of herself. "I read it in a book."

His tension melted, and he smiled. "Oh."

"Unlike some people in this bathroom, I haven't even been naked with anyone since you left, unless you count my obstetrician, Cliff."

Nat wasn't sure he could tolerate even that thought. He didn't know where this possessiveness was coming from, but it was very strong. "Is he single?"

"No."

"Good."

She wrapped her arms around his waist and laid her cheek against his chest. "And now that we have that settled, can we call the ranch?"

He knew the time had come. Although he didn't look forward to talking with Sebastian about the situation, he couldn't postpone it any longer. "Okay."

"Before you do, I need to tell you something."

His gut tightened. "What?"

"I wanted to make sure I was the one to tell you about Elizabeth, so I didn't tell Sebastian you're her father. When you call, he'll be hearing that news for the first time."

Nat grimaced. If he'd been dreading the phone call before, he purely hated the thought of having to make it now.

CHAPTER SIX

SEBASTIAN DANIELS got down on all fours so his wife, Matty, could prop Elizabeth on his back.

"Giddyap, horsey!" Matty said.

Elizabeth chortled and bounced as Sebastian whinnied and started off around the living room. Matty walked alongside to steady the baby and make sure she didn't fall.

Sebastian hated having only one week in three to spend with Elizabeth, but it was the only fair arrangement, and Sebastian valued fairness. When Jessica had named him the baby's godfather, she'd also included Travis Evans and Boone Connor in that honor. The kicker was that each of them thought they might be Elizabeth's daddy. All three of them had been pretty drunk the night of the avalanche reunion party, and each of them vaguely remembered making a pass at Jessica, who had stayed sober and driven them back to their cabin.

Ever since Jessica had left Elizabeth on Sebastian's doorstep eight months ago, the men had hotly debated the baby's parentage. Finally they'd submitted to paternity testing and discovered none of them was the baby's father. Trouble was, they and their wives had become so darned attached to the little cutie-pie. Until the real father showed up, or Jessica came back to clear up the mystery, they'd agreed to take turns with Elizabeth.

The baby trade always took place on Saturday morning, and whenever he picked up Elizabeth, Sebastian was on top of the world. The following Saturday, which happened to be today, was a different story. But both he and Matty tried to keep their sadness from Elizabeth.

Besides having to deal with Elizabeth leaving, Matty was extremely hormonal in this fifth month of her pregnancy. He loved the way her belly had begun to round out, and she seemed softer all over. She wore her blond hair loose all the time now, and Sebastian could barely keep his hands off her. But he'd noticed she could get weepy at the drop of a hat, and this morning he'd noticed her swiping at tears when she thought he wasn't looking.

Elizabeth seemed oblivious to their distress. Decked out in denim overalls and a bright red shirt, she laughed and bounced happily on Sebastian's back. Every so often she kicked his ribs with her moccasined feet, which was his cue to snort and pick up the pace. His knees were sore and his ribs were getting tender, but he didn't care a bit. He hoped that just this once Travis and Gwen would be late.

They weren't. The doorbell chimed at eleven, right on schedule.

"That'll be them." Matty lifted the baby off Sebastian's back.

"Travis never used to so damn punctual," Sebastian grumbled as he got to his feet and brushed off the knees of his jeans.

"I think it's Gwen's doing. Marriage to her has really domesticated that man." Matty propped Elizabeth against her hip and started toward the door.

"Here, let me take her," Sebastian said, hurrying after her. "You shouldn't be carrying—"

"I'm fine. Let me keep her a little longer," Matty said, a slight quiver in her voice.

Sebastian backed off. When she got that little tremble in her voice, he knew she was close to tears. He'd adjusted to her frequent crying, but she hated turning into a water faucet all the time. She'd cried more in the last couple of months than in the entire ten years they'd been neighbors, before they got married, and he knew it embarrassed her to be so emotional. It made him feel manly and strong, but he didn't dare tell her that, or she might whack him with the frying pan.

He was doing everything he could to stay on Matty's good side, because then he could enjoy one of the other side effects of pregnancy. Much to his surprise, Matty wanted to make love more often than ever, and he was quite happy to oblige.

He thought about that as Travis and Gwen came in, all smiles because they were about to make off with Elizabeth. Once they left, he'd coax Matty back to the bedroom. A hot session in the old four-poster would help ease the pain of having to be without the little girl for two weeks.

Gwen was dressed to emphasize her Cheyenne ancestry, with her long dark braid and a fringed outfit. Sebastian had seen the combination on her before, but for some reason he couldn't put his finger on, she seemed different today. Maybe she was trying out some new brand of makeup or something. Gwen was much more into that sort of thing than Matty.

Travis was his usual debonair self, strolling in with one hand behind his back. "Hey, Lizzie!" he said. "Lookee here!" He brought his hand out from hiding and waggled the raccoon puppet he held. "Hello, Mizz Lizzie," he said in a falsetto. "Wanna come home with me?"

Elizabeth squealed and wiggled impatiently as she held out both arms toward the puppet. Matty relinquished her to Travis.

Sebastian had always been a little jealous of the way Travis could charm the baby in two seconds. "Show-off," he muttered.

Travis whipped the puppet's head around toward Sebastian. "Spoilsport," he said in falsetto.

"Okay, you two," Gwen said, stepping forward. "Play nice."

"We always do," Sebastian said with a wicked grin aimed at Travis. Then he looked at Gwen. "Say, are you trying out a new shade of lipstick?"

"No." Gwen seemed taken aback.

"Lipstick?" Matty chuckled. "You are the last man on earth I expected to comment on a woman's lipstick color."

"I just think Gwen looks different today. I thought it might be the lipstick."

Gwen gave him a startled glance. "You really think I look different?"

"I'm probably imagining things."

Travis gazed fondly at his wife. "Oh, I wouldn't say that."

"Then there *is* something different."

Gwen looked at her husband and smiled. "In a manner of speaking."

Matty figured it out before Sebastian did, and she hollered with delight as she threw her arms around Gwen. "When? When did you find out?"

"About a half hour ago," Gwen said, hugging her back. "We wanted you two to be the first to know."

Sebastian eyed Travis and tried to pretend great seriousness. But inside he was jumping for joy. To his way of thinking, the more babies around, the better. "Seems to me the last time this happened, the guy responsible got tossed in a snowbank," he said. Travis and Boone had lost no time wrestling him out the door the night Matty announced she was pregnant.

"See, I plan these things better than you, Daniels." Travis looked ready to burst his buttons with pride. "I waited until the snow melted and I had a baby in my arms. Plus, you don't have Boone around to help, so I reckon I'm pretty safe."

"Don't count your chickens, buddy. The day's not over yet."

"This is so wonderful," Matty said. "Does your mother know, Travis?"

"Not yet. Like Gwen said, you two are the first."

"Luann will be out of her head with happiness," Matty said. "I'd love to see the look on her face when—" She stopped as the kitchen phone rang. "Excuse me a minute," she said as she started toward the kitchen. "That might be the vet. Stay right there until I get back, okay?"

"They will," Sebastian assured her. "Anybody for coffee? We have leaded and unleaded around here these days, so we can handle your new regime with no problem, Gwen."

"Thanks, but as soon as Matty gets off the phone, Travis and I need to get home. We have a ton of chores waiting, and besides, Luann counts the minutes until she sees Elizabeth again."

"I can relate to that," Sebastian said. "I—"

"Sebastian?" Matty hurried back in, a smile on her face. "You'll never guess. It's Nat! He's in New York!"

"He's back?"

Matty nodded.

"Hallelujah," Travis murmured.

"About time," Sebastian said. "This is turning out to be a real red-letter day." Relief and happiness washed through him as he started toward the kitchen. Nat's decision to help war orphans made some kind of crazy sense, given his background, but Sebastian had worried about his safety. They all had. Nat pretended to be so together, but inside he was one of the walking wounded. As a result, he took chances he shouldn't take, and it would be just like him to get himself killed doing something stupid and heroic. Apparently he'd escaped that fate…again.

"Tell him to get his sorry ass back to Colorado," Travis

called after him. "I want the sheepskin vest I loaned him, and I want it before the snow flies."

"I'll tell him," Sebastian said. He was grinning as he picked up the receiver and put it to his ear. "Hey, you crazy son of a gun. What the hell do you mean staying over there so long? We thought you'd gone native!"

"Hey, Sebastian." Nat's voice was thick with emotion. "It's good to hear your voice again."

"I'm glad, because I plan to run up your long-distance bill while I chew on your ear for being gone so damn long on that extended vacation of yours. When you finally show up at the Rocking D, I suggest you bring some identification. We've all forgotten what you look like."

"Yeah, I know I was gone too long." Nat sighed.

Sebastian's grin faded. He'd expected at least a chuckle out of Nat. A chilly finger of anxiety ran down his backbone. "Are you okay? Don't tell me you got shot up over—"

"No, no. I'm fine. But…look, Jess is here with me."

Sebastian almost dropped the phone. "She *is?*" He felt as if somebody had short-circuited his brain. "You mean *our* Jessica?" he repeated, his mind still not operating on all cylinders.

"Yeah. And that baby of hers you're watching is… mine."

"*Yours?*" Sebastian roared. "What the hell do you mean, *yours?* You weren't even *there.*"

Matty hurried into the kitchen followed closely by Gwen and Travis, holding the baby. They all stared at Sebastian, and Elizabeth started to fuss.

"Yeah, I was there, the night before you arrived," Nat said. "Is that her?"

The night before. Sebastian couldn't figure how Nat had been there and nobody had known about it. "Is what her?"

"I hear a baby. Is that her?"

Sebastian felt shell-shocked. And absolutely sure that Nat Grady was not Elizabeth's father. He couldn't be. "Yeah, that's her. But I don't know why you think—"

"I don't think. I know. After the avalanche I started seeing Jess. We had a...relationship...for almost a year, and—"

Pain sliced through Sebastian. "You were seeing Jessica for an entire year and you didn't tell me? I thought we were friends!"

"I'm sorry. I should have trusted you more. Should have trusted all of you more. But I was afraid you'd be after me to make a commitment, and I didn't think that was going to happen, so I asked Jess to keep it between the two of us."

Anger followed on the heels of Sebastian's sense of betrayal. Matty came forward, as if to offer her support, and he waved her off. Later he'd cling to Matty like there was no tomorrow, but at the moment he needed to concentrate on this conversation and make sure he understood what Nat was telling him. "Go on," he said to Nat in a tight voice.

"The week before the avalanche reunion party I went up to Aspen to spend some time with Jess before the rest of you arrived. The night before you guys came up, Jess and I had a big fight. She wanted to end the secrecy."

"Imagine that."

Nat sounded desperate. "She wanted marriage and a family, Sebastian! I knew I couldn't do that."

"Then you should have been a wee bit more careful, shouldn't you?" All the muscles in Sebastian's body clenched in denial. Shifting Elizabeth around every week wasn't a great solution, but at least he hadn't lost her completely. Now he might. He couldn't bear to look at Matty, and especially not at Elizabeth, so he stared down at the worn linoleum.

"Yes," Nat said quietly. "I should have been more careful."

"So now what?" Sebastian asked dully. "Are you coming back to pick her up? Is that what you called to tell me?"

"No. I'm still not sure what to do about the baby. I'll provide all the financial support Jess needs, of course, but I'm not a fit person to take on a little kid, as we all know."

"Why not? You've been over there taking care of nobody *but* little kids!"

"They had nothing. No one. And there were plenty of other people around, so I never worried that I'd do the wrong thing. But put me in a house with my own kid, and I don't trust myself."

"That's pure, unadulterated bullsh—" Sebastian caught himself as he remembered that Elizabeth was in the room. He'd vowed not to use those words around her, because in another seven or eight months she might start talking, and he didn't want…. Then he realized that in another seven or eight months Elizabeth could be gone.

"Call it what you want," Nat said. "It's the truth as I see it. I'm bringing Jess back to her baby, and we'll take it from there."

Sebastian fought so many conflicting emotions he couldn't think straight. He couldn't imagine a man turning away from Elizabeth, and he took it as a personal affront. Yet he wouldn't want a man to claim her if he wasn't planning to be an A-number-one dad. "When will you be here?"

"That's just it. I'm not sure. We might have to take a roundabout route. Jess has someone on her trail, somebody who's apparently trying to kidnap her. That's why she left the baby with you."

"Good God. Why would they want to kidnap Jessica?"

"Ever hear of a guy named Russell P. Franklin?"

"Why, sure I—" Then it all clicked into place. "Well, damn." He'd always suspected Jessica had come from money. Maybe it was the way she held a fork, or her posture, or her choice of words. Sebastian hadn't dreamed how *much* money, though.

He glanced over at Elizabeth in sudden fear. The child he loved so fiercely was an heiress, and that was potentially life-threatening. "Is the baby in danger?"

Travis frowned and wrapped his arms tighter around Elizabeth.

"Apparently the kidnapper doesn't know about the baby," Nat said. "Neither do Jess's parents. Now that Jess has been separated from Elizabeth for six months, she thinks it's safe to come back and see her." Nat lowered his voice. "She needs to, Sebastian. This has been really tough on her."

It's been tough on all of us, Sebastian thought. *And it doesn't promise to get any easier.* But complaining wouldn't get them anywhere. "Has she notified the police about this?"

"No. That would bring her parents into it. According to her, they'd swoop in and bring the baby back to New York to live on their estate. They could probably swing it, too, considering the legal firepower they have. Jess doesn't want that."

"I wouldn't want that, either," Sebastian said. "Unless it's our only choice to keep Elizabeth safe."

"I'd rather catch the bastard and not have to worry about him," Nat said.

Sebastian heaved a sigh. "Finally we have an area of agreement." Then he paused to think. "It's mighty strange that he's been following her all this time and hasn't snatched her yet."

"I've thought about that, too. Either he's crazy or inept."

"Let's hope he's inept. I don't suppose you have a weapon on you."

"You know I hate guns," Nat said.

"Yeah, I know. Listen, get here as best you can and as soon as you can. Be careful. Once you arrive, we'll find a way through this."

Nat didn't respond for a moment. Then he cleared his throat. "You're a better friend to me than I deserve."

Still smarting from Nat's betrayal, Sebastian was tempted to agree, but then he remembered the stories Nat had told of his childhood. Thinking of the cruelty Nat had endured made compassion easier to find. "You've always been too hard on yourself, buddy," he said. "Come on home and we'll straighten everything out."

"Home," Nat said, his voice husky. "That's how I think of it, too. Listen, Jess wants to ask you about the baby. Here she is."

Sebastian braced himself.

"Sebastian?" Jessica sounded very unsure of herself. "How…how is she?"

"Good." Sebastian discovered that the lump in his throat made talking difficult. "Big. Growing. She has four teeth."

"Four. Wow."

Sebastian could hear her swallow. Her struggle to stay composed touched him. "This must have been a nightmare for you," he said softly.

"Yeah," she murmured. "I hope you can forgive me for all I've put you through, but I couldn't think what else to do. And I didn't realize Nat would be gone so long."

"No kidding. None of us did."

"Is she…what color are her eyes now?"

"Blue." And now Sebastian could see it. They were Nat's eyes. "She has a sock monkey named Bruce," he added, not sure why he'd said it. "She dotes on that silly monkey."

"She does? That's…so cute. I wish—" Jessica broke off with a little sob. "Here's—here's Nat," she choked out.

Nat's voice was rough with emotion. "We'll be there as soon as we possibly can. Goodbye, buddy."

"Take care, Nat." His heart heavy, Sebastian slowly hung up the phone and turned to the little cluster of people waiting in the kitchen doorway. They all looked anxious except for Elizabeth. She'd stopped fussing and was playing happily with the raccoon puppet Travis had brought her.

Sebastian's chest grew tight as he looked at the baby. He'd known life couldn't go on indefinitely like this. He'd told himself hundreds of times that someday Jessica would turn up. But the longer she'd stayed away, the more he'd built a case in his mind for challenging her right to Elizabeth. Now he could see that she'd stayed away for a good reason, an honorable reason. She'd tortured herself in order to protect her baby, and he wasn't about to challenge her claim now. And that meant his days with Elizabeth were numbered.

"I think we'd better get Boone and Shelby over here," he said.

JESSICA HUDDLED on the bed and tried not to cry. No matter how hard she worked at it, she couldn't picture her little baby with four teeth. Four. And blue, blue eyes instead of the smoky gray-blue they'd been at two months.

Elizabeth was so different now, but all Jessica could imagine were tiny hands, impossibly tiny fingernails, a gummy smile. She didn't look like that anymore. And she'd found a favorite toy, a monkey named Bruce. Jessica had missed it all.

Nat hung up the phone and put his arm around her. "It'll be okay," he said gently.

"Will it?" She looked at him through eyes blurred with tears. "She's changed so much. If someone walked by me on the street holding Elizabeth, I probably wouldn't recognize her!''

"Sure you would." He gave her a comforting squeeze. "I'll bet she hasn't changed all that much."

The knot of misery tightened in her stomach. "Maybe that's true," she said, pushing each word out as if it were made of lead, "but even if I didn't know her right away, that's not really what I'm afraid of."

"Then what?"

She gulped back tears. "Oh, Nat, after all this time…*she* won't recognize *me!*"

CHAPTER SEVEN

JESSICA LONGED to hop on a plane and be in Colorado by nightfall, but in order to do that she'd have to use her real identity at the ticket counter. She didn't want to risk it.

"I think you'll have to rent us a car," she said as they ate a room-service breakfast, she wearing the hotel robe and Nat in jeans and a T-shirt. "I'll be glad to pay for—"

"Don't you dare start that." He put down his coffee cup and glared at her.

"Start what?"

"Assuming all the responsibility."

Even when he got gruff and bristly, she couldn't stop the surge of lust she felt every time she looked at him. When he talked, the movement of his mouth reminded her of his kiss, and everything he touched reminded her of his caress. "But I'm the one who should have known about antibiotics and how they affected birth control pills," she said. "If I'd been smarter, this wouldn't have happened."

"If you'd been smarter, you wouldn't have been involved with me in the first place." His tone was bitter. "I should have been proud to tell everyone that you...that you cared for me. Instead, I kept you hidden in the shadows."

"You didn't hold a gun to my head, Nat. I stuck around because I wanted to." She'd noticed that they were both avoiding using the word *love* to describe their feelings for each other.

For her part, she hesitated because she didn't want to saddle him with even more guilt. With Nat, it was probably a way to maintain some distance, despite their obvious sexual need for each other. He might figure that if he claimed to love her, she would expect certain things.

"Nevertheless," he persisted, "if our relationship had been out in the open, you might have gotten some advice from a girlfriend about those antibiotics."

"But then there would have been no Elizabeth."

"My point exactly."

Jessica could no longer contemplate a world without her baby in it, and the fact that Nat could imagine such a thing shocked her. She put down her fork and leaned toward him. "We need to get a few things straight. I don't regret one single minute I spent with you. I had a fabulous time. And I especially don't regret that I became pregnant with your child. But I assume you're not happy about the baby."

"You assume right."

Although she'd been expecting him to agree with her, his statement still hurt. She hurried on, not wanting him to know it. "That's why I want to take all the responsibility, as long as I can do it. I don't want Elizabeth's needs handled by a man who begrudges her existence."

"I didn't say that, damn it!"

She stood and tightened the belt on her robe. "Yes, you did. Do you want the shower first, or should I take it? We need to get on the road."

"Not until we settle this we don't." He pushed back his chair and nearly upset the breakfast tray as he got to his feet. "When you say I begrudge her existence, you make it sound like I'm upset because of the inconvenience. I don't give a damn about the inconvenience! What I regret more than I can say is bringing a child into the world by accident, when I have zero confidence in my abilities to be a father to that child."

So they were back to that. But things had changed since the last time they'd had this argument. She played her trump card. "If that's so, then what were you doing in some hellhole taking care of *orphans?*"

He flinched, and then his voice rose. "Maybe I was testing myself, okay? Maybe I wanted to see if I'd have the urge to get violent with those children."

She thought there was a lot more to his work with the refugees than that, but she wasn't going to question him on that point now. "And did you get violent?"

He looked away from her to gaze out the window. "No."

"Then you must know you'll be fine."

He swung back to face her. "I don't know that! You'd have to be a monster to lay a hand on those kids. They'd been through so much, patience was easy." He ran a hand over his face. "Some of them, especially the boys, tried so hard to be tough, but you could see that inside they were terrified."

Like you were as a child. Gazing at his anxious expression, she could picture the frightened little boy he must have been. She wanted to wrap her arms around him and let him know he'd never have to be that frightened again, but she didn't dare trespass on that minefield-strewn land. "It must have been terrible," she murmured.

"It was." He stared into the distance.

She guessed he'd seen his own experience in every child's face. Nat might as well have been orphaned, with no mother and totally at the mercy of a violent father who didn't know how to love. Living with a father like Hank Grady might not have been so different from living in a war zone. "You wouldn't have to worry about being violent around Elizabeth," she said gently. "I'll be there."

He snapped out of his daze and glanced at her. He looked so heartbreakingly vulnerable. "I don't know how to do this, Jess. With the orphans, it was easy. Get them clothes, get them food, find them a bed. Comb through the donations coming in and look for a stuffed animal they could hold.''

The picture of him doing that brought a lump to her throat. ''And did you hug them when they got scared?''

''Well, sure, but—''

''And when they were sad, did you tell them funny stories to make them laugh?''

''Once I learned the language, but—''

''And if they did something wonderful, if they were kind or generous or brave or smart, did you tell them they were great?''

''Of course.''

''Nat, that's all there is to it, whether you're talking about a refugee child in a faraway country or Elizabeth. That's all you have to do.''

''The hell it is! What if they do something stupid? How do you keep them from doing dumb things?''

She thought about her restrictive childhood in which she'd hardly been allowed to make a mistake. She'd broken free of that, and maybe she'd been stupid when she accidentally got pregnant. But as a result she had Elizabeth.

''Got you there, haven't I?'' he said.

She met his gaze. ''I think, within reason, you have to let them be stupid.''

He snorted in derision. ''Yeah, so they can get themselves killed, and maybe somebody else in the process.'' He said the words so automatically he seemed to be reciting a memorized lesson.

''Is that how your father justified beating you to a bloody pulp? That he was keeping you from killing yourself?''

''Sometimes.'' He glanced at her. ''Sometimes I think it was for the pure enjoyment of it.''

Talk about monsters, she thought. ''You have to know you're nothing like him.''

He didn't reply as he continued to hold her gaze.

"Nat, you're not like him! I'm sure of it."

"Better go take your shower."

She recognized the wall he'd just put up between them. She'd seen him construct it often enough in the year they'd been seeing each other. Once that wall went up, she had no hope of breaking through to him. But he hadn't seen Elizabeth yet. Jessica clung to the hope that the baby, *his* baby, might be the one thing that could breach that wall.

"Okay," she said.

"I'll call and arrange for a rental car, and I don't want to hear about you paying for it."

She hesitated. Letting him pay for things seemed almost as if she'd be giving him the easy way out. She didn't want his money. She wanted his participation in raising Elizabeth, or she wanted nothing.

"Please, Jess." His mask slipped a little. "It's what I can do for now. Can you accept that?"

She took a deep breath and nodded. "Okay. For now."

"Good. I'll call and get us a car."

As he walked over to the phone, she went into the bathroom and started the shower.

Nat was liable to break her heart all over again, she thought as she slipped out of the robe, tied her hair into a knot on top of her head and stepped under the hot spray. She wanted to believe that he would see Elizabeth and fall in love with the baby, so deeply in love that he'd be willing to rethink his position about marriage and children.

But that might not happen. He'd walked away once, and if the baby scared him enough, he would walk away again.

With that possibility hanging over her head, she probably shouldn't continue to make love to him. She was only setting herself up for a worse fall if she became accustomed to his sweet loving on a regular basis. If he couldn't cherish Elizabeth as she did, then she'd have to tell him goodbye.

But she'd better let him know they wouldn't be making

love. She needed to tell him before they started on their trip to Colorado. Considering her behavior up to this point, he would be justified in expecting to continue their physical relationship. After all, she hadn't made sleeping with him contingent on anything. She'd simply fallen into his arms at the first opportunity.

She didn't want to set up contingencies for when they would make love again, as if he had to agree to marry her before he could enjoy her body. That was too much like blackmail. But she had to create some distance between them. Surely he'd understand that she was only protecting both of them from worse heartache.

She turned off the shower, fumbled for a towel on the rack nearby and dried herself while standing in the warmth of the leftover steam. That's when she heard the steady snip of a pair of scissors.

Wrapping the towel securely around herself, she stepped out of the shower to find Nat standing there wearing nothing but his low-slung jeans. He'd propped a wastebasket up on the counter to catch the hair from his beard as he clipped it very short.

Apparently he'd just finished that part, because he set the wastebasket on the floor, lathered up the remaining stubble and picked up his razor. The spicy scent of his shaving cream brought back vivid memories of all the times she'd watched him do this little chore. Often he'd capped off a shaving session by making love to her and rubbing his baby-soft chin all over her body.

Yet she missed that beard already. Then she remembered the vow of abstinence she'd just taken in the shower. Whether he had a beard or not meant nothing to her now. "I see you're shaving it off," she said.

"Yep. I want to go out of here looking different from the way I came in, in case your friend saw us together."

"That's a good idea." And it was, but she still struggled

with disappointment as he stroked the razor over his chin. On the other hand, she liked seeing his strong jaw emerge from under the lather. And his skin would be very smooth after this first shave. He'd be heaven to kiss, all spicy scented and silky to the touch.

As he paused to meet her gaze in the mirror, his eyes seemed bluer than ever before. "If you stand there much longer with that look on your face, you won't be wearing that towel anymore," he said.

A familiar tingle of desire settled between her thighs. Keeping her vow wouldn't be easy. "We need to talk about that."

He continued to watch her as he shaved. "I wasn't thinking of having a conversation."

A deep, trembling need seized her. "All things considered, maybe it would be better if we didn't make love anymore."

He paused and narrowed his eyes. "Ever?"

"Well, at least not until...we know where we stand with...with each other, and the baby, and everything." That sounded like a contingency, after all, but she really didn't mean it that way.

"Mmm." He continued shaving, but his hand didn't seem perfectly steady. "Are you trying to bribe me?"

"Absolutely not!"

"Might work." He shifted his weight and stopped leaning against the sink. "I want you pretty damn bad."

"I don't operate that way." Heat sizzled through her veins as she realized he'd moved back from the sink because the edge of the counter was pressing into his erection. She swallowed. "I'm trying to think of both of us. Maybe we should protect ourselves."

"It might have been better if you hadn't made that speech while you're standing there wrapped only in a towel. Funny how when someone says you can't have something, that's the only thing in the world you want."

So did she. Right this minute. "I think it's for the best, don't you?"

"Jess, guys *never* think going without sex is for the best. But if that's the way you want it, that's the way it'll be."

Her glance took in the fit of his jeans from behind. She'd forgotten what a fabulous view that was. She licked dry lips. "That's the way I want it," she said.

"Then quit checking me out," he said in a low voice, "and go get dressed."

"Right." Heart pounding, she left the bathroom.

STEVEN DAMN NEAR MISSED Jessica leave the hotel. He'd known she'd have on another one of her crazy wigs. It was blond this time. He got a real high out of knowing she was going through all this trouble hoping to fool him, especially when he knew she'd lose in the end. The fact that he was playing with her gave him a buzz that was almost sexual.

Once he had her and got the money from Russell P., the challenge of the thing would be over. Maybe he'd be too rich to care about challenges at that point, but he wasn't altogether sure about that.

Her boyfriend might present some real obstacles, though, and the prospect of a new player in the game got his blood pumping. The boyfriend was obviously sharper than Steven had given him credit for.

Steven had been keeping an eye out for a scruffy guy with a beard. He'd noticed the tall, clean-shaven man who'd come out to claim a rental car, but he hadn't made the connection because everything was smooth about this character. His suit and hat were technically western in style, but the look was far more polished than Steven had ever seen on a cowboy. Even the longish hair looked avant-garde. He hadn't realized it was Jessica's boyfriend until she hurried out and hopped in the car with him.

In the past six months Steven had become an excellent carjacker. He had an instinct that allowed him to spot a car with the passenger door unlocked, and he found one now. No one on the busy street noticed when he got into the green sedan and quietly put a toy gun against the driver's ribs.

Once he'd explained to the gasping, quaking man that all he wanted was for him to follow the white rental car, the guy complied with Steven's request, as everyone so far had had the good sense to do. Once they were on the open road, he launched into his well-rehearsed covert-operations speech and showed the driver that the gun wasn't real. His altered press card looked official enough for most people. In all his carjackings, he'd never had to pull the .32 out of his boot.

He always made the drivers feel as if they were part of something really big, something top secret and connected with national security. When Jessica and her boyfriend stopped for gas, he let both driver and car go back home and he located another chauffeur. The routine worked like a charm, as it had for the last six months. So far no one had ever been hurt. Steven took pride in that.

NAT DROVE ALL DAY and into the night, ready to get this trip over with. Jess offered to take the wheel, but he knew once she did that, he'd fall asleep. Jet lag was playing havoc with his system, but he didn't want to sleep while she was driving and allow her to be at the mercy of whatever dangers were out there.

At a diner where they'd stopped for dinner, she'd said she thought the guy was around. She hadn't seen him, but she'd claimed to have developed a sixth sense about him, and Nat was willing to believe that. He'd kept his eyes open, but the man would be hard to spot. Jess had described him as average build with brown hair. He could look like a million other guys.

The best plan seemed to be to keep driving. They didn't talk much, for which Nat was glad. Even the sound of her voice got him hot. Her every movement was like the flick of a match against the dry tinder of his need. He wasn't sure how he'd travel with her all the way to Colorado without making love to her again. Exhaustion would help, he decided, so he pushed himself until he was afraid he was a hazard on the road. "We need to stop," he said about two in the morning as he took the exit to a motel right near the highway.

"Of course." She stretched her arms over her head and yawned. "I was beginning to think you'd decided to drive nonstop from New York to Colorado."

He pulled up in front of the motel lobby. "I didn't trust myself to stop for the night until I was totally wiped out."

"Oh."

He could see from her expression that he didn't have to explain himself any further. "We're getting one room, for the safety factor, but you don't have to worry about me attacking you. I'm too beat."

"I've never worried about you attacking me."

He glanced at her. "Maybe you should." He wasn't crazy about the blond wig and the elaborate makeup she'd included as part of her disguise, but in another way it was a turn-on. He'd never made love to her as a heavily made-up blonde, and it might be kind of fun. Her stretchy zebra-print dress was too tight to be fashionable, but it sure fueled the imagination. "Come on in with me. I don't want to leave you alone in the car."

"Don't worry. I wouldn't stay behind." As they started toward the lobby's front entrance, she chuckled. "You

know what they're going to think, when we come in at this
time of the night, with me looking like a—''

"Hooker?" he finished for her.

"I was going to say high-class call girl," she said primly.

"Hooker," he said, and opened the door for her.
Damned if his libido wasn't kicking in now that he was out
of the car and moving around. He wasn't tired enough.
Maybe there was no such thing as too tired where Jess was
concerned, especially when she was decked out like this.

But he didn't think he could drive another mile, so he
was stuck with this frustrating situation. He approached the
reception desk, where a sleepy-looking young man gave
Jess the once-over as she crossed the lobby to glance
through a rack of travel brochures. She'd slipped on her
coat over the stretchy dress, but hadn't bothered to button
it. She was dynamite.

Nat restrained the impulse to challenge the clerk's obvious assumption. He'd be wasting his breath, anyway. No
matter what he said, the clerk would think he knew exactly
what was going on.

Sure enough, the guy turned a coconspirator's gaze on
Nat, as if congratulating him man to man on his score.
"You folks need a room?" he asked, barely controlling a
smirk.

"Two double beds," Nat said. As if that would make a
difference.

"Oo-kay." The clerk typed a few things into his computer and took Nat's credit card. "Need help with luggage?" he asked as he slid the keys across the counter. He
looked as if he didn't expect luggage was part of this deal.

"No, thanks," Nat said. "We can handle it."

"Okay. Have a nice night." The clerk stopped short of
licking his lips when he gazed at Jess.

Once again Nat bit back a reprimand. Given the look of
things, the clerk couldn't be blamed for his behavior.

"We're all set," Nat said to Jess. "It's in the back. We'll drive around."

"Fine."

He held the door for her, and as she went through it looking for all the world like his playmate for the night, his temper began to fray. Then when he held the car door for her she managed to show quite a bit of leg getting in. She'd better not be teasing him. He closed the door with a little more force than was necessary.

"You slammed that door. Is anything wrong?" she asked as he got in and started the engine.

"Nope." He backed out and pulled around to a parking spot near their room on the second floor.

"Your face is all scrunched up, like you're upset about something."

"Just tired." He'd be damned if he'd admit that he felt randier than a teenager paging through a smuggled porn magazine. He was supposed to be more in control of himself than that, but damn it, she hadn't made life easy for him, wearing that getup of hers.

"I can understand you being tired. I wish you'd let me drive some of the time."

"It's better if I do it." He got out of the car and opened the back door so he could haul out their two backpacks.

She was beside him instantly. "Nat, let me carry my—"

"I've got it." He knew he sounded unfriendly. But he was too tired to be friendly and still keep his hands off of her.

"Okay." She lifted both hands and backed off.

He slung a backpack over each shoulder and they trudged up a set of outside stairs to the second floor of the motel. All the while, Nat was picturing that cozy room with two very available beds in it. He handed a key to Jess and she opened the door and flicked on the wall switch.

Moving into the plain but serviceable room, she glanced

around. "It might not be the Waldorf, but it's nicer than some of the places I've stayed in recently." She took off her coat and laid it on a chair. Then she walked over to the window and reached for the cord on the drapes.

He shoved the door closed with his foot and stood there holding the backpacks and watching those zebra stripes wiggle as she moved. Damn, but she was hot stuff. He slung the backpacks on the floor and when he spoke, his voice was razor-sharp. "Quit fiddling around and pick your bed. We need to get some sleep."

Surprise lifted her eyebrows as she turned toward him. "You are upset."

He laid his hat brim side up on the dresser and stripped off his suit coat. "I don't suppose you could have organized a different disguise for today," he said, an edge of sarcasm in his voice. He wanted the words back. He hated sarcasm. His father had used it all the time. Stress brought out those traits in him, which was why he worried about what he'd be like around a kid of his own.

She finished pulling the drapes closed. "What do you mean?"

He threw his suit coat on the nearest bed. "When you climbed into the taxi last night, you looked like a bag lady. Under the circumstances, couldn't you have come up with something more like that for this trip?"

"Circumstances? Oh! *Those* circumstances."

He allowed his anger to build. Maybe blowing off steam this way would keep him from doing something crude and unforgivable. "I mean, first of all you announce that we're not having sex, and then you put on a dress that looks like it came from Frederick's of Hollywood. Don't you think that's a little unfair?"

"For your information, I consider your outfit equally unfair."

"Mine?" He held out both arms and looked down at the

pearl buttons on his black western shirt. "What's wrong with mine?"

"When you said this morning that you had to go out and pick up a few things, I had no idea you were planning to buy that suit."

He'd been proud of the fact he'd found something decent to wear, given the short time he had to look for some clothes. He'd left all his spare shirts and jeans with the refugees, keeping only the sheepskin vest that belonged to Travis and the clothes on his back. On his quick shopping expedition that morning, he'd been glad to find something on short notice that he could actually wear once he started dealing with clients again. "What's wrong with it?"

"The cut of those western pants is so…blatant."

"They fit. What's the crime in buying pants that fit?"

"They fit like a glove, you mean! I've been watching you all day in those pants, and all I want to do is…" She paused, her color high. "Never mind what I want to do."

Oh, yeah. If she cracked first, then she couldn't blame him, could she? He began unsnapping his shirt. "You're the one who made the rules, darlin'," he said softly.

CHAPTER EIGHT

BOONE CONNOR HEARD the clock chime two-thirty in the morning as he lay staring into the darkness thinking about all that Sebastian and Travis had told him today. On the one hand, he was glad Elizabeth's father wasn't some stranger. On the other, it hurt to think that Nat hadn't seen fit to tell them that he was involved with Jessica for an entire year.

And the most troubling part of the news was that Nat wasn't enthusiastic about being a daddy to Elizabeth. Boone knew about Nat's crummy childhood and his fear that he wouldn't make a good father, but he should have tried to overcome that fear, in Boone's estimation. And marry Jessica, while he was at it.

But whether Nat decided to cooperate or not, Jessica was coming back to get her baby, which meant Boone wouldn't have the pleasure of playing daddy to Elizabeth every third week. He didn't like to think about that too much. He'd taken the little girl into his heart, and letting her go was going to be one of the toughest things he'd ever done.

Thank God he had Shelby and Josh to ease the pain. With a sigh he rolled to his side and gazed at his wife sleeping beside him. He couldn't see her clearly in the faint light, but he could see her clearly enough in his heart. He'd never known he could be this happy.

Having Shelby was wonderful enough, but now that they'd officially adopted her nephew Josh, Boone's world was nearly perfect. Josh's sociopathic father was behind bars awaiting trial for murder, and with the evidence against him, he wasn't likely to bother Shelby and Josh again.

Boone cherished the notion of having his own little family and thought Nat was a fool to turn his back on the chance to have one, too. A family steadied a man.

Shelby's hand, so small and delicate, lay on the pillow beside her cheek. Boone stroked it with the tip of his finger. He still couldn't believe that a tiny thing like Shelby wanted anything to do with a big lug like him.

Luckily she wanted a *lot* to do with him. They were trying for a baby and hoping for a girl. Another baby wouldn't replace Elizabeth, of course, but Josh had loved having a little sister. Boone and Shelby had both figured the day would come when they'd have to give up Elizabeth, so another baby seemed like a very good idea.

Trying to get Shelby pregnant had been an extremely satisfying project, although Boone was a tad bit worried about whether carrying his child would be too much for her small frame. She insisted that a woman's body was amazingly adaptable, and he'd have to say that sure was true when he made love to her. Despite the difference in their sizes, they fit together beautifully.

He hadn't realized she was awake until she spoke.

"You're thinking about this business with Nat and Jessica, aren't you?" she murmured.

"Yeah. I guess I woke you up with my tossing around."

"No." She snuggled against him, bringing with her the tempting scent of her body. "You woke me up with that feathery touch on my hand. For a big man you have the most gentle touch in the world."

He reached under her nightgown and cupped her sweet bottom with more force than he usually used. "Don't go making me sound like a sissy," he said, pulling her toward him.

Her low chuckle was rich with arousal as she wiggled closer. "No one could ever accuse you of that, Boone. You're gentle with the ones you love, but you're hell on anybody who tries to hurt them."

Holding her close, he stroked her blond hair and breathed in her special aroma, a blend of shampoo, cologne and woman. "That's what's bothering me. Nat's one of my best friends, but if he won't be a proper daddy to Elizabeth, that's going to hurt her. Maybe not right away, but down the line, she'll wonder how come he doesn't pay attention to her."

"I can't believe he's going to ignore her. She's too darned cute." She massaged the nape of his neck. "Each one of you worried yourselves sick about the responsibility until you laid eyes on her, remember? Once Nat sees her, he won't be able to help himself. He'll be a good father."

"I hope you're right, but he's going to have to prove himself before we just turn her over."

There was a smile in her voice. "Oh, I'm sure of that. Elizabeth definitely has her champions."

"Yeah." Holding her like this was having a predictable effect on him, which was just fine, because she was in her best time of the month for conceiving. And a man had to do his duty by his wife. His hot, sexy wife. His body throbbed with anticipation. "Well, enough of that," he murmured, easing her nightgown higher.

"I was wondering if you were going to talk for the rest of the night," she said.

"Nope." His mouth found hers in the darkness. As she kissed him with abandon, passion rose in him, blocking out every other thought but one. Maybe this time his seed would find fertile ground and Shelby would ripen with his baby.

JESSICA TRIED to remember all the reasons why she shouldn't make love to Nat as she stood in the motel room watching him strip off his shirt. Next, he hooked an arm over his shoulder, grabbed his T-shirt from the back and pulled that off over his head. Beneath a light pelt of dark chest hair, his muscles flexed as he tossed the T-shirt to the chair where he'd thrown his shirt.

No doubt about it, seventeen months of manual labor had sculpted him into a love god. He probably didn't realize it, but he'd gone from having a decent build to being calendar quality. Even his hair, which was longer than she'd ever seen it, added to his muscular appeal. And she had to find the strength to turn away from him.

His gaze challenged hers and his voice was dangerously soft. "Are you planning to get undressed for bed, or are you waiting for me to help you?"

Her pulse rate climbed. "I..." She paused and cleared her throat. "I'll undress in the bathroom."

"Suit yourself." He broke eye contact as he sat on the bed and pulled off one of his boots.

Without looking at him, she hurried across the room. She gave him as wide a berth as possible, which still meant she nearly stepped on his feet as she grabbed her backpack and ducked into the bathroom. She closed the door and leaned against it, breathing as if she'd run a footrace. Then she glanced at herself in the mirror and saw what Nat had seen—a blatant invitation.

She pulled off the blond wig and unpinned her hair. She hadn't been trying to tease him, she told herself while running her fingers through her hair and massaging her scalp. This was simply the next outfit in the rotation she'd developed.

She'd bought and discarded clothes and wigs along the way—this particular disguise was a fairly new addition to her bag of tricks. But as she shimmied out of the zebra-print dress, she had to admit that she'd been glad this was the outfit for today instead of another truly ugly one, especially after seeing how he filled out the shoulders of his western-cut suit.

Rummaging through her backpack, she found her teal sleep shirt. Usually that was all she wore to bed, but tonight maybe she'd better leave her underwear on, too. Oh, God, how she wanted him. The few hours they would be closed into this motel room would be so packed with tension she'd never sleep. He probably wouldn't, either. Maybe, for both their sakes, she should just go back out there and climb into his bed and be done with it.

No. She had to think of Elizabeth's welfare ahead of all else. Love me, love my daughter. Nat didn't seem at all prepared to do that, which meant she had to stay out of his bed.

After scrubbing all the makeup off and brushing her teeth, she started toward the closed door of the bathroom. The night before, she'd come out and he'd been standing right there waiting for her. If he did that again, and pulled her into his arms, she wasn't sure she could resist him. One kiss and she'd be a goner.

She opened the door slowly and peeked out. With a sense of disappointment, she realized he wasn't there. Apparently he wasn't planning to use any caveman tactics that would let her off the hook. That was just as well. Of course it was.

Turning off the bathroom light, she walked out into the room and discovered he was already in the bed closest to the door, lying with his hands tucked behind his head while he looked up at the ceiling. He'd left the lamp on between the two beds, and he'd only pulled the covers up to his waist, so his chest was bare.

She wondered if he had any idea of the picture he made. Probably not. He'd never been aware of his sex appeal. And damn it, she wanted to know if he was naked under the covers. She'd never known him to wear anything to bed.

Averting her gaze from the tantalizing sight of him lying there, she walked over to the far bed and pulled back the sheet.

"You're right, you know," he said.

"About what?" She got into bed and pulled the covers up to her chin.

"Not making love to me."

His tone of voice pierced her heart. "I don't know what's right," she said. "I only know what I have to do, for the baby's sake. I can't let myself be involved with someone who doesn't love her as much as I do."

He continued to stare up at the ceiling. "I knew you'd be a devoted mother, ready to sacrifice anything. That's good. You were meant to have kids, Jess. Too bad your first one had to be with me."

"As I said before, I don't regret that." She started to reach for the lamp switch and paused. Something had been nagging at her ever since the night before, and now she had to know. "Nat, why did you go to see my parents?"

He sighed. "Because I'm weak. Even though I'm the wrong guy for you, I keep thinking there must be a way for this to work, because I want you so much."

There is, if you can let go of your fear, she thought, but she didn't say anything. They were both tired, and this wasn't the time to get into it.

"I tried calling your apartment before I got on the plane in London, to tell you I was coming home," he continued. "When I found out the line was disconnected, I was determined to find you. I started with your parents."

The thought that he'd gone looking for her warmed her considerably. Maybe all wasn't lost. "And they agreed to see you just because you asked about me?" she asked. "That doesn't sound like them."

"They agreed to see me because I told them I wanted to talk about my foundation for helping the orphans in the refugee camps. I didn't mention you until later."

She propped herself up on one elbow to stare at him. "What foundation?"

Finally he turned his head to glance at her. "That was my main purpose in going over to that country, to see if I could set up some sort of program that would take care of the kids and find homes for them, either over there or over here."

"I had no idea."

"It'll be terrific." His tone grew more excited. "I have some great people lined up to administer it from that end, and I've used my own money to set things in motion, but this will be a huge project. Obviously I need more funding, but I think I can get—"

"I can't believe this." The injustice of it shot through her and she sat up in bed. "I vaguely remember you mentioned the idea of adopting an orphan at some time in the future, but I had no idea you were going to head up an entire operation."

"I'm already doing it," he said. "It's desperately needed, and once we clear up this situation with the person who's trying to kidnap you, I'm planning to give it my full attention."

"Are you?" Anger seethed within her. "Not that I don't think it's a wonderful idea, Nat. It is. I'm sure you'll be a hero. But how can you enthusiastically throw yourself into this program to save little children you don't even know, when you won't consider being a father to the one who belongs to you?"

His gaze was bleak. "You still don't get it, do you? I'm helping those kids because it's what I can do. I understand them, and because of that, I don't expect much from them. I can't relate to a little girl who's never known anything but loving kindness, because I'd probably expect her to be perfect. Hell, I might even envy her, and because of that I wouldn't cut her any slack." He paused. "I would ruin her, Jess."

She glared at him in frustration. "When you get an idea, you sure do clutch it to your breast forever, don't you?"

His glance flicked over her. "I've been known to. Now cover up."

She understood his implication and slid under the covers. "I'm too mad at you to make love, anyway," she said.

"Now, there's the difference between us," he said, reaching up to shut off the light.

"What difference?" she said into the darkness, knowing full well she should keep her mouth shut.

"I can get so mad at you I could chew nails, but at the same time I want to strip you naked and go at it until we're both moaning and soaked with sweat."

She gulped as the vivid mental image rocked her with desire.

"Sweet dreams," he murmured.

"Up yours," she said under her breath.

"We can try it any way you'd like to, darlin'. I'm open to suggestion."

With a groan, she turned her back to him. She would get no sleep tonight.

NAT DIDN'T EXPECT to sleep, considering that every rustle of the sheets in the other bed made him clench his jaw against a new wave of desire. When he closed his eyes he still saw her, sitting up so indignantly when she'd heard about his plans for the orphans. He'd thought she'd be pleased. He hadn't figured out how it might look from her perspective, and she probably had some justification for being angry.

In fact, she had every reason to be upset with him. He

wasn't giving her what she needed and deserved, and yet he wanted...all of her. In his imagination he could still see the proud thrust of her breasts under the cotton nightshirt and the wild tangle of her red hair as she challenged his behavior.

She might not remember, but some of their best times in bed had come about after a heated argument. That spitfire quality of hers really turned him on, maybe because he liked the idea that she'd never allow herself to be dominated by anyone or anything. A tiny voice told him that where he was concerned, her demands might be his salvation. But he didn't care to listen right now.

She'd come by her grit the hard way. After he'd met her father, he understood that she'd learned to be tough by having to go up against Russell P. Franklin. And maybe she was more like her father than she would like to think.

But she could be soft and vulnerable, too. Back in the days when they'd been together, he'd loved watching the transformation that took place as his lovemaking burned away her anger and left only molten passion surging between them.

Remembering, he lay in the dark and ached. If he'd hoped to get any sleep in this motel room, he'd probably wasted his money.

But finally exhaustion must have claimed him, because before he knew it, light was seeping around the edges of the closed drapes. Somewhere down the hall a vacuum cleaner whined. They needed to get back on the road.

He should just get out on the far side of the bed and go directly to the shower. Instead, he rolled to his side and lifted his head to glance over at Jessica, which was a definite mistake.

She was asleep, but she must have had a hell of time achieving that, because she was completely tangled in the covers. One smooth leg was revealed all the way up to the high-cut leg opening of her briefs. Irresistible.

Propping his cheek on his fist, Nat studied that bare leg way too long. He'd forgotten how much he loved her knees, which were small and finely shaped. He used to tease her about them, saying they were the most aristocratic part of her body.

And the backs of her knees were two of her most sensitive spots. Several times he'd driven her to the brink of orgasm simply by nibbling and licking those delicate creases.

He was punished for his reminiscences with a desperately rigid penis. If he knew what was good for him, he'd head for the shower now, before she woke up.

While he was still trying to gather the willpower to do that, she opened her eyes. The fiery belligerence that had lit those brown eyes the night before was gone. In its place was the soft acceptance of a woman wanting to be loved. He sucked in a breath, hesitating. Her pupils widened and her lips parted.

Heart pounding, he held her gaze as he started to get out of bed. But even before his foot made contact with the floor, he saw the change in her eyes as she became more aware of her surroundings. As memory, no doubt, returned. The welcome faded, to be replaced with grim determination.

"No," she whispered.

He groaned and flopped back onto the bed. "It was yes when you woke up, and don't try to tell me different."

"I can't control my dreams."

He looked over at her. "You were dreaming about me?"

She didn't answer, but he knew by the expression on her face that she'd been dreaming about him, all right. Hot dreams. He knew all about those kinds of fantasies. They'd been his constant companion the entire time he was over-seas.

He might still be able to force the issue and love her into submission, considering that she wasn't that far removed from those potent dreams. Her mind might be trying to shut down her desire, but her body would be slower to obey. She'd still be moist and ready, and he could break down her defenses easily enough if he climbed into that bed with her and ignored her protests.

But that wasn't his style. She'd told him to back off, and that's what he intended to do, unless and until she changed her mind. "Guess I'll hit the shower," he said.

"Okay."

Maybe his wounded ego was causing him to imagine things, but he could swear she sounded disappointed. Maybe she wanted him to override her objections. After all, she'd never said no to him before, so how the hell was he supposed to know if she meant it?

Damn, but she had him twisting in the wind. And if it was a game she was playing, he wanted to raise the stakes. He wanted her to twist a little, too. "And I'd appreciate some privacy while I'm in the shower," he said.

"You don't have to worry about that." She sounded huffy.

He realized she didn't get his implication, so he'd have to make his hint broader. "The thing is, a man can only stand so much before he has to find relief any way he can. I wouldn't want you to come in and be embarrassed by what's going on."

Her freckles stood out against the pink flush on her cheeks. She obviously got it now. "I wouldn't dream of barging in on you."

"Good." He had no intention of following through with what he'd hinted he might do in that shower, but he wanted her to think that's exactly what was happening. From the heat in her eyes, he had a good idea of how the concept was affecting her.

Later on he might be ashamed of himself for torturing her like this, but at the moment he couldn't seem to help it. He wanted her so much he could barely walk.

He rolled to the far side of the bed and swung his feet to the floor. Somehow he made it to the bathroom and closed the door. This was hell. If he'd thought living without her for seventeen months had been horrendous, that was only because he hadn't imagined what it would be like if she was right within reach...and forbidden.

CHAPTER NINE

THE MINUTE NAT closed the bathroom door, Jessica propelled herself out of bed and tore through her backpack looking for the most unattractive outfit she could find. When she heard the rush of water from the shower, she tried not to think about what might be going on behind the shower curtain.

He wouldn't really do it. He was only implying he would to mess with her head. But then again, she'd never been around a sexually frustrated Nat Grady. In fact, she and Nat had spent many hours in bed making sure that didn't ever happen. So maybe he *was* in the shower giving himself the pleasure she had denied him. The idea should repel her, but instead it made her hot.

Forcing her attention back to her task, she pulled what she needed from her backpack—faded, baggy overalls and a nondescript gray shirt to wear underneath. She was going to do her part to cut the sexual tension between them. In this getup she wouldn't look sexy and she definitely wouldn't feel sexy.

She could even get dressed right now and skip her shower. Then she totally would not feel sexy. She started to take off her nightshirt and paused. With the way Nat was driving, they'd probably make Colorado on this leg of the trip. Jessica didn't care what she was wearing when she saw Elizabeth again, but she'd like to be reasonably clean.

So she put her clothes in a pile and stalked back and forth in the small area between the beds and the double dresser while she listened to the drumming noise of the shower. He was taking too damn long in there. Probably he was shaving in the shower. That was it. He used to do that sometimes.

A quick whispering noise by the motel door made her turn in that direction and she noticed a piece of paper lying on the carpet in front of the door. Thinking it was the bill, she walked over and picked it up. The message was typed, and very short:

Don't think your boyfriend can protect you.

With a sharp cry she dropped the paper and backed away from the door, almost expecting to see the knob turn.

In an instant the bathroom door flew open and Nat came out, dripping wet with a towel held around his waist. "What? What happened?"

Shaking, she pointed toward the paper she'd dropped on the floor.

He snatched it up, read it and cursed. Dropping the note back on the floor, he whipped the towel from his body and grabbed his suit pants from the chair.

"What do you think you're doing?" she cried as he struggled into them and headed for the door while pulling up the zipper.

"Lock the dead bolt behind me," he said, "and don't open the door until you know it's me."

"No! You can't—"

"I won't debate this with you." He wrenched open the door. "Now lock it behind me!"

She could either do as he asked or run outside after him in her nightshirt. She didn't relish being kidnapped in her nightshirt. After bolting the door behind him, she scrambled into the gray shirt and overalls, her heart pounding in fear for Nat. Stupid fool. Stupid, impetuous fool. She was shoving her shoes on her feet when a knock came at the door followed by Nat's voice calling her name.

With only one shoe on, she hobbled quickly to the door and opened it. He looked to be in one piece, and she sighed with relief.

He came in, breathing hard, his hair still damp and his pants spotted with the moisture he hadn't bothered to towel off before he put them on. Locking the door, he leaned over and put his hands on his knees while he got his breath back.

"Couldn't find him," he said at last, glancing up at her, his hair falling down in his eyes.

"You shouldn't have tried! What did you think you were going to accomplish, racing out there half dressed like that?"

"The element of surprise. Even if I didn't find him, he might have seen me. And that's good."

"How do you figure?"

He straightened and combed his hair back with his fingers. "I know his kind, Jess. He's a bully, and there's nothing he likes better than to know someone is scared. I've been thinking about this. Sebastian wondered if the guy is inept, considering he's been after you for this long and still hasn't caught you."

That got her dander up. She braced her hands on her hips. "Did it occur to Sebastian that I might be outsmarting this jerk and that's why he hasn't caught me?"

A faint smile touched his lips. "Oh, I'm sure that's part of it. Your disguises make it tougher for him, and you've let him know by your actions that you're smart. He understands that when he makes the snatch, he'd better make it a good one or you'll get away. But I think there's something else going on here."

She was proud of her efforts so far, and didn't much appreciate Nat's comments. "Such as?"

"If he's the bully I think he is, he's getting such a charge out of scaring you that he hates to finish the job too soon. That would put an end to his fun."

Jessica's indignation faded and she shivered. "That's sick."

"Yeah, well, sick people are out there. Sometimes they appear to be perfectly normal, too."

She gazed at him and knew without a doubt that he was talking about his father. He understood bullies because he'd been raised by one.

"We'd better get on the road," he said. "The sooner we pull into the Rocking D, the better. This guy's had a field day stalking you while you've been running all over the country by yourself. He won't have it so easy when a bunch of us are around to protect you."

"Do you think there's a chance he'll forget the whole thing?"

"No. Sorry. I'm sure you'd like to believe that, but anybody who's this persistent will want the pot of gold at the end of the rainbow. Maybe, when he realizes you're less accessible at the Rocking D, his frustration will cause him to make a mistake."

"You think so?"

"I kind of figure it that way." The corner of Nat's mouth tilted up. "I know a bit about frustration, too."

That reminded her of their previous conversation, and suddenly she wondered what activity she'd interrupted when she cried out.

His expression softened. "Aw, hell, Jess. Don't look at me like that. Nothing X-rated was going on it that shower. Now let's get moving. We need to hit the road." He glanced at her outfit, as if seeing it for the first time, and started to laugh. "Is that the plan for today?"

"It's not *that* funny."

"It's not funny at all. It's cute as the dickens. Is it for my benefit?"

She bristled. "You said yesterday's outfit was too sexy, so—"

"Jess, I appreciate the effort. I really do. But I realize now I gave way too much credit to your outfit yesterday. It wasn't the tight dress turning me on, it was the body inside it. And covering it up with those overalls only makes me want to take them off so I can get a better look. You can't win this one."

She threw out both arms. "Then what am I supposed to wear?"

"Anything you want, darlin'. The guy already knows what room we're in, and he'll probably watch us come out. I'd say a disguise isn't going to do you much good today. Got any ordinary clothes in that backpack?"

"Some jeans and a sweater." She'd kept them with her during the entire six months. The jeans were her favorites and she'd needed their familiar comfort for days when she'd felt as if she was losing her identity. And the sweater—well, Nat had given it to her for Christmas.

"Then wear those," he said gently. "And get ready as quick as you can. I'll call Sebastian and tell him to expect us late tonight."

Her stomach began to churn. "For sure?"

"We can make it if we eat on the run."

"Okay." She wanted to see Elizabeth desperately, but now that the moment was so close, she was even more afraid of Elizabeth's reaction to her after all this time. She'd never intended for the separation to be this long, but the weeks had slipped by while she waited for Nat to come home. "It's a long way," she said. "Are you sure you're up to it?"

"I'm up to it. You need to see your baby, and another night in a motel room with you would probably kill me."

She picked up her backpack and started for the bathroom. "Same here," she said over her shoulder.

NAT'S DRESS PANTS were damp and uncomfortable after he'd pulled them on straight from the shower, so he put on the only other clothes he'd bought when he'd made the quick shopping trip before leaving New York, jeans and a collarless knit shirt. The jeans were new and stiff, so he'd do well to keep his mind off Jess during the drive today or he'd do his privates some serious injury.

Once he was dressed, he sat on the bed and reached for the phone. Punching in his credit card information, he dialed Sebastian's number. He got Matty again and wondered why she'd answered Sebastian's phone both times he'd called.

"Is Sebastian in the neighborhood?" he asked after assuring Matty that he and Jess were fine. He decided not to relay the information about the note slipped under the door. No use worrying people who couldn't do a damn thing about it.

"He's down at the barn. Do you want me to go get him?"

"That's okay. I just wanted him to know we'll be rolling in tonight, but it might be late. I hate to make him wait up for us, but with this bozo running around loose he'd better not leave a key under the mat."

"Don't worry about keeping us up," Matty said. "In fact, we might—"

"Uh, Matty?"

"Yes?"

"Has there been a…change in living arrangements while I was gone? You keep saying 'we' like you're, um…how can I say this without being offensive?"

Matty laughed. "You want to know if we're shacking up?"

"I guess I do." Nat found himself grinning. "Are you?"

"That's one way of putting it. I guess Sebastian didn't get around to telling you the news. We're married."

"Seriously?" Nat's grin widened. What a perfect match. It was amazing that nobody had thought of it before.

"The truth is, we're hardly ever serious," she said, her voice teasing. "We save that for when we have to worry about you."

"God, I know this has been a mess." The burden of the problems he'd caused his friends settled heavily on his shoulders. "I hope someday you'll forgive me. In the meantime, I'm sure happy for you, Matty. That's great news. When did you tie the knot?"

"Five months ago. We have Jessica and Elizabeth to thank for bringing us together, as a matter of fact. Sebastian desperately needed help with the baby, and I wasn't much more knowledgeable than he was, but we muddled through together, and in the process figured out we couldn't live without each other."

"Hot damn." The knowledge that Sebastian and Matty were together lightened his load of self-blame. "I'm glad to know something good came of all this."

"Oh, lots of good came from it. Having Elizabeth around has changed quite a few lives. While we went on our honeymoon, Travis took care of her, and when she caught a cold, he went to Gwen Hawthorne for help, and now—"

"Evans having a new girlfriend isn't news, Matty." Nat leaned back against the headboard. "It'll blow over, like every other love affair he's ever had."

"I doubt it. Not considering they've stood in front of a preacher and are expecting a baby."

"What?" Nat sat up straight. "You're kidding. Are you sure we're talking about the same Travis Evans?"

"One and the same. He's domesticated, Nat."

"I find that hard to believe. Next you'll be telling me that Boone—"

"Ah, yes. Boone. On his way up here from New Mexico to see about Elizabeth, he met Shelby McFarland, who became, as of two months ago, Mrs. Boone Connor."

"My God." Nat rubbed his temples with his free hand and tried to take it all in. He focused on the first bit of information she'd given him about Boone. "Why would Boone be coming up to see about Elizabeth?"

"Jessica didn't tell you what she did?"

"Well, yeah. She left the baby with Sebastian." He glanced up as Jessica came into the room in the green sweater he'd given her two Christmases ago. The sight of her in that sweater did funny things to his heart.

"She didn't tell you about the letters she wrote to each of the guys?"

"Not that I remember." He watched Jessica move around the room collecting any stray belongings. The forest-green sweater was cashmere, he remembered. He'd loved stroking her breasts through the soft material. He wanted to do it now. "What letters?" he asked to be polite, although he was fast losing interest in the conversation.

"She wrote a letter to each of them, asking them to be a godfather to Elizabeth."

"That's nice." Nat liked the soft drape of the sweater on Jess, but it was even more effective combined with the snug fit of her jeans. He remembered that combination had seduced him quite thoroughly the last time she'd worn it.

"I don't think you understand," Matty was saying. "They were so drunk that night of the avalanche reunion party that Jessica drove them to their cabin and tucked them in. Elizabeth was born nine months later, so they each assumed the godfather label was a smoke screen."

Finally what Matty was saying penetrated his erotic musings about Jess. His gut clenched when he realized her implication. "Wait a minute. What do you mean, a smoke screen?"

"I mean that every last one of them thought he was the baby's father."

Nat stared at Jess as jealousy washed over him in uncompromising waves. "Why the hell would they think that?" he said much too loudly.

Jess closed a dresser drawer and turned to gaze at him in alarm.

"Oh, you know," Matty said. "Because they each vaguely remembered making a pass at her in their drunken stupor. Stealing a kiss. Harmless stuff, I'm sure, but they imagined they'd gone beyond that and fathered this kid."

Nat could barely breathe. The fact that none of his friends had known a thing about his involvement with Jess was a point of logic that didn't matter right now. He still wanted to wring each of their necks for even *thinking* of touching her.

"It's sort of funny, looking back on it," Matty said. "But believe me, it wasn't funny at the time. And now that I realize this is all news to you, I should probably warn you that these guys still feel very fatherly toward that little girl. They're extremely possessive. They've found out they're not her father, of course, but the bond is formed, and I doubt it'll ever go away."

"I see." New and strange emotions coursed through Nat. He should be happy that his friends were so attached to Elizabeth. That took some of the responsibility off his shoulders. Hell, they probably didn't need him around at all, with three of them ready to take over as the baby's father figure.

So why was he feeling as if he needed to charge in and trumpet his claim like some wild stallion warning off rivals?

"I'm glad I had a chance to talk to you," Matty said. "I'm guessing that everybody will be here when you arrive tonight. You should be prepared. They'll probably give you the third degree regarding your intentions toward Elizabeth." Her voice softened. "She's cute as a bug's ear, Nat. Once you see her, you'll understand why the guys are so protective. Why we all are."

Nat's head began to ache. "I appreciate the information, Matty," he said. "We'll get there as soon as we can."

"Don't break any laws doing it," she said. "Bye now."

"See you soon." Nat put the receiver back in the cradle and gazed at Jess, who was standing motionless by the dresser. "You failed to mention the letters you wrote to my friends."

"Did I? Well, that was part of my plan to make sure Elizabeth had plenty of protectors. I asked Sebastian, Travis and Boone to be her godfathers. I thought it was ingenious of me."

"Oh, it was that."

"Then why are you looking like a thundercloud?"

He stood and walked toward her. "Because each of them assumed he was Elizabeth's father, that's why!"

Her jaw dropped.

"What went on the night of the avalanche reunion party, Jess?" He prayed she'd laugh and give him a logical answer. "Why would all three of them think that?"

She didn't laugh. Instead, her eyes grew bright with anger. "What in hell are you implying?"

"I'm not implying anything." He drew closer. He desperately wanted her side of the story. "Matty said they all got smashed and remembered making passes at you. I just want to know—"

"How can you even *think* to question me about this?" She trembled with rage. "Is that the sort of opinion you have of me?"

"No!" He lifted a hand as if to touch her cheek, but after seeing the look in her eyes he thought better of it. "I just—"

"You just want my word that I didn't go to bed with all three of your best friends in the same night!" Her voice quivered. "Well, you're not getting it. Only an insensitive idiot would ask the question in the first place, and I will not stoop to explaining myself."

"Damn it, Jess. Less than a minute ago I found out that three other men thought they were the father of my baby. Any guy would want to know what that was all about!" Deep in his heart he knew she hadn't done anything wrong, but jealousy had him by the throat. *Something* had gone on that night. He wanted her to tell him it had been nothing, like Matty said. Harmless. He wanted her to assure him that she felt nothing but friendship for each of those men.

"*Your* baby? As I recall, you don't want anything to do with her."

"That's beside the point. She's my baby, and those guys have no right—"

"All of them rushed to take care of her, as I hoped they would," she said. "While *you* were out of the country and completely out of touch. In my book that gives them a ton of rights."

"I didn't know about her!"

"You ran away, so how could you know?"

"I didn't run away." But he had and he knew it. So did she. Then he remembered the rest of Matty's news. He delivered it with some relish, knowing it would shock her as it had him. If she'd secretly thought one of his stalwart, responsible friends would be a backup if he bowed out, she could forget that fantasy. "Well, they're all married now."

"They are?"

"Surprised at that, aren't you?"

"I sure am! I had no idea—"

"So if you had some plan that included roping one of them into marriage in case I didn't work out, you can forget it. They're taken."

Her open palm stung as it connected with his cheek. He resisted the urge to put his hand against the spot, which hurt like hell. They stared at each other, both of them breathing hard.

"We need to get going," he said.

"Fine. Let's go. The sooner I'm rid of you and your

insinuations, the better.'' She spun on her heel, snatched
up her backpack and headed for the door.

"Don't go out there by yourself, damn it!'' He hoisted
his backpack and charged after her.

"Maybe you should let me be kidnapped,'' she replied
harshly, flinging open the door. "Shoot, if I play my cards
right, I might even be able to bribe the guy into marrying
me. After all, any man will do, so long as I have a ring on
my finger.''

He slammed the door and caught up with her, grabbing
her by the arm. God, the cashmere was soft. The first time
she'd worn it, she hadn't put on a bra, and when he'd
rubbed his palms over her breasts, her nipples had puckered
instantly under the material. She'd said it was like being
stroked with mink. He really didn't want to fight with her.

He took a breath. "Maybe I shouldn't have said that,''
he murmured. "But I think you still owe me some explanation for—''

"I owe you *nothing*.'' She pulled her arm away and
marched down the balcony toward the stairs.

Nat didn't know where the creep might be hiding, but
letting Jess get so far ahead could be the invitation the guy
was waiting for. He caught up with her again and took her
arm. When she struggled, he gripped her harder than he'd
intended. Seventeen months of digging ditches had given
him that kind of strength.

"Let me go.''

"No.'' He lowered his voice as he propelled her down
the stairs so fast she nearly stumbled. "You may not owe
me anything, but I owe you something, and that's to see
that you get safely back to Elizabeth. Now, don't pull away
from me again.''

She struggled for breath as they hurried across the parking lot toward the car. Her voice was sharp with fury. "I'll
bet you're finally mad enough not to want me.''

He opened the car door and practically shoved her in.
"You'd lose that bet,'' he said.

CHAPTER TEN

As THEY RODE in silence, speaking only when they stopped to order a fast-food breakfast to go, Jessica tried to control her curiosity. She was dying to know who each of the guys had married, and whether it had happened before she'd dropped off the baby or after. But she'd be damned if she'd strike up a conversation with a man who, however briefly, thought she was capable of engaging in some sort of orgy the night after he'd dumped her.

She hadn't been able to gather any personal news about Sebastian, Travis or Boone during her quick calls to the Rocking D in the past six months. She hadn't dared spend any time on the line when she'd phoned for fear the kidnapper would somehow trace the call and go there to find out what the fuss was about. Even now she worried that she was leading him to Elizabeth, but now that Nat knew he was the baby's father, Jessica was ready to make a stand.

So all three men were married. The idea caused her to smile. Each of them in his own way would make some woman very happy, even a confirmed bachelor like Travis. Jessica had always suspected there was more to Travis than the playboy image he projected, which was why she'd wanted him to be part of the group watching out for Elizabeth.

If three women had joined Elizabeth's chosen circle, so much the better. They'd have to be fantastic ladies if they'd hitched up with three of her best friends. She could hardly wait to meet them.

She peeked over at Nat. His expression was grim and he'd pulled his Stetson down low over his eyes, which was always a sign he didn't feel like having a conversation. Not that she had much to discuss with him, after what he'd said.

But the drive seemed endless with no communication between them and all the questions hanging in the air. She gazed out the window at the stubble of harvested fields and willed the time to go faster.

They picked up more fast food for lunch. Continuing to drive was fine with Jessica, but she began to feel sorry for Nat, who bore the brunt of the task. She shouldn't feel sorry for him. After all, at the first hint that all was not fitting and proper, he'd practically accused her of being a tramp. If he didn't trust her any more than that, she didn't want to have anything to do with him.

That was a lie. The only reason he'd been able to hurt her with his questions was that she was in love with him. From the feel of it, she wouldn't ever be in love with anyone else. She'd hoped to fall out of love with him sometime during the seventeen months he'd been gone, but it hadn't happened.

And he still loved her. He might not *trust* her completely, but he still loved her. She could see it in his eyes every time he looked at her.

Before they reached the western border of Kansas, he apologized. "Look, I'm sorry," he said quietly. "You're right, I shouldn't have even asked the question."

She sighed and relaxed against the seat. She hadn't even realized how stiffly she'd been sitting until the last of the anger flooded out of her in one big gush. "Thank you for that." She glanced at his tense profile. That apology had cost him a lot of pride and she admired him for sacrificing it. She could do no less. "Would you like to hear about that night?"

"Doesn't interest me in the least."

"Liar."

The corner of his mouth tilted up. "Okay, I want to hear every last detail, but you don't have to tell me a damn thing."

She couldn't ever remember wanting to kiss him as much as she did now. But they were driving, and even if they weren't, she'd said no lovemaking, which naturally meant no kissing, either. "I guess I should be flattered that you're jealous."

"You can be flattered if you want, but I'm furious with myself."

"Jealousy's a natural emotion."

"That could be, but in my opinion, the only men who can treat themselves to jealousy are would-be husbands, so that lets me out."

The words hurt, so she tried to make light of them. "Oh, I don't know. It seems to be the in thing these days."

"No kidding."

"Before I tell you about what happened that night in Aspen, will you tell me who the guys married? I'm dying of curiosity."

He glanced over at her.

"Nothing but curiosity, I swear," she said with a smile.

"I wouldn't blame you for being attracted to any of them. They're good men, and I guess they're okay-looking." His grin was genuine this time. "Not as handsome and manly as me, of course."

"Of course. But obviously someone found them irresistible. Who was it?"

"Sebastian married his neighbor, Matty Lang. Her husband was killed a while back, flew his Cessna into a mountain, and she's been running her ranch by herself, except for Travis helping out in the summer. Now that I think about it, she's the perfect match for Sebastian. But I guess now I'll never be able to buy his ranch. He's probably there to stay."

"You wanted to buy a ranch? You never told me that."

"It's a beautiful piece of property." He straightened his arms against the wheel and flexed his shoulders, stretching the kinks out. "I could sell it for a huge profit someday, but that wasn't my motivation. I'm not sure what my motivation was."

"You grew up on a ranch. Maybe you'd like to get back to that."

He shook his head. "Probably not."

"Maybe you'd like to run a ranch for kids with no place to go," she suggested gently.

He gave her a startled glance. Then he returned his attention to the road. "You sure have a way of getting inside my head, Jess. I hadn't put it all together, but you might be right. The orphans in the refugee camps aren't the only ones without a home. But it was a place to start."

Such noble dreams, she thought. How she'd love to be a part of them. But she came with a kid attached. How ironic that he wanted to save all the children of the world except one. She'd been upset about that at first, but she was slowly beginning to understand his reasoning, and it didn't seem so contradictory now.

"So who did Travis marry?" she asked.

"Gwen Hawthorne, who runs a bed-and-breakfast in Huerfano, the little town down the road from the Rocking D."

"I know where it is." Just hearing the name of the ranch brought back the pain of the night she'd abandoned her child.

"Do you know what the town's name means in Spanish?" Nat asked.

"No. I took French in college."

"It means *orphan*."

"Really?" She wondered if that had been one of the reasons he'd been attracted to the area in the first place. "Maybe it's fate that you're supposed to start something like that near Huerfano."

"If I do, I'll have to find a piece of property besides the Rocking D to do it on."

"Guess so." She tried to sound as if where he ended up didn't really concern her, when in fact it concerned her tremendously. If he chose not to link his life with hers, then she wanted to locate far, far away from him. "What about Boone, then? Who did he find?"

"A woman named Shelby McFarland. He met her on the way up from his folks' place in New Mexico to the Rocking D."

"You mean both he and Sebastian got married *after* I left Elizabeth at the ranch? That's weird."

He nodded. "Travis did, too. Matty said it was the baby that pulled each couple together, in a way."

"Wow." She'd never anticipated causing such havoc, even though it seemed to be a good kind of havoc. "And each one of the guys thought he was Elizabeth's father. That blows me away. It never occurred to me they'd think such a thing. I only wanted to surround Elizabeth with people who would watch out for her. I knew I could trust them to do that."

"So what did happen that night?" Nat asked the question as if he was only mildly curious.

She smiled at his obvious attempt to sound casual. "Your friends assembled in the bar at the lodge and got totally plowed, that's what." She still chuckled whenever she thought of the raucous drinking songs, the arm-wrestling contests and the corny jokes that made them all laugh until their sides hurt. They'd pledged eternal friendship to each other that night, but she'd never expected to put that pledge to such a test.

"I gathered they got smashed. Then what?"

"They'd booked that same little cabin you guys had the year before, which is about two miles from the lodge, if you remember. It was nasty out, and I didn't dare let any of them behind the wheel, so I drove them back to the cabin.''

He glanced over at her. ''You didn't have anything to drink?''

''Somebody had to stay sober and keep them out of trouble.'' She didn't want to admit she'd been so heartbroken that even one drink might have caused her to lose control and start sobbing in the middle of what was supposed to be a celebration. She shouldn't have continued to feel an obligation to keep her relationship with Nat a secret, but she had—all this time.

''So you drove them home and that's it?''

''Well, of course not. I knew they'd be miserable in the morning, so I made them take some vitamin C and B-complex. I tried to get them to drink some chamomile tea with honey, but they wouldn't hear of it. Said it was a sissy drink and they were studly cowboys who could hold their liquor, by God.''

Nat chuckled. ''Good for them.''

''I'm not surprised to hear that from you, considering how you've reacted whenever I've tried to guide you to some natural cures.''

''You wanted me to drink stuff made with weeds!''

She bristled. ''Those *weeds,* as you call them, are loaded with nutrients. People have no idea what a bountiful harvest they have in their own backyards! Why, if only everyone would—''

''I think I've heard that lecture a few times, Jess.''

''And it's had zero effect.''

''If I promise to drink the next cup of weed tea you offer me, will you finish your story?''

''There's not much more to tell. I helped them out of their clothes and into bed, and then I went home. The next morning—''

''Hold it. Back up the hay wagon. What do you mean, you *helped them out of their clothes?*''

Her anger from their morning argument threatened to return. "I don't like your implication, Nat."

"Okay, okay. I'm not implying anything was wrong, but I'm getting a mental picture here, and it's bugging me. Be fair, Jess. You weren't too happy when you found out I had my tongue in another woman's mouth."

"I *never* had my tongue in any of their mouths."

"But you undressed them."

"Down to their T-shirts and shorts! They were in sad enough shape the next day, without adding the discomfort of sleeping all night in their clothes."

"I guess," he mumbled. "Did any of them try to kiss you?"

"Sure they did. So what?"

The muscles in his jaw bunched. "I'm going to strangle them."

"Nat, they didn't know about us! They were drunk, and goofing around." She paused. "But I sure never imagined any of them thought they'd done more than try to kiss me. Is that even possible? To do the deed and not remember the next day?"

"That's never happened to me, but I guess it's possible." He blew out a breath and glanced at her. "None of this would have happened in the first place if I'd been there that night. I should have been there. But I thought I was doing you a favor by leaving."

"A *favor?* By walking out of my life completely? By putting yourself totally out of reach in a country across the ocean with no reliable phone or mail service? How was that supposed to be a favor?"

"I thought if I was out of the picture, you would find someone else."

Her throat tightened. "Is that what you want?"

"Hell, no, that's not what I want! I'm going crazy thinking of you in the clutches of my friends, even though I know it was all completely innocent. I don't dare imagine you in bed with another man. It would drive me nuts.''

"I can't imagine that, either,'' she said quietly.

He groaned. "I love hearing that, and I shouldn't love it. I should want you to go out and find yourself a nice, marriage-minded guy who loves the idea of having children of his own.'' He slapped the steering wheel. "I am beyond selfish to want you, when I'm not capable of giving you everything you need.''

She felt bathed in warmth, and absolutely sure he was wrong about himself. He had no idea what he might be capable of, given a chance. "But you do want me?''

His jaw clenched again. "Every minute of every day.''

She restrained herself from reaching over to touch him, although she ached to do that. One touch and they'd be exiting the freeway and parking on some side road so they could climb in the back seat together. Exciting as that sounded, she believed that making love now would only confuse the issue. Nat thought sex was all he could give her, and she wanted to show him they had far more going for them that that.

Because she dared not touch him, she could only reach out with words. "Don't give up on us yet,'' she murmured.

He responded with silence, and although she would have preferred more encouragement, she was glad that at least he didn't argue with her.

MANY LONG, frustrating hours later, Nat drove down the dirt road leading to the ranch turnoff. The sun had set hours ago, and he thought he deserved a medal for making it all the way to the Rocking D without swerving onto some dark back road and finding a place to make love to Jess. He felt certain she wouldn't have stopped him if he'd tried that.

The closer they came to the ranch the more nervous he was. While he was overseas he had imagined reuniting with his buddies would be a homecoming of sorts, but Jess's bombshell of an announcement had changed all that. He desperately needed the sense of safety that making love to her would bring, but she'd chosen to pull the rug out from under him on that, too.

Her decision to stop having sex was a shaky one, and they both knew it, but his pride wouldn't let him challenge her decree. He wasn't entirely clear on what would have to happen before she'd take him back into her bed, but he figured it hinged primarily on his attitude toward Elizabeth. A marriage proposal would probably do the trick, too.

She'd be amazed if she knew how much he'd thought about marrying her, and how close he'd been to asking— right up to the moment he'd found out about the baby. He'd worked it all out somewhere over the Atlantic. He'd planned to propose, and when she inevitably brought up the idea of kids, he would then suggest adopting one of the orphans from the refugee camp as a first step.

That process would have taken some time, time he desperately needed to adjust to the concept of being a father. If he'd managed okay with an orphan child, then he'd have been ready to consider having a baby of his own. It had been a carefully thought-out compromise that he'd believed he could live with.

Of course, once he was in a hotel room alone with Jess, he hadn't been able to think at all. Making love to her had taken top priority. And then he'd been hit with the news about Elizabeth.

He wasn't ready. He didn't know if he'd ever be ready, but he didn't have the luxury of more time to find out. Everything was on the line right now, and he felt as if he'd been told to take an exam he was doomed to fail. Worse yet, he would fail in front of his three best friends, men whose respect he wanted.

They had a head start on him with his baby thing, too. During his work at the refugee camps, he'd steered away from the really tiny ones, leaving them to the women volunteers. He'd concentrated on the ones who could walk and talk.

The vulnerability of a baby terrified him. He knew damn well that if his mother hadn't been around during the first three years of his life, his father would have killed him for doing something as innocent as crying. Then he'd gained another couple of years' advantage while his father drowned his grief in the bottle.

By the time Hank Grady had looked around and noticed he had a son to bear the force of his rage and frustration, Nat was old enough to run and hide most times. A smart kid could usually avoid the worst of the abuse, but a little baby had no defense at all.

As he turned down the lane leading to the ranch house, he took a deep breath. He wasn't much of a praying man, but he found himself praying now. It wasn't a specific prayer, just a general plea to somehow have things turn out okay for everyone concerned.

Stands of juniper trees dotted the approach to the ranch house, shielding it from view until the final bend in the road. The place was lit up as if it was a holiday. He'd driven up here at night many times, and the first glimpse of the rustic log house with its wide porch, large windows and native-rock chimney was usually a welcome sight on a chilly night. Tonight Nat was intimidated by it. All those lights blazing from the windows seemed to be announcing the coming of Judgment Day.

"Nat, I'm scared," Jess said.

"Me, too."

"What are those other pickup trucks doing here at this hour?" she asked, sounding easily as nervous as Nat felt. "It looks like they're having a party or something."

"Matty warned me about that." He pulled into the circular driveway and parked behind a purple truck he didn't recognize. Travis's fancy black rig was in front of that, and Boone's battered king-cab was in the lead. Nat looked around for Sebastian's Bronco and saw it parked down by the barn.

"What'd she warn you about?" Jess asked, her eyes wide.

He turned off the rental car's engine. The little sedan looked out of place in the lineup of cowboy Cadillacs. For the first time ever in his visits to the Rocking D, Nat felt out of place. "Matty said everybody would probably be here—all the guys and their wives. I gather they've become very protective of Elizabeth, and they're not...well, they're not eager to give her up."

"That's too bad!" A frantic note crept into her voice. "I'm her mother, and I—"

"Hold it." He reached over and put a reassuring hand on her shoulder. Dealing with her panic would help him push aside his own. "I didn't say they weren't going to do it. But when you think about it, they've spent more months with Elizabeth since she's been born than you have. It's understandable that this will be tough for them. I'm sure once everyone gets used to the idea that you're ready to take her back, they'll be fine with it."

Jess gazed at the house and her lower lip trembled slightly. "This show of strength doesn't indicate they're going to be fine. They could take me to court, you know. They could charge me with abandoning her, and they'd have a pretty good case, too."

He gave her shoulder a gentle squeeze. "They're not going to do that," he said quietly. "Come on. Going in to face everybody will be the hardest part. Let's get it over with."

She turned to him. "Nat, I've said this before, but I want to say it again. Whatever happens in there, however this gets screwed up, I want you to know that I don't regret the pregnancy. I don't regret that you and I brought a little girl into this world. I realize we've caused a lot of people a ton of trouble, but I would do everything the same, just to have Elizabeth.''

He loved her so much at that moment that the feeling was painful in its intensity. ''That's all the people in there will have to hear,'' he said, his voice gruff with emotion. ''Now, let's go face the music.''

CHAPTER ELEVEN

As JESSICA REACHED for the handle of the car door, a familiar tickling at the back of her neck told her she and Nat were being watched. She'd learn to dread the sensation, but she was grateful for it, too. It left her less vulnerable. "I think he's followed us here," she said.

Nat tensed. Then he turned to look through the back window of the car.

"You won't be able to see him unless he wants you to," she said. "I've always had a feeling that when he shows himself, he means to do it."

"The guy's a damn psycho," Nat muttered as he continued to peer into the shadows. Then he looked over at Jessica, and his words took on an edge of steel. "And you know what? I'm glad he followed us. Now that we're here, we can figure out a way to catch that son of a bitch."

She was grateful for a champion, and now that they were at the Rocking D she would have four of them. Until the moment that she sensed her stalker was watching, she'd been nervous about going into the house and facing Sebastian, Boone and Travis. Now she wanted to be close to all that protection. "Let's go in," she said, opening the car door.

"Close the door and lock it. Then wait there until I come around and get you out."

"Help is close by, if he tries anything."

"Doesn't matter. Before I could get there, he could use

you as a hostage and we wouldn't be able to do anything about it. Wait there."

"Okay." After closing and locking the door, she kept her attention on Nat as he rounded the car. Then she unlocked the door and took his hand as he helped her out.

"I can't imagine how you've lived this way for six months, having to be afraid all the time," he said.

"Simple. You can't stay afraid all the time. You can get used to anything, if it goes on long enough. I—" A movement on the path coming up from the barn caught her eye. "Nat."

His grip on her hand tightened and he glanced over his shoulder. "What?"

"Over there." She pointed toward the barn. "Someone's—"

"I see him." Then his grip relaxed and he blew out a breath. "It's Sebastian. And Fleafarm."

"Fleafarm?" In her relief, she found that name funnier than it might have been otherwise.

"She was a stray, and Sebastian's ex-wife named her that. Sebastian wanted to change it once he found out what a great dog she is, but it's tough to change a name once it sticks." He tugged on her hand. "Let's walk down to meet him. I wouldn't mind breaking the ice by talking to Sebastian first."

"Good idea." Her feeling of being watched had begun to fade, and trusting the instincts she'd developed over the past few months, she decided that her stalker had retreated for the time being. She became more aware of her surroundings—the clean scent of juniper mixed with wood smoke, and the faint sound of country music and male laughter coming from the house. "I think the guy's gone now, anyway."

"You're that tuned in to him?"

"After six months, it's become a habit." Not a pleasant

one, she had to admit, but a necessary one. "Now let's go meet Sebastian."

As the sense of danger passed, she once again had the luxury of being nervous about facing Sebastian. Watching him walk toward them, she didn't know how she'd ever mistaken his purposeful stride and solid build for her stalker. There wasn't a sneaky bone in Sebastian's virile body.

When she'd made that fateful decision to leave Elizabeth at the Rocking D, she'd been blind to every concern except protecting her tiny child. Yet the arrival of the baby had drastically changed Sebastian's life, as well as the lives of the people waiting inside the house. She had to take responsibility for that. No matter how noble her motives, she'd created chaos.

She felt it whirling inside her, too. In a short time she'd see her child again. Logically, Elizabeth couldn't be expected to know her. Illogically, Jessica prayed that she would recognize her mother, that something about Jessica's voice, her touch, her scent would awaken memories. But even if that happened, Elizabeth would be hesitant at first. She'd prefer the people she'd lived with since March to some vaguely familiar woman. The pain of watching Elizabeth choose someone else over her own mother would be excruciating.

Sebastian spotted them and quickened his pace. "Nat? Jessica? I thought I heard a car drive up."

"What are you doing down here?" Nat asked as he drew closer. "Did Matty banish you to the barn?"

"I'll thank you not to say that in front of her and give her ideas," Sebastian said, his grin flashing in the darkness.

Fleafarm bounded forward with a bark of welcome.

"Hey, Fleafarm," Nat said, leaning down to scratch behind the dog's ears. "I'm surprised you remember me."

"I'm surprised *I* remember you," Sebastian said as he

reached them. He grabbed Nat's outstretched hand and clapped him on the back. "How the hell are you?"

"Surviving," Nat said with a faint smile.

"That's a start." Sebastian gave him a level look before turning to Jessica. "How about you, little one?"

She'd forgotten he used to call her that, and the endearment brought tears to her eyes. "I'm okay, Sebastian. But I'm afraid I caused quite a ruckus around here."

"You could say that." He stepped toward her. "But that doesn't mean I'm not glad to see you. I'm happy you're safe, Jessica." And with that, he enfolded her in his arms for a bear hug, just like old times.

Tears dribbled down her cheeks at his uncomplicated welcome. "I'm sorry for what I've put you all through," she murmured as she hugged him back. "I had no idea you'd all think that you might be Elizabeth's father."

"You didn't?" Releasing her, he tipped back his Stetson with his thumb and gave her a puzzled look. "By the way you dropped her off, asking us to be godfathers and everything, I thought you meant for us to think one of us was."

"Oh, God, no." She put a hand to her chest. "That would have been diabolical, to lead you to believe that and then keep the real father a secret. Did you really think I was capable of something so mean?"

"Well, no." Sebastian looked uncomfortable as he glanced over at Nat. "But then I didn't think Nat would carry on a yearlong relationship with a woman and not tell me, either."

Nat squared his shoulders as if ready to take whatever blame might be heaped on him. "Like I said on the phone, I was wrong to keep that from you."

"Then why did you?" Sebastian asked quietly, hurt shining in his eyes.

"Because I have a yellow streak a mile wide running down my back," Nat said, glancing at Jessica before he returned his attention to Sebastian.

"I wouldn't put it like that," Jessica said. Her heart went out to him. This moment was difficult for her, but it had to be sheer hell for Nat. In her experience, men didn't like to admit their vulnerability and mistakes to other men.

"I don't know. I think it sounds about right," Sebastian said evenly.

Nat met his friend's steady gaze without flinching. "Not going to cut me any slack, are you, Sebastian?"

"Not when I stop to consider that little baby in there."

Jessica heard the warning loud and clear as the men faced each other like two bucks vying for the same territory. Either Nat agreed to take full responsibility for Elizabeth, or Sebastian, Travis and Boone would step in and do the job. But she didn't want Nat to be bullied into doing his duty. Then they'd all lose.

She took a deep breath. "Is Elizabeth awake?"

"Probably not," Sebastian said, his glance softening as he turned toward her. "She generally goes to bed about eight. She must have picked up on the excitement, because we had a little more trouble than usual getting her to sleep tonight. Then again, it could be another tooth coming in." His voice was filled with love as he spoke about Elizabeth.

Jessica battled a surge of jealousy. She was being extremely petty to be jealous. After all, having everyone become so attached to her baby was the best she could have wished for. But she *was* jealous—of all the time and experiences they'd shared with her daughter and the strong bond that had been created as a result. She couldn't stand her own separation from Elizabeth a moment longer "I want to see her," she said. "I promise not to wake her up."

"I expected you'd want that. We need to get on in, anyway, before Matty organizes a search party."

"Why were you down there?" Nat asked again as the three of them started toward the house. "You never did say."

"Just jumpy, I guess. Ever since your call I've been on edge, thinking about the guy you told me about. I was probably imagining things, but about twenty minutes ago I had the biggest urge to go out and take a look around. I didn't see or hear anything, so I'm sure it was just nerves."

"I'm not so sure," Jessica said. "I think the guy's around here somewhere."

Sebastian paused and gave her a sharp look. "What makes you think so?"

"After all these months, I've developed a sixth sense about when he's nearby and when he's not. When we pulled up tonight I had the definite feeling that he was watching us."

"And now?" Sebastian asked, glancing around him.

"Now I think he's gone again, but I'm guessing he knows I'm here."

"And you're sure he doesn't know about the baby?" Sebastian sounded agitated.

"Yes, I'm sure."

"That's good." Sebastian started up the path again. "As far as I'm concerned, his days are numbered, anyway."

"They sure as hell are," Nat said. "He's not getting near Jess or Elizabeth."

Jessica drew comfort from those words, but as she approached the house she had a horrible thought, one that would explain a great deal. "I'm not really sure he doesn't know about the baby," she said as anxiety churned in her stomach. "In the beginning he might not have, but he might have found out, somehow. Maybe that's why he's waited all this time, so he could snatch Elizabeth and me together. With both the Franklin child and grandchild, he could demand anything he wanted from my parents and expect to get it."

"Doesn't matter," Sebastian said, "because he's not getting either one of you."

"I know, but…" She paused at the steps leading up to

the wide front porch and her stomach twisted as she remembered the agony of leaving Elizabeth there. The sacrifice had seemed necessary. It might still be necessary. "Maybe the best thing for me to do is go away again," she said softly. "I've kept him distracted so far. Maybe I should—"

"No!" Nat gripped her arm as if he thought she might run off into the woods at any minute. "You can't do that."

"I second the motion," Sebastian said. "I love that baby as much as I would my own kid, but the fact is she's *not* my kid, and she belongs with her mother." He paused and sent Nat a challenging look. "And her father."

Before Nat could respond, the front door opened and Travis came out looking handsome as ever, a grin on his face and a longneck in his hand. A tan Great Dane bounded out with him and began to cavort around the porch with Fleafarm.

"I thought I heard somebody carrying on out here!" Travis said. "Thanks for letting us know, Sebastian, old buddy. Sadie, cool it."

"They just got here," Sebastian said.

"Yeah, yeah, yeah." Travis crossed the porch in two quick strides. "Admit it, you were monopolizing them." He bounded down the steps and swept Jessica off her feet as he kissed her loudly on the cheek. "So you finally decided to show up, Jessie-girl. If you weren't so damn pretty and I didn't like you so much, I'd tan your hide for what you've pulled."

Same old Travis, she thought, smiling in spite of herself. "I—"

"Don't you be mauling that woman, hotshot," Boone said as he came thundering down the steps looking even bigger than Jessica remembered. "Not all females appreciate that kind of treatment."

"Name one," Travis said as he set Jessica back on her

feet. "Hey, Nat." He stuck out his hand. "Hope you don't mind me giving your girl a friendly hug."

Nat cleared his throat. "She's not my—"

"Hello, Boone," Jessica said, wanting to cut off Nat's denial of their relationship. Sebastian, Travis and Boone might want to argue the point, and this wasn't the time to get into it. "I'm so sorry for all the trouble I've caused you." She stood on tiptoe, put her hands around his neck and placed a kiss on his cheek.

Boone returned her kiss with a brotherly hug. "I don't blame you," he said. "You were trying to protect your baby, is all."

"Thanks for understanding." With all four men gathered together, her fears eased. These guys were a match for anyone. That's why she'd left Elizabeth here in the first place.

"Everything's gonna work out." Boone gave her a reassuring smile before turning to Nat. "It's good to have you back home, buddy," he said as he shook Nat's hand.

"I'm glad to be home."

Jessica wondered if he really was glad, or if he regretted leaving the refugee camp.

"I'll bet he is glad, at that," Travis said. "Looks like they were short of barbers over there."

"They were short of a lot of things," Nat said. "And barbers were—"

"Well, I have two things to say," Boone cut in. "First off, I want you to know I'm real proud of what you did, going over to help those orphans. And the length of your hair is of no concern to me."

"Thanks," Nat said.

"I wanted to say that first off," Boone added, "because the second thing is of great concern to me." His cheeks reddened, but he soldiered on. "If you won't try and be a real daddy to this baby, I'll kick your butt from here to the New Mexico line."

Jessica was amazed that someone as mild-mannered as

Boone would make such a threat, but she'd had enough of this coercion talk. "Listen, I don't think anybody should be forced to—"

"Now, Jessie-girl," Travis said, "Boone and me, we have a point to make with our buddy Nat, so don't be implying that he'll be let off the hook. In fact, we asked the ladies to wait inside so we could get a few things straight with him before he goes in to see Lizzie."

Lizzie? Jessica's groan of protest was out before she could call it back.

"What's wrong?" Travis asked.

"Um, I...uh, didn't expect you'd all be calling her Lizzie," she said.

"Don't worry," Sebastian said. "Travis is the only one who calls her that. She's Elizabeth to the rest of us."

"Oh." Jessica told herself to be reasonable. A nickname wasn't the worst fate that could befall her baby. But she loved her daughter's name, and didn't like someone fooling with it. Still, it was probably a small matter. "I suppose in the grand scheme of things it isn't important, but I'd always thought—"

"There's not a thing wrong with the name Lizzie," Travis said. "Considering she's smart and funny and loves to play, I'd say it fits her personality a lot better than a long handle like *Elizabeth,* which sounds like somebody in one of those movies made in England."

Jessica winced. She'd been a fan of such movies in college. She'd chosen the name Elizabeth *because* it sounded elegant and British.

"I happen to like her name the way it is," Sebastian said. "It sounds pretty to me."

"Me, too," Boone said.

"Nope, way too formal," Travis said. Then he glanced at Jessica. "No offense. I figure you named her that because it's flexible, and you can make a lot of names out of it.

There's Beth, and Betty, and Liza, and just plain Liz. But the way she's turning out, Lizzie fits best. You'll see."

"She's not going to see a damn thing unless we let her go into the house," Sebastian pointed out.

"I guess we can go in now," Travis said, "as long as Nat understands our position on this baby thing."

"Oh, I understand it," Nat said. He gave the impression of great nonchalance. "But I'm afraid you've raised the bar too high for this ol' boy. I tried to tell Sebastian that I—"

"Hey." Boone clapped a big hand on Nat's shoulder. "Listen, I don't talk about it much, but my old man whupped me when I was growing up, too."

"Yeah," Nat said, "but I'll bet it wasn't the same."

"No kidding," Travis said. "Boone probably outweighed his dad by the time he was ten."

"Doesn't matter if it was the same or not," Boone insisted stubbornly. "He still beat us, but I'm not like my dad, and you aren't like yours, either. I'd lay money on it. So don't give up on this program so quick, before you ever see her."

"Yeah," Travis added. "She'll melt your heart, buddy."

"That's a fact," Sebastian said.

Uncertainty shone in Nat's eyes as he glanced around at his three friends.

Jessica put a comforting hand on his arm, and when he looked down at her, she gave him a reassuring smile, in spite of the butterflies fluttering in her stomach. "Let's go see our daughter," she murmured.

NAT DREW what strength he could from Jess's gaze. He wished he could hold her for a minute before they walked through that door, but that wouldn't be happening.

He glanced once more at his three friends, but their expressions had no give to them. They expected too much, but he couldn't bring himself to tell them so, straight out.

He already felt like a failure for getting Jess pregnant and leaving her to face the experience alone.

"I'll do the best I can," he said.

"In that case," Sebastian said, "everything will work out just fine. Now let's get in and enjoy that fire!"

As they all trooped into the house Nat had come to consider his second home, he was bombarded with the many changes there. A mesh-sided playpen filled with soft baby toys was set up behind the old leather sofa. He noticed a floor loom in a corner and remembered that Matty was a weaver. A new picture hung over the fireplace, and a pretty display of pinecones and autumn leaves decorated the mantel. Sebastian would never have thought to do such a thing.

Matty greeted him and Jess with all the confidence befitting the lady of the house. And she was definitely that, pregnant belly and all. But he had no time to comment on that development. As Matty took their coats and began the introductions, he sensed Jess's tension as she waited for the moment she'd be able to go see their baby. *Their baby.* The reality still hadn't hit him.

But before they could take that long walk back to the bedroom, it was only right that they acknowledge the women who had helped nurture that baby for six months. They met Travis's wife, Gwen, a tall brunette he vaguely remembered as one of Matty's good friends, and Shelby McFarland, Boone's petite, blond wife. They learned that Shelby and Boone had recently adopted Shelby's three-year-old nephew Josh and that he was also asleep in the room with Elizabeth.

The big surprise was Travis's mother, Luann, a tiny, gray-haired woman in her fifties who'd come to live at Gwen's bed-and-breakfast. Nat had always assumed Travis's playboy existence had continued when he'd returned to Utah every winter. Apparently he'd gone home to watch over his widowed mother.

At last the introductions were complete.

"I'd like to go see her now," Jess said quietly.

"Of course." Matty started down the hall, and everyone followed, bumping into each other as they tried to squeeze into the hallway. Jess and Nat brought up the rear.

Matty turned and held up her hand, like a traffic cop. "Hold on, here. We can't all go. In fact, Jessica should be allowed to go alone, if she wants."

Amid mumbled agreement, everyone backed out of the hallway.

Nat could live with Jess going in first. He wouldn't mind taking it slow, easing into the situation a little at a time.

"I'd like Nat to go with me," Jess said.

So much for taking it slow. With his buddies giving him the evil eye, he had no choice but to agree. "Okay. Sure. Good idea."

Everyone stepped aside.

"She's in the guest room, Nat," Sebastian said. "The room you used to use when you came down from Denver. Matty redecorated it."

"And I just want to add that Sebastian picked out that girly crib," Matty said. "I wanted something plainer."

"We left a night-light on," Boone said. "Josh likes that, especially when they're together, so if he opens his eyes he can see Elizabeth over there in her crib."

"Oh, and about the pacifier," Travis said. "Some people purely hate them, but Doc Harrison said it wouldn't hurt her, and so we use it sometimes."

"I hope you like her sleeper, Jessica," Gwen said. "Travis and I couldn't decide which one to put on her when we brought her over tonight. We went with Winnie-the-Pooh."

Jess turned to her with a look of surprise. "Brought her over? I thought she stayed here all the time."

"Oh, no," Shelby said from her position beside Boone. "We all take—I mean, we all *took* turns. You see, everybody…'' She trailed off and glanced around nervously, as if afraid she'd spoken out of turn.

"Everybody wanted her," Sebastian finished, his voice rough with emotion.

Oh, God. Nat had never seen his friend so emotional. It made him feel about an inch tall, knowing he'd helped cause this fiasco.

Jess swallowed, and her voice shook. "I don't know how I'll ever be able to thank you all, or make it up to you for…for…''

Feeling the need to do something of value, Nat reached for her hand, which was ice-cold. "Let's go," he said gently.

She blinked rapidly, swallowed again, and nodded.

Nat started down the hall. Through their linked hands, he could feel Jess trembling. He laced his fingers through hers and gave her hand a squeeze. If he could have forced words past his tight throat, he would have said something reassuring, but all he could give her at this point was the comfort of touch.

Ahead of them, the guest-room door was open a crack, and a faint light showed around the edge. It wasn't often, Nat thought, that stepping through a door could so completely divide ignorance from knowledge. This was one of those times. Once he went through that door, he would never be the same.

CHAPTER TWELVE

AS NAT GENTLY PUSHED open the door, Jessica gripped his hand and vowed not to cry. Crying would only wake Elizabeth and little Josh and frighten them both. Besides, as long as Elizabeth stayed asleep, Jessica could hang on to the fantasy that her child would remember her.

A zoo of stuffed animals covering every available surface, and bright cartoon wallpaper left no doubt this was a beloved baby's room. The crib was against one wall and a double bed against the other. Jessica barely spared a glance for the small boy in the bed as she started toward the crib, heart pounding so loud she thought the sound might wake Elizabeth.

She was so big! Tears swam in her eyes and she wiped them away swiftly. She wanted to see.

Oh, God. Her daughter was so beautiful. Jessica pressed her fist against her mouth to stifle the sob that rose in her throat as tears rushed down her cheeks. Beautiful. The pain of being separated from this child, this flesh of her flesh, rolled through her unchecked. Until now she'd refused to give it room in her heart, but now, at the sight of Elizabeth, it blasted past her defenses, threatening to engulf her.

She fought for control, reminding herself that the separation was over. No more time apart. Now she could mend the rift between her and this precious child. Elizabeth would be confused, so it was up to Jessica to be strong, to be up to the challenge.

Elizabeth slept on her tummy with her bottom up in the

air. Jessica had never seen her do that. But then, she'd never seen her crawl or pull herself up, and she probably could do both of those things now. Her dimpled hand lay over the tail of a sock monkey with black-button eyes. Her favorite toy, Sebastian had said. Jessica's heart grew heavy as she thought of all she'd missed.

The baby's hair, which used to be so wispy and light brown, looked redder now and more abundant as it curled in ringlets all over her head. She had Jessica's hair. *Her child.* Possessiveness flowed hot in her veins. *Hers.*

Before she knew it, she'd dropped to her knees in front of the crib and was reaching through the bars. She stopped herself just in time. No, she didn't want to wake Elizabeth. Not yet. To keep herself in check, she gripped the bars while she peered into Elizabeth's face.

Oh, yes, she was older and bigger all over, but the same. Same uptilted nose, same rosy cheeks, same Cupid's bow mouth. Jessica's breasts ached with the memory of how sweet it had been to nurse her and how agonizing to switch her to the bottle.

She heard a steady *plop, plop, plop* and finally realized it was the sound of her tears, dripping on the edge of the crib mattress. Drawing back, she felt the imprint the crib bars had made against her cheeks as she'd tried to eliminate the barrier between her and her daughter.

When an arm came around her shoulders, she jumped.

"It's me," Nat whispered, crouching beside her. "Only me."

She turned her head in surprise. She'd forgotten he was even in the room.

He stared at Elizabeth as if totally amazed by her. When he glanced at Jessica, even the dim lighting couldn't disguise the wonder in his expression.

"We did this?" he murmured.

She nodded, unable to speak.

His attention returned to the baby, as if drawn by a magnet. "Amazing."

Hope swelled within her. Maybe, if he was as awestruck by this miracle as he sounded, he would find a way around his fears. She looked back at Elizabeth and her craving to hold the baby was like a live thing she had to wrestle every moment she stayed near the crib. Her mouth grew moist with the need to touch her child. Not yet. Soon.

"She's so small," Nat said quietly. He kept his arm around Jessica and kneaded her shoulder gently.

Jessica swallowed hard and managed a whispered comment. "I was just thinking how big she is."

"She looks like you."

"A little." She battled the urge to snatch this baby up and never let her go. "Her eyes are the same shape as your eyes." Jessica had fantasized this scene a million times— picturing how it would feel to be gathered inside the protective circle of Nat's arm as the two of them watched Elizabeth sleep. "And look at her fingers," she said. "They're long and graceful, like yours."

He made a brief noise of protest. "My fingers aren't *graceful*."

"They are." Her emotions pooled like wax around a candle flame, ready to spill over at the slightest tremor. "Especially when you're—" She caught herself.

"When I'm making love to you?" he asked softly as he increased the pressure of his easy massage.

She'd thought Elizabeth had laid claim to all her needs for the moment, but she discovered Elizabeth's father had a grip on his share, after all. She glanced at him. He was gazing at her with that primitive glow in his eyes that told her exactly what was on his mind.

She shook her head. "I didn't mean to say that."

"How can you help it, when right in front of us is the evidence of me being deep inside you," he murmured.

She tried to be rational. "This isn't the time to be thinking of…that."

"Maybe not. But I don't think I've ever wanted you more than I do right this minute."

His gaze was mesmerizing in its intensity. She could no more stop her instinctive response to him than deny her need for this baby. He leaned down, as if to kiss her. Then a rustling from the crib broke the spell.

Elizabeth smacked her lips and heaved a sigh.

Jessica froze in place, sure their whispering had caused the baby to wake up. Now she'd have to bear the heartache of watching those eyes open and show absolutely no recognition. Jessica felt too fragile to deal with that yet.

But the baby's eyes remained closed, her lashes creating a pale, feathery crescent against her soft cheek.

"We'd better go," Jessica whispered. "Before we wake her."

"Yeah." Nat stood and then helped Jessica to her feet. He held both her hands, and for a moment it seemed he might pull her close. Then he squeezed her hands and released them. "Let's go back to the others. It's been a long night, and they'd probably like to get home."

IT TOOK SOME DOING, but finally Matty and Sebastian hustled everyone out the door, including a very sleepy Josh. Nat could see that nobody was happy about leaving Elizabeth, knowing that once they returned, Jess would be in charge as the baby's mother.

Finally the last vehicle pulled out of the driveway, and Nat brought in his and Jess's backpacks. He wasn't sure what to do with them because their sleeping arrangements hadn't been decided, so he leaned them against the wall by the front door. Matty had just eased into the rocker and she looked glad to be off her feet for a change. He decided not to ask where to put the backpacks and risk sending her into her hostess mode again.

While Sebastian made the rounds checking the locks on all the doors and windows, Jess stood warming her hands by the fire. Because Nat couldn't be near her without wanting to put his arms around her, he roamed the living room, examining all the feminine touches Matty had added.

From her position by the fire, Jess turned so she could look at Matty. "I want to thank you for bringing everybody together tonight and giving me a chance to let them know how much I appreciate all they've done."

Matty smiled. "You're welcome, but I probably couldn't have kept them away with a loaded shotgun." A small sigh of weariness escaped her as she laid her head back against the rocker.

"But you're exhausted," Jess said. "I feel terrible that this has been so much work for you."

"I'm a little tired," Matty admitted, laying a hand over her rounded tummy. "But don't feel guilty. I wouldn't have missed any of it for all the tea in China. Besides, being tired at this stage probably goes with the territory."

"I'm afraid it does," Jess said. "I never slept so much in my life as when I was pregnant with Elizabeth. I even took naps, and I never do that."

Matty nodded. "Around this place we've turned into Naps 'R' Us. It's embarrassing how much sleep I need these days."

As the two women exchanged an understanding glance, Nat felt cheated that he hadn't been there to experience Jess's pregnancy, naps and all. As a man, he couldn't be expected to know what it was like to be pregnant, but if he'd gone through it with Jess, he'd at least have some reference point.

Instead, he felt shut out. But it was his own damn fault that he hadn't made sure she was all right before he left the country. "I didn't get a chance to congratulate you before, Matty," he said. "But I think it's great. When's the baby due?"

"We're hoping for Valentine's Day," Matty said.

"We're *planning* on Valentine's Day," Sebastian said, coming into the room and moving behind the rocker. He reached over and began massaging Matty's shoulders. "Little Rebecca will be right on time, like the sweetheart she is."

"You already know it's a girl?" Nat said.

"No, we don't," Matty said.

Sebastian continued to massage his wife's shoulders. "Yes, we do. I don't mean we've looked at an ultrasound or anything. I just know in my bones we'll have a girl."

Matty chuckled. "I sure hope your bones aren't misleading you. A boy isn't going to be happy wearing that hand-tooled belt you're making that says *Rebecca* across the back."

"Sounds like you really want a girl, Sebastian." Nat was fascinated by the concept. He would have sworn Sebastian would want a boy, at least the first time around. Not that Sebastian was sexist, exactly, but the female of the species had always puzzled him. He'd be on firmer ground during the raising process with a boy.

"I surely do want a girl," Sebastian said. "Baby girls are something special, Nat. You'll see."

"Guess so." By now Nat had a good idea how attached Sebastian had become to Elizabeth. Insisting that Matty would have a girl probably helped him cope with giving Elizabeth back to Jess.

"I thought you two could take that double bed in Elizabeth's room for now," Matty said.

Nat tensed and decided not to look at Jess. He didn't know which way she'd choose. She'd asked him to be with her when she'd gone into the bedroom to see their daughter, so maybe she'd want all three of them to be together tonight, too. He could go for that. Having the baby in with them would be nerve-racking, but he'd brave it through if it meant being with Jess.

But she had to know that if they shared a double bed, they'd end up making love, even if they did it softly and quietly so as not to wake the baby. After what she'd said that first morning about no lovemaking, this was her call, not his.

"You might be a little cramped," Matty continued, as if she'd decided their silence meant they weren't happy about the size of the bed, "but it should do until we've worked out…" She paused as if searching for the right words, and glanced up at her husband.

"Well, until we figure out…" Sebastian didn't seem any more able to define the situation than his wife.

"Is that the only spare bed?" Jess asked, her question tentative, as if she didn't want to sound rude.

So she didn't want to share the bed with him, didn't want to feel his arms around her. Nat was bitterly disappointed, but he accepted her decision with as much gallantry as he could muster. He glanced over at her. "There's a daybed in Sebastian's office. Why don't I take that and give you the bed in Elizabeth's room?"

She met his gaze, and her expression was carefully neutral. "I'd appreciate that," she said quietly.

No one spoke for a moment, and finally Matty stood. "Well, guess I'll get some sheets for the daybed."

"I'll make it up," Nat said. "You and Sebastian go on to bed. We've put you to enough trouble as it is."

"Better yet," Sebastian said, "*I'll* get the sheets for the daybed, while the mommy-to-be goes nite-nite." He steered his wife toward the hall.

"It's no trouble. I—"

"I want you horizontal, woman. You've been on your feet long enough. Go on now. You can warm up the sheets for me." Sebastian gave her a quick kiss. "See you in a little while."

Matty's gaze flicked from her husband to Nat. "Okay. Don't be too long."

"I won't."

"Guess I'll turn in, too." Jess walked over to pick up her backpack.

"Here." Nat crossed to her. "Let me take that in for—"

"That's okay." She stepped out of reach. "Thanks, anyway. I can handle it. Good night, and thanks again for everything, Sebastian." With that, she headed down the hall toward Elizabeth's room.

Nat's heart twisted. He wanted to be able to pamper her a little, the way Sebastian pampered Matty. But you couldn't pamper a woman if she wouldn't let you, he thought sadly.

He'd also noticed the eagerness in her eyes as she'd turned to go down that hall. She wanted to be with her baby, and he didn't blame her for that. The idea of spending the night in the same room with her daughter probably thrilled her as much as it would have terrified him. But he would have done it, if that had meant he could hold Jess all night long.

He watched her walk quickly to the end of the hall and nudge the door open. Then she slipped inside and closed it behind her. The whole procedure felt very wrong to Nat. He should be in that bedroom with her.

"I'll get you those sheets," Sebastian said.

"Thanks." Feeling totally unnecessary, Nat walked over to the fireplace and set aside the screen so he could rearrange the coals with the poker. It didn't particularly need doing, but he had the urge to busy himself with something.

He had to maneuver around the dogs, who were asleep on the braided rug in front of the hearth. They both raised their heads, gave him a look as if they thought he was making a fuss for nothing, and went back to sleep.

"You wouldn't understand if I explained it," he muttered to the dogs, who didn't stir.

Crouched next to the fireplace, he looked at the elegant tool in his hand. Boone had made the set five years ago, using his blacksmith's skills to create a gift for Sebastian's thirtieth birthday.

How things had changed in five years. Sebastian had been married to Barbara then, and Matty's husband had still been alive. Come to think of it, Gwen had been at that party with the guy she used to be married to, Derek somebody or other. Travis had brought a date, and so had Nat. He could barely remember who he'd been seeing then. Maybe it was Marianne, or then again, he might have brought Tanya to that party.

Funny how not a single woman from his past stood out in his mind except for Jess. Until he'd met her, he'd never believed in the concept of soul mates. He still didn't, not really. She might be the only woman for him, but he wasn't right for her at all.

"Somebody gave Matty and me some very old, very expensive brandy for a wedding present," Sebastian said.

Nat glanced up to see him standing by the sofa, the day-bed sheets folded over one arm. "That's nice," Nat said.

"I thought so, but Matty hates brandy. Besides, she's on the wagon until after the baby's born. I've got a hankering to try the stuff."

"That's okay, Sebastian." Nat flashed him a brief smile. "You don't have to stay up and keep me company. Go on to bed with your wife."

"Or to put it another way, you don't have to stay up with me." Sebastian tossed the sheets on the sofa. "I'm opening that brandy, but if you don't want any, I guess I'll have to drink alone. Which would be a hell of a thing, when you consider it. A man hasn't seen his friend in seventeen months, and that friend would rather go to bed than share a little brandy and polite conversation. Did I mention that it was old and very expensive?"

Nat grinned and pushed himself to his feet. Sebastian obviously wanted to talk and it wouldn't be very gracious of him to refuse, especially considering that he hadn't been much of a friend to Sebastian recently. "Yeah, I believe you did mention it." He returned the fireplace poker to its place on the wrought-iron rack. "A man would be dumb to turn down an offer like that."

"Then come on in the kitchen and I'll get you a glass. Or a snifter, as the trendsetters say."

"You've got snifters?" Nat hadn't realized how much he'd missed Sebastian and his wry sense of humor.

"Hell, no. Years ago Barbara tried to talk me into getting some. She even bought me a box of Cuban cigars and a smoking jacket."

Nat laughed at the mental picture of Sebastian in jeans, boots, a Stetson and a smoking jacket. "She never did get you, did she?"

"Guess not." Sebastian reached into a cupboard and took down two juice glasses and the promised bottle of brandy, which he carried over to the scarred oak kitchen table. "Did you know she had an affair with Matty's husband, Butch?"

Nat stopped dead in the middle of the kitchen. So that nasty little bit of information had come to light at last.

Sebastian poured the brandy into the glasses before he looked up. "You did know, didn't you?"

"Yeah." Nat didn't like admitting that. He was getting a real reputation for being secretive. Maybe the best thing to do was to get it all out in the open. "She told me about it, and you might as well know the circumstances. She propositioned me, too, and when I turned her down, she said it didn't matter because she always had Butch to fall back on."

A flicker of anger came and went in Sebastian's gray eyes. "Now I wonder who else she came on to. What about Travis?"

Nat sighed. "Yeah, she tried to get something going with Travis, too. Barbara was a real alley cat, and neither of us knew how to tell you. I have a hunch she went after Boone, as well, but he's the kind of guy who wouldn't mention that fact to a soul, even if you put a branding iron to his feet.''

''I guess I can see why you wouldn't tell me. A man tends not to want to believe a thing like that about the woman he married. Instead of waking me up, it probably would have come between you, me and Travis.''

''That's what we figured. So we kept quiet.''

Sebastian took one of the glasses and handed it to Nat. Then he picked up his own. ''To friendship.''

Nat saluted him with his glass. ''To the best damn friend I know.''

Sebastian sipped the brandy and grinned. ''Not bad. Not bad at all.''

Nat had to admit the dark liquid felt good going down. He took another sip and felt himself begin to relax. ''Real good, in fact.''

''Now that we've discovered it doesn't taste like rat poison, pull up a chair,'' Sebastian said, taking a seat at the table. ''We don't charge extra for that.''

''Don't mind if I do.'' Nat settled into a wooden chair worn smooth by countless denim-covered butts. After another swallow of the brandy, he felt the tightness loosen in his chest. ''This really is good stuff. So you scored this just for getting married?''

''That's all I had to do. Here, let me top that off for you.''

''Why not?''

Sebastian poured Nat's glass nearly to the brim and set the bottle down. ''That oughta put lead in your pencil.''

''Now there's a problem I don't have. I have just about every other problem you can name, but lack of interest in sex isn't one of them.''

Sebastian eyed him. ''I was only being a smart-ass, but as long as we're on the subject, how do things stand between you and Jessica, anyway?''

"I figured you'd get around to that." Without the relaxing effect of the brandy, Nat might have been more defensive, but the more he relaxed, the more he felt like talking. Of course, Sebastian had planned it that way.

"How you're getting along with Jessica is pretty damn important," Sebastian said. "If you two are fighting, then Elizabeth will know it right off. That's not good for a little kid."

"We're not fighting," Nat said. "At least, not like you think. We've had a few heated words, but mostly…mostly I need time to get used to this whole situation, which I told her. At this stage of the game I can't make promises. So she decided we shouldn't sleep together."

Sebastian nodded. "That sounds logical."

"Oh, it's *logical* as hell. But logic doesn't keep me from wanting her."

That made Sebastian smile. He took another swig of brandy and set it down carefully on the table. Then he swiveled the glass back and forth between his fingers, staring at the contents as he spoke. "You dated her for a year, right?" He glanced up. "That's quite a long time for a free spirit like you."

Nat met his gaze as another wave of remorse washed over him. "Yeah, and I should have told you guys about it."

Sebastian shrugged and leaned back in his chair. "Hey, forget it. That's water under the bridge. We've established that you're a regular chickenshit when it comes to matters of the heart." He grinned to take the sting out of his words. "Besides, you thought we'd try to interfere, and you were right about that. I would have told you to marry that woman if you'd enjoyed each other's company for an entire year. Lucky for you that you get another opportunity."

"You know, when I was on my way home, I'd pretty much decided to ask her to take a chance on me. I figured that if I loused things up in the first few months because

I'd reverted to being like my father, then she could divorce me." That concept of divorcing Jess soured his stomach when he said it out loud. He took another sip of brandy. "But now, with the baby, it's more complicated. And I don't want to put that little kid at risk."

"From you?" Sebastian gazed at him.

"Yeah, from me."

"That's—"

"Don't tell me it's ridiculous. It's not. I've seen what happens to people under pressure. They do things they wouldn't otherwise do."

Sebastian stared into the depths of his brandy. "What was it like over there?"

"Rough." Nat wondered how Sebastian would have reacted to seeing a child of three sobbing over her mother's body, knowing that the mother's death had been the result of a senseless act of violence. It might have broken Sebastian's big heart beyond repair. Sebastian liked to believe the best of people.

"It was hell, in fact," he added. "But it some crazy way it was heaven, too. The measure of a person working or living in the camps wasn't how they dressed or how much education they had or the size of their bank account. It was all about character."

"And you thrived there, didn't you?"

"I guess I did." Nat had always valued the way Sebastian could help him sort out his thoughts. "I know I felt worthwhile for the first time in my life." He looked over at his friend. "I have a project under way to get some of those war orphans adopted, but that's a short-term thing. On the way here Jess brought up the idea of me running a ranch for kids in this country who have no place else to go. I kind of like the idea."

Sebastian looked interested.

Encouraged, Nat continued. "I could still broker real estate on the side, to keep the cash coming in, and I could use whatever I've learned about sales to get some backers. What do you think?''

''I think that if you don't hook up with a woman who has that much insight into what you need to make you happy, you are the biggest fool who ever sat in this kitchen.'' He chuckled and drained his glass. ''And that's saying a mouthful, because I'm no Einstein when it comes to relationships, either. Now, let's go to bed. I've learned what I came in here to learn.''

Nat chuckled. ''Which was?''

''That you're pie-eyed in love with the mother of your baby. If we have that to work with, we'll be all right.''

CHAPTER THIRTEEN

JESSICA DIDN'T WANT to sleep. She wanted to lie in the double bed and listen to her baby breathe. Whenever sleep started to claim her, she'd wake herself up, get out of bed and pad barefoot over to the crib. She'd stand there watching Elizabeth until the urge to touch her became too strong, and then she'd go back and crawl into bed again to listen to her breathing.

And all the while she carried on a silent conversation with her daughter. *Mommy's here now, sweetheart. When you wake up, I'll be able to lift you out of your crib, the way I used to do. I can change your diaper and play those little tickle games that we used to play. You can show me your new teeth, and how you've learned to sit up, and crawl, and pull yourself up. Mommy's here.*

She lay in bed planning how she would approach Elizabeth when the baby woke up. Obviously she should take it slow and let Elizabeth get used to her again. Knowing that the baby had been swapped between three couples made her feel more confident that Elizabeth wouldn't be as inflexible as she might have been if Sebastian had kept her at the Rocking D the whole time. Still, Jessica didn't kid herself that the transition would be easy.

For now, though, she was content to be in the same room with her child at last. Nat hadn't been happy about sleeping elsewhere, but having him in this bed with her would have overloaded her circuits. For one thing, she wouldn't have been able to concentrate on her child, and right now, that was very important.

Besides, she really believed in the ban on lovemaking she'd imposed. If Nat had shared this bed with her tonight, he would have made love to her. It would be ridiculous to suppose otherwise, with both of them crammed into the double bed together for hours.

The thought was not without appeal, however. She breathed in the scent of wood smoke that pervaded the house and snuggled under the down comforter. No, the idea was not without appeal.

Although she would have sworn that she hadn't slept at all, she opened her eyes and realized the room was filled with the gray light of dawn.

"Ba," cooed a soft voice. "Ba-ba."

Her pulse rate skyrocketed. Elizabeth was awake. Cautiously she moved the comforter aside so that she could peek over at the crib.

On her hands and knees in her footed Pooh sleeper, Elizabeth faced her. Oh, yes, she had her daddy's blue eyes. But they were fringed with light eyelashes, not dark ones like Nat's. Her tousled hair was a riot of coppery curls, and her cheeks were flushed pink from sleep. Jessica could have looked at her forever.

She was staring intently at the bed, and Jessica smiled at the puzzle she must have presented to the baby. When Elizabeth had gone to sleep, a little boy had been in this bed. Now he'd been magically transformed into a grown woman.

"*Ba*-ba," Elizabeth said again, and drooled. Keeping her attention on the bed, she used the bars to pull herself up until she was standing. *Standing*.

Jessica stayed perfectly quiet and watched, fascinated by the developmental strides Elizabeth had made in her absence. She swallowed a lump in her throat. So much had happened while she'd been away. Too much.

With a firm grip on the railing, Elizabeth began to rattle the crib. "Ba!" she called, exposing her new teeth as she rattled the crib some more.

"Hi, baby," Jessica murmured. Seeing those teeth made her eyes blur with tears. Her little girl was so grown-up.

Elizabeth stopped rattling the crib and stared some more.

"It's me, your mommy," Jessica said softly.

Elizabeth didn't seem alarmed, only curious.

"You sure are a pretty girl." Moving slowly, Jessica propped herself up on one elbow. "Do you remember me at all?"

A flicker of worry settled in the blue eyes.

"It's okay." Jessica kept her voice low and soothing as she sat up and pushed the covers back. "You'll get used to me again. "You'll—"

Elizabeth's screech of fear froze Jessica's blood.

"I won't hurt you, darling," she pleaded as Elizabeth began to cry. Instinct drove Jessica out of the bed and over to the crib. "Don't be afraid." She reached for the baby. "Please don't be afraid. It's me. Your mommy."

With an even louder wail, Elizabeth flung herself backward to escape Jessica's extended arms and banged her head on the far side of the crib. Then she began to cry in earnest.

"Oh, no." Jessica released the latch on the railing and leaned over. "Oh, sweetheart! Please let me—"

"I'll get her." Matty hurried into the room and over to the crib, lifting a squalling Elizabeth out of the crib and out of Jessica's reach, as if she were a menace.

Jessica knew Matty didn't mean to make it seem that way, but it did, anyway. Tears streamed down her cheeks. "She hit her head," she said. "P-please check her and m-make sure she's okay." The fact that she couldn't comfort her own child was the worst pain she'd ever endured. "I didn't mean to scare her. I didn't mean to."

"Of course you didn't." Matty ran her hand over the

back of Elizabeth's head. "And she's fine. There, there, little one." Matty held the baby against her shoulder and rubbed her back. "Easy does it. You're fine."

"What happened?" Sebastian appeared in the doorway, fastening his jeans.

"I—" Jessica found she didn't have the power to tell him. Her throat was closed with grief and shame. Her baby didn't want her.

Then Nat came up behind Sebastian. He, too, was wearing only a pair of jeans. "Is everybody okay?"

"I think Elizabeth got a little spooked, seeing Jessica for the first time," Sebastian said.

"She'll be okay," Matty murmured as she continued to stroke the baby. "We'll have to ease into it, that's all."

"Oh, Jess." Nat's eyes clouded. "I'm sorry."

She was more than sorry. She was destroyed. And she couldn't stand to be in the room a minute longer. She managed to choke out an excuse that she needed to go to the bathroom. Then she pushed past everyone, went into the bathroom across the hall and shut the door.

Once there, she grabbed a towel and buried her face in it while she sobbed. Elizabeth didn't want her anymore.

Eventually the tears slowed, although she didn't think the pain in her heart would ever go away. She'd lost her baby. Because of that horrible man who was after her, she'd lost Elizabeth. She was ready to search him out and kill him with her bare hands. He'd robbed her of her child.

A light tapping on the door was followed by Nat's voice. "Jess? Can I come in?"

"No."

"That's what I get for asking," he muttered, opening the door.

She turned away and made herself busy hanging the towel on the rack and making sure it was aligned perfectly. "I don't know what ever happened to the concept of privacy," she said in a voice still thick with tears.

He came in and closed the door behind him. "You don't need privacy right now." He took her by the shoulders, eased her around and wrapped her in his arms, tucking her head against his chest.

She was too weak to resist. "How do you know I don't?" Her words were muffled against his shirt. Apparently he'd taken the time to put one on before coming to see about her. She appreciated that. As needy as she felt right now, his bare chest against her cheek might cause her to do something unwise.

"I know because I saw the look on your face when you ran in here to hide. You only think you need privacy. What you really need is somebody to hold you."

He was absolutely right. Her arms had gone around him automatically, and she was clinging to him like a burr. "And you're some sort of expert?"

He laid his cheek against the top of her head. "As a matter of fact, I am."

Come to think of it, he probably was, considering all the times he must have been called upon to comfort grief-stricken people in the refugee camps. His own knowledge of grief was hard-won as a small child.

"I don't know much about this baby stuff," he said, "but Matty told me that Elizabeth will get over this, and I figure Matty knows what she's talking about. She blames herself for setting up the sleeping arrangement that way. She didn't think about how Elizabeth might react when she woke up and found a str—uh, someone she wasn't...well, wasn't used to, in the room."

"I'm her *mother*," Jessica wailed, tightening her grip on him. "And she's afraid of me."

"She'll remember," Nat said softly, rubbing her back in the same way Matty had rubbed Elizabeth's.

"Maybe not." Jessica felt the tears welling up again. "Maybe I'll have to start all over, and it'll be as if I adopted her. Oh, Nat, why couldn't you have come home sooner?"

He groaned. "I wish to God I had. Oh, Jess. It's going to take me a hundred lifetimes to make it up to you for the pain I've caused. And may still cause. Damn it."

Immediately she regretted making a scapegoat of him. She held him close. "Nat, I shouldn't have said that. This whole problem is mine. I'm the one who got pregnant. I'm the one who thought I could keep my wealthy background a secret."

"If we're passing blame around, I should have walked away from you the minute I laid eyes on you. I knew it, too. But I was weak, and I kidded myself that if we kept everything quiet and sort of contained, it wouldn't get messy."

"It's messy."

"I'm aware of that. The Exxon *Valdez* has nothing on us. We could probably qualify for a Superfund."

She surprised herself by chuckling.

"Now, that's music to my ears." He kissed the top of her head. "Any more where that came from?"

She leaned back to gaze up at him and realized her heart no longer felt like a stone in her chest. "You did it."

"No doubt. Name any crime you want and I'm probably guilty."

"Oh, for heaven's sake!" She took his stubbled face in both hands. "Must you always think the worst of yourself? I only meant to say that—"

"Don't try to whitewash the situation, Jess. Everybody knows that birth control fails sometimes. I made love to you…a lot. I should never have left the country without making sure you were okay. If I'd done that, none of this would have happened."

"I would still have this creep on my trail."

He shook his head. "Nope."

"No?"

"I would have eradicated the guy long before now."

She sighed. "You're a good man, Nat." She continued

to cradle his face between her hands. "And thank you for comforting me so well. I do feel better."

He held her gaze, and the anxiety in his blue eyes cleared. "That's good." There was a husky note in his voice as his attention strayed from her face. For the first time he seemed to be taking inventory of the scooped neck of her sleep shirt and the obvious fact that she wore no bra underneath. He swallowed and looked into her eyes again. "Sleep well?"

"No."

His tightened his grip on her. "Jess—"

"No." The look in his eyes set off fireworks in her tummy.

"I'm going crazy."

So was she. She felt her resolve slip a little as heat licked through her. "Nat, we're in the bathroom, for heaven's sake."

"That counter would support you," he murmured. He cupped her bottom and snugged her up against his erection. "I'm a desperate man, Jess. Give me five minutes. I know we can manage in five minutes. We once did it in four, remember?"

She remembered it all, and those memories weren't helping keep her strong.

"I need you. Need to be inside you," he coaxed, seducing her with a rough-edged tone that never failed to arouse her to a frenzy.

And she wanted him there, too. But she shook her head. "Not a good idea," she said, although her breathing was no longer steady. "Besides, you don't have birth control."

He kneaded her bottom through the material of her sleep shirt. "That's what you think. I guess you've forgotten that I was a Boy Scout."

"You actually have a—"

"I do, and I will. At all times. In case you change your

mind.'' He gave her one last nudge and released her. ''See you at the breakfast table.''

FORTUNATELY FOR NAT, when he left the bathroom no one was in the hallway. He ducked into Sebastian's office where he'd spent a miserable night longing for Jess and worrying about Elizabeth. After taking a few deep breaths to get his raging hormones under control, he put on his boots, grabbed his jacket and Stetson and left the room.

The living room was empty but he could hear Matty, Sebastian and the baby in the kitchen. He whistled for Flea-farm and got Sadie, Matty's Great Dane, in the bargain as both dogs trotted out of the kitchen.

''I'm taking the dogs out for a run,'' he called, and didn't wait for an answer before heading out the front door. He needed some time alone before he dealt with that baby again. Or with Jess.

He crossed the front porch and bounded down the steps while the dogs cavorted in front of him like a couple of puppies. Pausing in the circular driveway, he filled his lungs with cool mountain air. Nothing matched the pine-scented air of Colorado.

Damn, but he'd missed this country. And how it loved to show off in October, with cobalt skies and mountains splashed with gold from the stands of aspens turning color. The two white-barked trees Sebastian had planted in his yard beyond the driveway shimmered in the light breeze, the leaves dripping from the branches like coins from a pirate's treasure.

The dogs glanced back at him as if wondering which direction he planned to take. Nat longed to get a good horse between his thighs and ride until he was saddle-sore. But he hadn't stopped long enough to ask Sebastian about tak-ing a horse, and he couldn't presume to do that without asking, even if the answer was sure to be yes.

So he set off toward the trees on foot. He hadn't been

much used to walking before he volunteered to go overseas, but he'd done a lot of it in the refugee camps. Vehicles were in short supply, and if the refugees had owned any horses they probably would have eaten them instead of riding them. Sebastian knew he would never take the basic comforts of his life for granted again.

Fleafarm and Sadie frisked along ahead of him, pausing every now and then to glance back and make sure he was still following. The dogs reminded Sebastian of some other plans he'd made for when he came home. He'd decided to get a dog. But the dog had only been part of the plan.

While living among the refugees, he hadn't missed his luxury apartment in Denver or his well-run real estate office or dealing with clients. He'd missed spending time at the Rocking D. And although he didn't want to go into ranching, he wanted to own a piece of land like this, maybe not quite so large, but big enough that he could have a barn, some horses and a dog.

He'd hoped Jess might like that idea, too, because he'd pictured her there with him. Her suggestion of opening a ranch for orphans intrigued him, but he didn't know if she had any interest in being part of something like that. And there was also the matter of the baby.

This constant, pounding need for Jess made thinking about anything else nearly impossible, though. Nothing was clear to him except that he needed to make love to her. Then maybe he'd be able to consider the other aspects of his life. But obviously she thought he should figure out his life first, and then, depending on what he'd decided, they might be able to make love again.

She wasn't being unreasonable. Even Sebastian thought her decision not to go to bed with him until he knew his own mind made perfect sense. But neither of them understood that trying to sort through his feelings while he needed Jess so desperately was like trying to learn to cook while the kitchen was on fire.

A jay flew across his path in a flash of blue, and from
the cloudless sky above, a hawk cried out as it circled,
looking for breakfast. A chipmunk bounded out of Nat's
path and scurried into a hollow log so it wouldn't *be* breakfast.

Life was so simple for these creatures, Nat thought. Instinct told them when to hide, when to mate and how to
take care of their young. He wondered when, in the evo-
lution of humans, the act of breeding had become so surrounded with land mines.

The breeze blew down from the hillside in front of him.
The dogs paused to sniff the air at the same moment Nat
saw a movement ahead, up higher in the trees. The dogs
barked and headed in that direction. At first Nat thought it
might be a deer, but then sunlight glinted off something
metal.

"Fleafarm! Sadie! Come!" His stomach lurched. "Come
here!" he called again, and fortunately the dogs turned
around with great reluctance and started slowly back to
him. "Good girls!" He patted his thighs enthusiastically
while he kept an eye on the spot where he'd seen movement.

All was still now. Although he had a premonition that
wouldn't quit, logically he didn't know who was up there.
Could be a hunter trespassing on Rocking D land, or a bird-
watcher with a pair of binoculars that caught the light of
the sun. Or it could be Jess's stalker. He needed to get the
dogs to safety and then alert Sebastian. If they saddled up
a couple of horses, they could take a look around.

Once the dogs were with him, he started back toward the
house, glancing over his shoulder often to see if he noticed
anything more on the hillside. Nothing. If it hadn't been
for the reaction of the dogs when they'd obviously caught
the scent of something, he would have wondered if he'd
imagined the whole thing.

Then he heard the rumble of a vehicle on the road, and

before he reached the driveway, Travis pulled up in his shiny black muscle truck.

Travis hopped down from the cab and gave Nat a grin. "Out for a morning stroll, cowboy? What's the matter, did you forget how to ride a horse while you were over there?" His grin faded as Nat drew closer. "What's the problem? Is Lizzy—"

"The baby's fine. At least she was last time I saw her. I need to get these dogs inside and grab Sebastian. I think I might've seen the guy up on that hill. If we saddle the horses and ride up there, we might get lucky."

"Did he know you saw him?"

"I'm not sure. Maybe. But we have to try."

"I'm on it. You get Sebastian and I'll start saddling the horses." Travis hopped back in his truck and spit gravel as he shot off toward the barn.

NAT HEARD the shower running when he walked in the door. He headed for the kitchen, where he found Sebastian feeding Elizabeth cereal, and Matty measuring coffee into the pot. Nat looked into the baby's blue eyes and felt his heart get all tangled up in that gaze. Quickly he looked away. He didn't have time for that now. "Is Jess in the shower?"

Matty glanced up. "Apparently. She hasn't come into the kitchen, and I'll bet she's afraid to. I was wondering if you'd go convince her to—"

"No can do." Nat looked over at Sebastian. "Our guy may have been up on the hillside just a minute ago. Travis is saddling the horses."

"Right." Sebastian put the spoon into the cereal bowl and set it on the table out of Elizabeth's reach. "Matty, take over here, and set the alarm once I'm out the door."

Matty was by his side instantly, grabbing his arm. "I don't think you should go charging up there without a plan."

"I have a plan. I'm getting my rifle." He pulled away from her and brushed past Nat as he headed through the living room.

"Watch the baby, Nat," Matty said as she ran after Sebastian. "Listen, cowboy, you can't just ride up there like the Three Musketeers, you know!"

Sebastian's voice drifted back as he kept going down the hall toward his bedroom. "Don't argue with me, Matty. We don't have time to waste if we want to catch him."

"He could pick you off!" She charged down the hall after her husband.

Nat glanced over at Elizabeth sitting in her high chair with cereal smeared all over her mouth. She was staring at him with wide eyes. He sure did recognize the color in those eyes. He saw it every morning in the mirror. Then her face scrunched up like someone was squeezing it, and she let out a howl of protest.

"Aw, don't do that," Nat said. "Matty will be back soon."

Elizabeth only cried harder and spit out whatever cereal she'd had in her mouth.

Nat panicked. For all he knew, she might choke or something if she kept crying like that. He could still hear Matty and Sebastian arguing back in the bedroom, and here was this kid who might be in serious danger, and he didn't have the foggiest idea what to do. "*Matty!*" he bellowed.

And just like that, Elizabeth stopped crying. But the look on her face was no improvement. She looked petrified. Of him. Nat's insides twisted as he remembered how he'd felt whenever his father had yelled like that. And here he was, scaring his daughter the same way.

"I'm sorry," he murmured. "I'm sorry, baby."

She gazed at him, and tears quivered on her lower eyelids.

"I won't yell at you anymore," he promised, looking into those big blue eyes. Oh, God. She was getting to him.

His chest grew tight and his throat felt clogged up. That little face, that tear-streaked, cereal-smeared little face, was getting to him.

"Let's go." Sebastian came into the kitchen wearing a jacket and carrying his rifle.

With relief, Nat turned toward Sebastian.

"You are idiots, all of you!" Matty said, coming in behind him. "We should call the sheriff."

"By the time we do, Jessica's stalker will be long gone," Sebastian said. "Now set the alarm once I leave, and if we're not back in an hour, then you can call the sheriff."

"Peachy," Matty said. "Should I ask him to bring body bags?"

"Stop it. We'll be fine." Sebastian glanced at Nat. "Ready?"

"Ready," Nat said. As he started out the kitchen door behind Sebastian, he chanced one more look over at the baby. She was still watching him. "See you later, Elizabeth," he said softly.

CHAPTER FOURTEEN

JESSICA HAD NEARLY FINISHED her shower when she heard the commotion in the hall as Matty and Sebastian came by arguing about something. With guilt her constant companion, she couldn't help wondering if it had to do with her. She needed to come out of hiding and find out.

Toweling off quickly, she dressed in jeans and an ivory long-sleeved T-shirt. Then she ran a comb through her hair. As she left the bathroom she heard the kitchen door close.

"Men!" Matty's disgusted voice carried down the hall from the kitchen. "I tell you, Elizabeth, most guys don't have the brains God gave a goat."

Jessica approached the kitchen doorway with caution. "Matty?" she called out before she showed herself. "Do you think I should come in the kitchen?"

"Absolutely," Matty said. "Elizabeth and I need reinforcements, don't we, sweetheart? The guys just took the morning train to Stupidville."

"Ga!" came the delighted response.

Jessica's heart hammered as she edged into the kitchen doorway. From her wooden high chair Elizabeth looked her way, and Jessica braced herself for more tears. Instead, the baby almost seemed to give a mental shrug as she returned her attention to the spoonful of applesauce Matty was holding out.

Indifference was better than fear, Jessica told herself. "What did you mean about the guys?" she asked, keeping her voice low and nonthreatening. "Where did they go?"

"Nat thought he saw your stalker up on the hill."

Jessica put her hand over her mouth to stifle a gasp that would probably scare the baby.

"Travis arrived when Nat was coming back to tell us, so those three dimwits saddled up and rode out to find him. Sebastian took his rifle." Matty continued to feed Elizabeth, but the line of her back was rigid.

"Oh, dear."

"I've set the alarm, so we'll know if the fellow shows up here, but I think we should have called the sheriff. The guys didn't agree."

Despair washed over Jessica. Calling the sheriff would inevitably lead to the sheriff contacting her parents, but she couldn't continue to avoid that if people were placing themselves in danger. "Maybe I should just call my parents and be done with it. I can't have all of you risking yourselves like this."

Matty glanced at Jessica before resuming the feeding as she slipped the spoon neatly in Elizabeth's mouth. "If you come in slowly and sit at the table, I think that would be a good way for this little gremlin to become used to you again. Then you can tell me about this situation with your parents."

"All right." Jessica eased herself over to the table. She resented every second she had to spend carefully and cautiously renewing the bond with Elizabeth. She wanted to scoop the baby up and smother her with kisses. Of course, it was normal for a baby her age to be fearful of strangers, but Jessica shouldn't be one of them. The world was out of kilter and she wanted to blink her eyes and make it right again.

Elizabeth watched her warily as she came to the table and sat down about four feet from the high chair.

"Elizabeth," Matty crooned. "Have another bite of applesauce, sweetie pie."

The baby turned back toward Matty and banged her

hands on the high-chair tray while Matty fed her. Matty expertly used the edge of the spoon to scoop up the excess applesauce from around her mouth and tuck that inside, too.

Jessica took note of the procedure with more than a touch of envy. She'd never fed a baby before, but if she and Elizabeth had learned together, Elizabeth wouldn't have noticed that her mother was clumsy at it. Now she'd immediately sense Jessica's lack of experience.

"I take it your parents don't know about the baby or the stalker," Matty said, keeping her tone conversational as she continued to feed Elizabeth.

"That's right. I've been hoping to keep Elizabeth from growing up the way I did, a virtual prisoner because my father was afraid someone would try to snatch me for a huge ransom."

"I guess he had a point," Matty said.

"Unfortunately, he did." Jessica sat gazing at her daughter, her heart breaking. "The way I see it, I can either call my parents and get their protection from this guy, or... assuming the jerk doesn't know about Elizabeth yet, I can take off again before he finds out about her."

Matty turned, her gaze extremely alert. "And then what? Leave her with us indefinitely?"

Jessica didn't miss the barely disguised eagerness in Matty's voice. She didn't blame Matty for ignoring the question of what would happen to Jessica in that scenario. Matty was primarily concerned with Elizabeth's welfare, which was as it should be.

"I would leave her with you forever," Jessica murmured as pain sliced through her at voicing the unthinkable. "If I go away again, I wouldn't come back for her. That wouldn't be fair to anyone, most of all her."

Matty swallowed, but she didn't speak. Then she put down the spoon and picked up a damp cloth that had been lying on the table. Slowly, tenderly, she washed Elizabeth's face while the baby tried to grab the cloth and made little gurgling sounds.

Then, still holding the cloth, Matty looked over at Jessica. Tears shimmered in her eyes. "Of course I would love to have this child forever. Sebastian would be ecstatic. So would everyone—Travis, Gwen, Boone, Shelby, Luann and little Josh." She cleared her throat and continued. "Before I was pregnant, I might not have understood the sacrifice you're suggesting, but now I do, and I can't let you make it."

Jessica gulped back her own tears. "If it's the best thing for Elizabeth—"

"It's not," Matty said firmly. "Did you ever sing to her?"

Jessica blinked back her tears. "Sing? Why?"

"It might be a way back."

"Oh." Jessica had never known a kinderhearted woman than Matty Daniels. Any fool could see how she'd bonded with Elizabeth, and the thought of losing the baby had to be painful. Yet Matty was trying to help Jessica connect again. "Yes, I sang to her," she said.

"I thought so. Most of us do that instinctively, I guess."

Most of us. Jessica wondered if Matty knew she'd unconsciously included herself in the category of mother, even though her own child hadn't been born yet. Well, she should include herself, Jessica thought. She'd been Elizabeth's mother for several months, along with Gwen and Shelby.

"Why don't you try singing now?" Matty suggested.

"Here?" Jessica felt self-conscious singing while her child sat in a high chair four feet away and Matty was still in the room. When she'd sung to Elizabeth before, the baby had been wrapped snugly in her arms. The moment had been cozy and intimate with only the two of them. This would be like a performance.

"She's full and pretty happy right now," Matty said.

"With me right here, she's not threatened by having you around. And she's not being distracted by anyone else at the moment. What do you say?"

"Okay." Jessica gave Matty a tiny smile. "But I'll feel like a Vegas nightclub act."

Matty smiled back. "I promise to be a good audience."

Jessica knew exactly which song she wanted to sing. She could still remember her mother singing it to her when she was a little girl. Jessica had never learned the song's title, only the words, which told of a train bound for dreamland. It ran on a peppermint rail, and only stopped at ice-cream stations to pick up Crackerjack mail.

She'd loved that concept as a child. Although Elizabeth wasn't old enough to understand the words yet, she would be, sooner than Jessica could have imagined.

Blocking out memories of her mother and father had been more difficult for Jessica recently. She'd assumed all along that her parents would be critical and punishing when they eventually discovered Elizabeth's existence. Now she wasn't so sure.

She gazed at her baby as the little girl sat playing with her fingers and experimenting with shoving different combinations into her mouth. Absorbing the beauty of Elizabeth's coppery curls, pink cheeks and innocent blue eyes, she couldn't imagine her parents feeling anything but love for this child. Yet how could she bring them into Elizabeth's life and not expect them to overprotect the baby in the same way they'd overprotected her?

She couldn't. Taking a long, shaky breath and feeling very self-conscious, she began to sing.

Elizabeth looked over at her immediately. With two fingers thrust into her drooling mouth, she focused intently on Jessica's face.

Jessica continued to sing and gradually forgot Matty was there as she searched the baby's expression for the slightest evidence of recognition.

Elizabeth seemed fascinated by being sung to, but maybe she was that way with everyone.

"Keep singing and trade places with me," Matty said.

As Jessica and Matty got up, alarm showed in Elizabeth's eyes. She looked quickly from one to the other while they switched seats, which placed Matty farther away and Jessica right in front of Elizabeth.

Jessica panicked when the baby scrunched up her face as if to cry. Then Matty, who obviously had heard enough of the song to get the melody, began to hum along with Jessica. She couldn't carry a tune in a bucket, but Jessica didn't care. The ploy worked to unscrunch Elizabeth's face.

Elizabeth's attention rotated from one woman to another as the makeshift duet continued, and the look of amazement on the baby's face nearly made Jessica laugh. But she kept singing. She must have started smiling without realizing it, though, because all at once a miracle happened. Elizabeth looked at her and grinned.

Jessica's throat closed and she couldn't sing anymore. But as Elizabeth's grin faded and she began to cloud up again, Jessica made a superhuman effort and began singing again. She even managed a smile, although it quivered at the edges.

Matty began adding words to her humming, but they weren't the words of the song. *"We're doing great,"* she sang. *"How about if you—"*

The sound of hoofbeats came from outside.

Matty bounced out of her chair and looked out the kitchen window. "They're back." She poured a truckload of relief into those two words.

Jessica's heart began to pound. Breaking eye contact with Elizabeth, she went to the window, almost afraid of what she might see. "They're okay," she said with a sigh.

"Looks like." Matty went to shut off the alarm system and then stood on tiptoe to get a better look out the kitchen window. "I don't see any blood."

"Me neither." Jessica couldn't stop looking at the easy way Nat sat his horse. She kept forgetting he'd been raised on a ranch and was a genuine cowboy from the brim of his hat to the tip of his boots. He certainly looked the part now.

She watched the three men dismount and tie their horses to the hitching rail by the back door as if they were part of a western movie. She'd only seen these guys at a ski lodge, where they were out of their natural element. No doubt about it, they were in their element at the Rocking D.

Elizabeth started banging on her tray with both hands.

Matty glanced over at the baby. "I think someone misses the floor show."

Jessica followed her gaze and was gratified that Elizabeth's mood still seemed cheerful. "Do you think we really made progress?"

"I would bet on it. I think singing is the ticket. You should keep that up. Sorry about screwing up your act with my caterwauling, by the way."

Jessica had been brought up to be reserved with people until she knew them well, but it seemed like the most natural thing in the world to put an arm around Matty's shoulders and gave her a quick hug. "Are you kidding?" she said with a chuckle. "Your backup singing saved the day."

Matty laughed. "Be sure and tell Sebastian that," she said as the kitchen door opened and the man in question came through it. "He's threatened to pay me not to sing."

"No, you have that wrong." Still carrying his rifle, Sebastian walked over and gave his wife a swift kiss. "I've said I'd pay you to dance *instead* of sing. I think we should all stick to what we have a talent for, and your talent is definitely dancing." He left the kitchen to put his rifle away.

"Wait a minute!" Matty called after him. "Did you find anything up there?"

"Ask Travis," Sebastian called back.

"So?" Matty asked as Travis came in, followed by Nat. "What happened?"

"We located some tracks," Travis said, shucking his jacket and hanging it on one of several pegs by the back door. "We followed them for a while, but we lost the trail when we hit the rocky section."

Jessica turned toward Nat. "Did you get a look at him before? Do you think it could have been the man who's been following me?"

"Don't know. I only knew somebody was up there, but I didn't get a good look. It could've been anybody, I guess." His grim expression reminded Jessica of the one he'd had when he first got off the plane, a don't-mess-with-me look. There was definitely a harder edge to Nat than there had been before he'd gone overseas. She found it incredibly sexy.

"Might have been one of the neighbors out for a ride," Travis said. "Except if it was, you'd think they'd have come on down to the house for some coffee instead of heading off in the opposite direction."

"I still say the guy deliberately rode across those rocks," Nat said as he took off his jacket and hung it next to Travis's. "He meant for us to lose his trail."

"Could be," Sebastian said as he came back into the kitchen. "But whether he meant to or not, he succeeded." He glanced at Travis. "I thought you were some sort of tracking wizard, hotshot."

"Aw, I just told Gwen that to impress her, considering she has that Cheyenne ancestry and all," Travis said. "I can lose a trail in the rocks the same as the rest of you."

"Wonderful." Sebastian looked at his head wrangler and shook his head. "And for this I pay you the big bucks."

Elizabeth banged on her tray and started gurgling.

"No, you pay me the big bucks to change this little gal's diaper," Travis said with a grin. "Right, Lizzie? Nobody does it like the Diaperman, right?"

The baby laughed and held up her arms to Travis.

"Want me to spring you from that chair, don't you, sweet-cheeks?" Travis unlatched the tray and scooped Elizabeth up in his arms. "Hey, little girl, I do believe you need my services right this minute." He nuzzled her neck until she laughed. "Come with me, darlin'."

As Travis left the kitchen carrying a smiling Elizabeth, Jessica gazed after them in frustration. How long before the baby held up her pudgy little arms to her mother?

NAT WONDERED if he'd ever be able to be as relaxed and charming as Travis was with Elizabeth. Probably not. Ah, but he ached to be. He'd expected to be afraid of the baby, and he was, to some degree. But fascination was quickly overtaking his fear. And he was developing a hunger to hold the little girl and see if he could coax a dimpled smile from her.

"I think Jessica and I made progress with Elizabeth while you three were gone," Matty said. She handed her husband a mug of coffee and poured another, which she gave to Nat.

Sebastian blew across the top of his mug. "Yeah? What did you do?"

"It was Matty's idea." Jess murmured her thanks as she took the coffee Matty poured and held out to her. "She suggested I sing to Elizabeth, thinking she might remember the song and start getting used to me again." She took a sip of coffee. "I think it helped."

"Great idea." Nat figured he was the only one who noticed Jess's slight grimace as she drank the coffee. She would have preferred herbal tea, but under the circumstances, she probably didn't want to ask if there was anything like that in the house. He wished he could have been here to watch her sing to Elizabeth. That would have been a scene to add to his memories.

Damn, but Jess looked good in her T-shirt and jeans. He

would love to be able to go over and sling an arm around
her shoulders the way Sebastian felt free to do with Matty.

But he didn't dare. She probably wouldn't appreciate him
making such a gesture in front of Matty and Sebastian, and
he might lose whatever ground he'd gained earlier that
morning in the bathroom. Despite her rejection, he'd been
encouraged by the look in her eyes. He still saw a little of
that fire now whenever she glanced his way.

"Having you sing to her is a great idea," Sebastian
agreed. "But shouldn't you keep that kind of thing up?"

"You want her to go around singing all day?" Matty
asked.

"No, although there's nothing wrong with that, either. I
meant the contact with Elizabeth." He looked over at Jess.
"You could go in and help Travis change her. Then
she might start getting the idea that you'll be around all the
time, and eventually you could try doing the job and she
might not think anything of it."

"You're right." Immediately she set her coffee down on
the counter and turned toward Nat. "Do you want to—"

"Let's not have a convention in there," he said, although
he wouldn't have minded going. He wanted an excuse to
follow Jess around like a puppy, to breathe in her scent and
watch the way the light played in her red curls. "Too many
of us might overwhelm her."

"He has a point," Matty said. "We'll work him into the
rotation later."

"For sure." When Jess glanced at him this time, there
was no mistaking the look in her eyes.

His pulse accelerated. Oh, for a few minutes alone with
her. But it wouldn't be anytime soon. With a flicker of a
smile, she left the kitchen, taking his heart with her.

"And I'll warn you, Travis doesn't sing any better than
I do!" Matty called out after her.

Once she was out of earshot, Nat looked at Matty. "Do

you think Elizabeth's really getting over her fear? Or are you trying to make Jess feel better?''

"Elizabeth will get over her fear mainly because Jessica loves that baby more than life itself, and she's willing to do whatever it takes.'' She smiled as the sound of Travis's off-key baritone blending with Jess's more musical voice drifted down the hall from Elizabeth's room. ''When she was singing to that baby, I darn near started bawling, it was so touching.''

"It's been tough on her," Nat said. And he longed to find a way to ease her pain, one that wouldn't land them both in bigger trouble.

"I'm sure," Matty said. "While you three were gone, she began to worry all over again about the danger presented by this character that's been tailing her. She figured her choice was to call her parents and get their protection, or leave now before the guy gets wind there's a baby in the picture.''

Nat's stomach clenched. "She actually said she might leave?''

"Yes, and let me tell you, contemplating that was killing her, but she's willing to consider it if Elizabeth will be better off as a result.''

"She can't leave," Nat said, his voice betraying more emotion than he'd intended.

"Whoa, son," Sebastian said. "Nobody's gonna let her do that.''

"Couldn't we call the sheriff and get him out here?'' Matty asked. "I'd feel a lot better if we had some law enforcement working on this instead of you guys running around like some posse out of a grade-B western.''

Sebastian gave her hair a playful tug. "Watch how you talk, woman. The boys and I command a heap of respect in these here parts.''

"Joke about it if you want," she said. "But I—''

"While we were out trailing the guy, we talked about

the possibility of calling the sheriff's office, Matty,'' Nat said. "I know this makes you nervous. It makes me nervous. But the problem with going to the authorities is that they'll want to run down leads if they can, and the logical place to start is with Jess's folks."

"Would that be so terrible?" Matty asked. "It seems as if they ought to know about this. Jessica said she was afraid they'd be overprotective, like they were with her, but Jessica is Elizabeth's mother. Surely she could control the extent to which they did that."

Nat thought about the iron gates with the scrolled initials *FH* worked into the elaborate design, and the iron-willed man who lived behind those gates. "I met her father a few days ago, before Jess—well, before she and I hooked up. I can believe that Jess is right about how he'd react if he found out about this situation, and the man's got clout. He'd commandeer the ranch. And Elizabeth would be shipped back to New York so fast it would make your head swim. I'm not sure any of us would ever see her again."

"Oh." Matty glanced up at her husband. "Then I guess we have to come up with a different plan, huh?"

"'Fraid so," Sebastian said. "I'm not about to let some New York bigshot tell me how to run things on the Rocking D. And we're sure as hell not letting him make off with that baby." He leveled a glance at Nat. "Right?"

"Right." Nat had no trouble meeting Sebastian's gaze on that one. Before he'd seen Elizabeth he might have briefly imagined that having her tucked safely inside the gates of Franklin Hall would be the best solution all the way around. Now he knew that was unthinkable. He wasn't sure what part he might end up playing in the little girl's life, but he didn't want either her or her mother hidden away in the Hudson Valley.

"But at the very least we're going to have to beef up security around here," Sebastian said. "I'll have our local expert Jim add a few wrinkles."

"Unless you want me to call the guy who does the security for some of my clients," Nat said, thinking about one particular sale in which a Hollywood star who'd bought property near Colorado Springs had used Seth's expertise to secure his estate.

"Oh, yeah," Sebastian said. "I remember you telling me about him. He's based in L.A."

"He could do a job for us," Nat said. "But he's expensive and slow. Most of the people who hire him are putting in a system they plan to leave in place forever, whereas this would be temporary."

"That's true." Sebastian sipped his coffee. "Let's see what Jim can come up with for now, and keep your guy in reserve in case we need more expertise."

"Sounds reasonable," Nat said. "And in the meantime, we have to convince Jess that she can't leave."

Matty grinned. "I figure that's your job, Nat."

Nat felt the heat climb up from his collar. He rubbed the back of his neck and gave her a sheepish smile while he considered how to explain that he was willing, but Jess wasn't letting him use all the weapons at his disposal. "Well, the thing is, I—"

"Come on, buddy," Sebastian said, obviously taking pity on him. "Let's go unsaddle those nags while Matty cooks us up some of her famous bacon and eggs for breakfast."

CHAPTER FIFTEEN

JESSICA HAD ALWAYS thought of her childhood as lonely, and had supposed she'd love living in a house bustling with people and activity. To her surprise, she didn't love it. After several days of constant visits from all the people who had a stake in Elizabeth, the lack of privacy at the Rocking D began to wear on Jessica's nerves.

Although Matty and Sebastian had moved Elizabeth's crib into their room so there wouldn't be any more scenes when the baby woke up, Jessica had graduated to being able to hold Elizabeth for short periods of time. Still, someone Elizabeth trusted had to remain in the room. If that person started to leave, Elizabeth would begin crying.

Under normal circumstances Jessica would have suggested that they tough it out and see if Elizabeth stopped fussing, but these circumstances were far from normal. Jessica didn't feel she could demand control of the situation and tread on the toes of the people who had been so wonderful to her and her baby.

Because she wanted to spend as much time as possible with Elizabeth, she was forced to have someone else around constantly, too. She'd shared her baby with Matty, Sebastian, Gwen, Travis, Luann, Shelby, Boone and even little Josh.

And most frustrating of all, the third person in the room couldn't ever be Nat. He had to be person number four, or else Jessica was obliged to leave so he could have a chance to hold the baby, too. Jessica had noticed something else.

Whenever she held Elizabeth, changed her diaper or fed her, no one told her how to go about it. But when Nat took his turn, everybody had an opinion.

The women weren't as bad as his three buddies, who were constantly making suggestions and offering to demonstrate a particular skill for Nat. Sebastian, Boone and Travis were definitely guilty of hovering. As a result, Nat had developed no confidence in his abilities with the baby.

He kept trying valiantly anyway, and that was the important thing. He hadn't rejected Elizabeth, but learning to feel comfortable with her while everyone coached from the sidelines might be an impossible task.

Jessica's heart went out to him. And the rest of her body wanted to follow. Sleeping alone in the double bed with Nat right down the hall was becoming increasingly difficult to tolerate. Yet the pattern had been established, and to change it now would cause comment in the household. If and when Jessica invited Nat back to her bed, and she was very inclined to do so, she wanted a more private setting.

Everywhere she turned these days she met with frustration, but she felt ungrateful for having such negative thoughts. Matty and Sebastian had leaned over backward for her. They wouldn't even let her help pay for groceries, and she knew when this was all over she'd have to come up with some way to repay them, to repay all of them. If they were a little possessive of Elizabeth, if they didn't want to rush the moment when Jessica could take care of the baby by herself, that was understandable.

Besides, she was reunited with her child, even if she couldn't be alone with Elizabeth yet. And she felt safe. Now that Sebastian's friend Jim had increased security around the ranch house with a more extensive lighting system, it seemed as if her stalker had grown discouraged and left. After so many days had passed and she no longer had the sensation of being watched, she was daring to hope that the guy had given up.

All in all, her life was going as well as could be expected, she thought as she stood beside Matty at Elizabeth's changing table late in the afternoon of another busy day. They were sharing the job of dressing the baby for Gwen's thirtieth birthday party.

Freshly bathed and diapered, Elizabeth lay on the changing table clutching her sock monkey and chewing vigorously on its arm. Jessica had braced herself for another evening of watching Nat's friends instruct him in the art of baby care.

Earlier she and Matty had decorated the ranch house within an inch of its life. The number thirty had been taped to the walls and hung from the beamed ceilings. They'd even spelled it out on the dining table with Elizabeth's alphabet blocks. Sebastian and Matty had vowed not to let Gwen slide past this milestone without "raising a ruckus," as Sebastian had put it.

"I'm running behind," Matty said as she put on one white lacy sock and Jessica put on the other.

"What's left besides getting Elizabeth ready?" Jessica figured it would take less than ten minutes to put on the baby's ruffled lavender dress and tie bows in her curls. Sebastian was in the shower and Nat was out stringing thirty colored lanterns along the porch railing.

"I still need to stick the candles on the cake and wrap those thirty bottles of Geritol we're giving her."

Jessica glanced over at Matty. "I could finish dressing Elizabeth while you do that."

Matty hesitated.

"We have to keep testing to see if she's adjusted yet."

"I know, but this might not be the best time. Maybe Sebastian's almost finished. He could—"

"Matty." Jessica gave her a level look. "I think she might be ready."

Matty's eyes grew moist. "So do I. I've thought so for

the last couple of days. I just didn't want to admit it, not even to myself.''

Jessica's heart went out to her. With a gentle smile she put her arm around Matty and gave her a hug. ''I'm not going to jerk her out of here right away, and even when we eventually go, I won't take her completely out of your life. I promise. We'll come back a lot.''

Matty swallowed. ''I know that. But it will never be the same.''

''Oh, Matty, I never meant to hurt—''

''Hey.'' Matty gave her a wobbly grin. ''You did nothing but make our lives better around here when you left Elizabeth at the Rocking D. Without this little girl I wouldn't be married to Sebastian. Travis wouldn't be with Gwen and Boone wouldn't have found Shelby and Josh.'' She reached for a tissue in her pocket and wiped her nose. ''I'm very grateful we had her for a little while, but I won't lie to you. When you finally take her, I'll miss her like the devil.''

''Rebecca will help.''

Matty patted her tummy and attempted to look brave. ''You bet she will. And Jeffrey, too.''

''Who?''

''Rebecca's brother. Sebastian's so sure we're going to have another one, and it'll be a boy, that he's started on a second belt. He's using a darker leather, and—'' She stopped talking and glanced at Elizabeth. ''Okay, I'm stalling.'' She took a deep breath and tweaked Elizabeth's foot. ''See ya, toots.'' Then she turned and left the room.

Elizabeth twisted her head to watch Matty leave. Then she glanced up at Jessica.

''Just you and me, kid,'' Jessica said, her stomach churning as she waited to see if Elizabeth would cry. ''Think you can handle that?''

Elizabeth stared at her, as if thinking things over.

The knot in Jessica's stomach began to loosen as she concluded that Elizabeth wasn't going to cry. The baby was definitely evaluating the situation, but apparently she'd decided that Jessica was to be trusted. Finally.

"Just you and me, kid," Jessica said again with a smile. "Sounds pretty good, doesn't it?"

Elizabeth waved her sock monkey in Jessica's face. "Da!" she said loudly.

"I stand corrected." She felt like dancing and singing for joy, but she didn't want to get too wild and alarm the baby. The baby who was finally hers again. "Just you, me and Bruce."

"Any room in that equation for another interested party?"

At the sound of Nat's voice from the doorway, Jessica's heartbeat quickened. Keeping one hand on Elizabeth, she glanced over her shoulder at him.

He leaned casually in the doorway, but there was nothing casual about the way he was looking at her. He'd bought a deep blue western shirt for the party, and it brought out the brilliant color of his eyes. She could have eaten him up with a spoon.

"Is this the first time you've been alone with her?" Nat asked.

"Yes." She glanced down at Elizabeth and saw that she was watching her father with great curiosity, but no apparent fear.

"Then maybe I'd better not come in."

Flushed with triumph, Jessica was ready to be bold. "I'd love you to come in." The three of them hadn't been alone together since the first night, when she and Nat had gone into the bedroom to watch Elizabeth sleep. She still remembered the magic of that moment, and she wanted to experience it again.

"I could stay over here, to play it safe."

Jessica looked back at him. "You know what? I'm sick to death of playing it safe."

A smile flitted across his chiseled lips. "Yeah?"

"Yeah."

He pushed away from the door frame and came slowly across the room as his gaze flicked over her outfit, a pale green sweater dress she'd picked up during a quick trip to town with Matty and Sebastian. If she were honest with herself, she'd have to admit that in buying it, she'd been hoping to incite the lust she saw in Nat's expression.

"Is that why you're wearing that dress?" he asked. "Because you're sick of playing it safe and you want to push me right over the edge?"

"Maybe." Her breathing quickened at the flame that leaped in his eyes. Suddenly not sure if she'd bitten off more than she could chew, she returned her attention to Elizabeth and reached for the ruffled dress hanging from a hook above the changing table.

"Did I hear you say maybe?" he murmured, coming to stand beside her. "That's a country mile from no. Are you aware of that?" He wasn't quite touching her, but electricity seemed to arc between them.

"Yes. No. Oh, Nat, I don't know what I think." Her heart was pounding and she could feel heat spreading through her body and warming her cheeks. "Except that I miss you so much."

"Missing me's a good sign." His voice was gruff with emotion.

Elizabeth waved her monkey in the air. "Da-da!"

Nat went very still. "Did she say what I think she said?"

Jessica glanced over at him. She didn't have the heart to tell him that Elizabeth probably didn't know what she was saying, and that she'd said it before when no men were on the scene at all. It happened to be a syllable she could pronounce, but it didn't necessarily mean she was labeling him. Still, Jessica didn't know that for a fact, now, did she?

He gazed at the baby, his heart in his eyes. "Do you know who I am, Elizabeth? Da-da?"

She waved the monkey again and smiled. "Da-da!"

"My God." Nat looked thunderstruck. And proud, as if he'd been given first prize in some lofty competition.

Jessica took the moment and tucked it away in her memory. No matter how things turned out, she would always remember Nat's expression as he gazed at his daughter. She longed to close the bedroom door and prolong the intimacy of this little group for...for a very long while.

But there would be no closing of bedroom doors. The party would start soon. "We'd better get her clothes on her," she said gently. "Sit her up and hold her steady while I put this dress over her head."

"You're sure she won't get upset?"

"Why should she? After all, you're her da-da."

"My hands are cold." He blew on them and rubbed them briskly together. Then he held them against his cheeks. "Still cold."

"Okay, I'll hold her and you put the dress over her head." She handed him the ruffled outfit and propped Elizabeth up in a sitting position.

"But she likes to play peekaboo when you put something over her head." Nat sounded as if the assignment was way beyond his abilities.

"I'll bet you can play peekaboo."

"I'm not sure if I—"

"Nat." She glanced up at him. "I don't know much about your experience with little children, but I do know what a tender, sensitive and creative lover you are. I'm sure you can manage a game of peekaboo with a little baby."

His gaze grew hot. "You're flirting with me, Jessica Louise."

She smiled and nodded toward the outfit he held in one hand. "Put the dress on the baby."

"Yeah." Without warning, he grasped the back of Jessica's head and kissed her hard, thrusting his tongue firmly into her mouth in a blatantly aggressive gesture. A possessive gesture, a branding gesture. Then, just as quickly, he released her.

She stood there trembling, her mouth tingling and moist, and she was unable to say a word. If she had been able to speak, she could only have uttered one syllable. *More.*

Nat gave her a slow, sensuous smile before turning to the baby. "Hey, Elizabeth, ready for this?"

Jessica hadn't been ready for the kiss, that was for sure. Either her memory of his potent kisses had faded a little or he'd upped the emotional ante. Nat's kisses had been dizzying, arousing, playful, erotic. But she never remembered a kiss that had said forcefully, *Mine.*

Nat carefully lowered the dress so that the material settled softly over Elizabeth. "Where's Elizabeth?" he asked. "Where's that baby?" Then he opened the neck wider and popped it over her head. "There she is!"

Elizabeth laughed happily, showing off her teeth.

"Peekaboo, I see you!" Nat said.

"Da-da!" Elizabeth beamed at him.

"And so I am," Nat said quietly.

"And so you are," Jessica said, looking up at him.

He met her gaze, his eyes glowing with happiness. "Jess, I—"

"How's everything going in here?" Sebastian asked as he strode into the room. "Looks like you nearly have that munchkin dressed. Tying those ribbons in her hair can be tricky, though. I thought I'd see if you needed any help."

Much as Jessica loved her good friend Sebastian, at that moment she could have cheerfully decked him.

Sure enough, Nat's bright expression dimmed and he backed away from the changing table. "Maybe you should take over for the rest of it. I'll see if Matty needs any help in the kitchen."

"Or Sebastian could help Matty in the kitchen," Jessica said, although she had little hope Nat would stay, now that Sebastian was here.

"That's okay." Nat was already halfway out the door. "I'm no good with little ribbons. I'd probably pull her hair or something."

Sebastian glanced from Nat's retreating back to Jessica's face. "Did I just screw up?"

Jessica gave him a halfhearted smile. He was a dear man, but he could be so dense. She started getting Elizabeth's arms through the sleeves of her dress.

"I did screw up, didn't I?" Sebastian said as he came over to the changing table. "I'll bet the three of you were—you know—bonding."

"Sort of. Could you hold her while I button the back of this?"

"Sure. Hey, peaches." He took hold of Elizabeth and kissed her on the cheek.

"Da-da!"

"Did you hear that?" Sebastian said with obvious pleasure. "What a smart little dickens."

"Uh-huh." Jessica finished the buttoning and gathered her courage. "Sebastian, do you really want Nat to take on the job of being Elizabeth's father?"

"You know I do! Why would you even ask?" He leaned down and rubbed his nose against Elizabeth's. "Nosy, nosy."

Elizabeth chuckled and made a grab for his nose.

"You're very good with her," Jessica said.

"It's easy. I love her. Don't I, sweetheart? Love this little bundle to pieces. Yes, I do." He scooped her up from the changing table and nuzzled her again until she laughed.

Nat would never have had the courage to pick Elizabeth up so spontaneously, Jessica thought. "You're all good with her," she said, "and it's been wonderful to watch because I know how well she's been cared for all these months."

Sebastian glanced at Jessica. "Where are you going with this, little one?"

She was so afraid of sounding ungrateful. But something had to be said. "I'm afraid if you three godfathers don't back off a little, Nat's never going to feel comfortable taking on the role of Elizabeth's daddy."

Sebastian stared at her. "But we're only trying to help him get acclimated. He doesn't know about babies, and—"

"And the more you tell him that, the less confidence he has in himself as a father. And he didn't start out with a whole lot to begin with."

"Neither did I!"

Elizabeth laughed and made another grab for his nose.

He gently pried her hand away. "Neither did I," he repeated more quietly. "When you dropped this little girl off, I was scared to death, afraid I'd do something wrong and cause serious damage. At least Nat's got us to help him."

"And that's good, up to a point. The thing is, you didn't have the kind of father Nat had, and his insecurities about being a parent run a lot deeper than yours. None of you had experience with babies, but I don't think any of you seriously doubted you could do it once you put your mind to it. I was sure you could, as long as you had a list of instructions and a book to read."

"You must have spent hours on those instructions."

"Oh, I did. I had to throw away the first set because they were all tear-spotted."

Sebastian's gaze was soft. "You've been through so much. Tell me what I can do to help this get fixed the way you need it to be."

"I'm...I'm not sure. But I think that when Nat sees how competent all of you are, he despairs of ever making the grade."

"I'll talk to Travis and Boone tonight."

She touched his arm. "If you do, please tell them that I love the way they are with Elizabeth. I treasure it. But right now, it doesn't give Nat much room to maneuver."

"We'll come up with a plan," Sebastian promised. "I

want the three of you to be a family. Do you think that could happen?''

"I don't know. But for a moment there, right before you came in, I began to believe it might.''

"And I spoiled that moment. I'm so sorry, little one.''

Jessica wrapped her arms around him and gave him a hug. "It's okay. There will be other moments.'' Then she crossed her fingers and prayed she was right.

THE PARTY WAS boisterous and fun. Jessica found herself feeling guilty that she'd begrudged any of these wonderful people constant access to Elizabeth. As far as Nat was concerned, they'd only been trying to help, and maybe they'd been planning to ease up on their own. Maybe she shouldn't have said anything to Sebastian, after all.

While she was helping clear the table after the meal, she noticed Sebastian in a quiet huddle with Travis and Boone. It looked as if they'd deliberately chosen a time when Nat, Shelby and Gwen were hunched over a game of Candyland with Josh. From the way the men kept glancing in Nat's direction, Jessica was sure they were discussing her earlier comments to Sebastian.

Dear God, if she'd messed up the relationship among those men she would never forgive herself. Maybe Travis and Boone would be offended that she thought their attempts to help had been interfering. She had a strong urge to set down the pile of plates and go tell them to forget what she'd said to Sebastian.

After all, she was the newcomer in this group. They'd all known each other for many more years than she'd been in the picture. Maybe she'd read the situation wrong.

But in the end, she carried the plates into the kitchen. Then, acting on her own renewed confidence regarding Elizabeth, she lifted the baby from the playpen Matty had put in the corner of the kitchen for the duration of the party.

"I'm going to change her and get her ready for bed," she announced to Matty, who was working at the sink.

"Good idea." Matty glanced over at Jessica. "I think she's getting tired."

Luann put away the glass she'd been drying. "Does she have to go down already?" Then she looked at the kitchen clock. "Goodness, I didn't know it was so late."

Jessica had a real soft spot for Travis's mother, who so obviously adored the concept of grandchildren. Although Jessica had been relishing the idea of being alone with her baby, Luann looked so wistful that she relented. It was a darn good thing Luann's daughter-in-law, Gwen, was also pregnant.

"Would you like to help me with Elizabeth?" she asked. "I'm sure Matty could spare you for a few minutes."

"Of course I can," Matty said.

"Then I'd love to help with that precious little girl." Luann couldn't hang up her dish towel quickly enough.

With two of them working, it didn't take long before Elizabeth was in her sleeper and ready to collect her good-night kisses from the houseful of people. Being with Luann always made Jessica think of her own mother and how she would have enjoyed spoiling a grandchild. Regret that things couldn't be different prompted Jessica to give Luann the privilege of carrying the baby back into the living room.

She followed Luann down the hall and was surprised to notice that everyone was assembled there as if they were waiting for something. At first Jessica thought it might simply be time for the cake, but Matty was there, as well, so no one was available to bring the cake in.

Nat no longer sat on the floor by the coffee table playing the game with Josh. He stood with his back to the fire and gazed intently at her as she walked into the room.

Her stomach rolled. They were all waiting for her. She had overstepped by speaking to Sebastian this afternoon.

Someone was about to deliver a lecture on the subject of ingratitude.

"Sebastian has come up with a plan, Jess," Nat said. "He passed it by me, and now we need to know what you think of it."

Jessica clutched her hands in front of her stomach. "I shouldn't have spoken up. Forgive me, all of you. I couldn't have asked for a warmer, more wonderful—"

"Oh, sweetheart." Matty came forward and put an arm around Jessica's shoulders. "You were right, and everybody knows it. I can't imagine how we expected you, Nat and Elizabeth to form a unit in the midst of all this hubbub."

"You need privacy," Sebastian said.

"Privacy and security," Boone added.

"And atmosphere," Travis said with a wink.

Jessica looked from one to the other, not understanding.

"There's an old but serviceable line shack on the Rocking D," Sebastian said. "We're going to check with Jim and see if he can rig up a good enough security system out there, although this might be the time we have to call in Nat's security guy from L.A."

"A line shack, huh?" Jessica was beginning to get the idea, and she hoped she was hearing it right.

"It's not fancy, but it's clean," Sebastian said. "Once the place is secure, Nat can drive the Bronco out there with you and Elizabeth and enough supplies to last a week or so." He smiled at her. "No interruptions. Should make for some of that bonding stuff."

Her glance flew to Nat as her heart began to pound. "That's okay with you?"

His gaze burned into hers. "It's okay with me. How about you?"

She couldn't hold back her grin. "It sounds great to me," she said.

CHAPTER SIXTEEN

As NAT HAD SUSPECTED, Jim didn't have the know-how to do an adequate job on the line shack, so Nat had called Seth Burnham. But securing the shack had taken three endless days, and Nat had wondered if he'd make it. Following the decision that they were literally going to "shack up" together, Jessica had turned shy on him, almost going out of her way to avoid him.

He'd spent a fair amount of time wondering why that was. The most promising explanation was that she didn't trust herself to be around him and stay in control of her desire. Now that they were facing a situation in which they could make love again, the anticipation might be driving her crazy, too. Any other explanation for her behavior was too depressing, so he decided to go with the one he liked.

Because he was suffering intense sexual frustration, he'd paid an unholy sum to get Seth on site ASAP. Then he'd spent his days out at the line shack with Seth, helping him install the system.

"This is the best technology has to offer," Seth had said when he was finally finished. "But it's no damn good if you forget to turn it on. So don't forget."

"I won't," Nat had promised. But as he'd driven Seth back to the ranch house in Sebastian's Bronco, his mind hadn't been on security systems. He was thinking about the double bed in the cabin, the one he'd made up fresh with clean sheets. He was thinking of the other preparations he'd made—the folding screen he'd constructed to give them a little privacy in the one-room shack, the flowers he'd put in an old mason jar, the herb tea he'd stocked because he knew she was probably getting sick of coffee.

He was thinking about the following day when he, Jessica and Elizabeth would be driving the Bronco out to the line shack. And he was hoping Elizabeth would take her usual two-hour afternoon nap.

AFTER THE CLOSE CALL he'd had that first morning, Steven Pruitt hadn't ventured so near the ranch house again. He had no intention of facing three pissed-off cowboys, especially when one carried a rifle and looked as if he could use it.

So Steven had marshaled his considerable news-gathering skills to get information out of the citizens of Huerfano. His drama training had come in handy, too, just as it had when he'd worked for the Franklin Publishing Group. Franklin had lost a hell of an undercover investigative reporter when he'd had the stupidity to order Steve Pruitt fired.

It might turn out to be the most costly mistake Russell P. had ever made. The residents of Huerfano liked to talk, and they'd told many tales about the mystery baby who'd been living out at the Rocking D for the past six months. It didn't take a genius to figure out whose baby it was, although Steven knew his test scores put him within genius range.

Waiting to make the snatch had paid off in ways he'd never dreamed. Besides the visceral pleasure he'd enjoyed for six months while he stalked and intimidated Russell's precious daughter, he now had a shot at scooping the Franklin grandchild into his net at the same time he nabbed Jessica.

And he would succeed. Luck was definitely on his side. He'd happened to be in the Buckskin, a local watering hole, when a guy named Jim had come in for a beer. Turns out

Jim's nose was out of joint because Sebastian Daniels had brought in some expert from L.A. to set up a security system for a line shack on the Rocking D. Jim couldn't figure out why they wanted such a high-falutin' system for a line shack in the first place.

Steven had made a hot journalism career out of acting on hunches. He'd seen how tight Jessica had become with that boyfriend of hers. No doubt he was the father of that kid. Steven would bet his bottom dollar the three of them were going off to play house in that line shack. At last, the opportunity he'd been waiting for.

"TAKE MY .38," Sebastian urged the next morning as he and Nat loaded the last of the boxes into the Bronco. "I'll feel a hell of a lot better if you have something out there with you."

Nat wondered if he was being foolishly stubborn. He hated guns with a passion, but he knew how to use one thanks to the endless target practice his father had forced on him. And Jess and the baby were depending on him to keep them safe.

Sebastian closed up the back of the Bronco. "I know you believe in all that newfangled technology you and Seth installed, but I'd still feel better if you had a backup."

"Okay," Nat said with a sigh of resignation. "Do you have a locked box or something secure I can put it in? I don't want to take any chances with that baby."

"I'll give you a locked box, but I'd advise you to put the gun on a high shelf and not lock it up. I'm as concerned about Elizabeth as you are, but she can't climb to the top of those cabinets in the line shack."

Nat gazed out at the hillside where he'd seen the flash of metal on the morning he'd taken the dogs for a run. "He could be gone, you know. Any guy who would follow a woman around for six months has to be weird. Maybe he got his jollies doing that, and now that she's not running, he's picked out another target for acting out his strange fantasies."

"If she were just any woman, I'd say you were possibly right." Sebastian rubbed the back of his neck and glanced at Nat. "But you've hooked up with an heiress, my friend."

Nat gave him a startled look. "Yeah, but she doesn't want—"

"Doesn't matter. She may hope to live a secluded life, but I think she's kidding herself on that score. Look at the Kennedys. Look at your Hollywood clients. Eventually some reporter digs up some information on one of the relatives and the whole family's in the headlines again, even if they work to avoid it."

Nat hadn't really thought about that aspect of his relationship with Jess. He'd thought his main concern was whether he'd be the kind of father Elizabeth deserved and whether he dared take a chance on being the kind of husband Jess deserved. The idea of living in a fishbowl didn't sit well with him.

"I can see you haven't thought much about that," Sebastian said. "You know how dearly I want you to make a life with Jessica and Elizabeth. But I wouldn't be a very good friend if I didn't point out that there's a negative side to that program. She can't change who she is."

"For some reason I never thought of Jess like that. As an heiress." Nat considered the homely little line shack he was about to take her to and winced. She'd probably tolerate it with good grace, the way she'd tolerated drinking coffee for days because she didn't want to make a fuss.

"It's been on my mind ever since you told me," Sebastian said. "When we were deciding whether to call her parents or not, I told you I didn't want to turn things over to some bigshot from New York. That's true, but the other thing I didn't want was the media circus that would result."

"Yeah, it would." Nat glanced around. The log ranch house, the sturdy barn and the horses frisking in the corral created a postcard-pretty view of country living. Then he imagined the area swarming with TV vans, reporters, even helicopters overhead. Sebastian's treasured peace would be shattered.

Filled with remorse, he faced Sebastian. "We shouldn't even be here. I should take Jess and Elizabeth and head out, away from the Rocking D. I've known about her background almost from the beginning, but you haven't. It's not fair to expect you to take this kind of risk with your whole way of life when you had no way of knowing what you were getting into."

"Whoa, son!" Sebastian chuckled. "God, but you do manage to focus on the cloud instead of the silver lining, don't you? I intended to give you a little reminder about the hazards on this road, not send you charging off in another direction entirely."

"But—"

"Never mind your buts. I was only saying that I think it's probable this kidnapper hasn't given up, and yet I'm not in favor of calling Franklin if we can help it. I would gladly entertain the whole crew of *60 Minutes* if that meant I could spend more time with Elizabeth, though. I'm crazy about that kid, in case you haven't noticed."

"Yeah, and that's also my fault. You should never—"

"Listen." Sebastian actually shook a finger in Nat's face. "Whether you and Jessica like it or not, we're in this rodeo with you, and we're gonna be part of that baby's life. All of us—Boone, Shelby, Josh, Gwen, Travis and Luann, besides Matty and me. The fact that her granddaddy's a billionaire is something we'll have to accept and find a way to deal with. But we're not letting that baby get away. At least not very far away. Got that?"

Nat grinned. "Got it."

"And I'm not ready to see the last of your sorry carcass, either, despite the fact you are a heap of trouble."

Nat's grin broadened. "I realize that."

Sebastian handed over the keys to the Bronco. "Here come the ladies with Elizabeth. I'll go get the .38."

"I sure wish I didn't have to take it."

"You're taking it." He started back toward the house.

Nat turned to watch Jess come out toward the Bronco carrying Elizabeth. Heiresses, both of them. When he tried to be objective, he could see the evidence of privilege in Jess. Someone had probably coached her, from a young age, how to walk, how to hold her head, how to remain gracious when everything wasn't exactly as she'd like it to be.

He'd made what most people would think was a lot of money as a broker, but his bank balance was laughable compared to her father's. That hadn't been a factor before, partly because Jess had insisted she wanted no part of her father's wealth because she hated that life, and partly because he'd never intended their relationship to go this far.

Now it was too late to consider whether he was an appropriate person for Jess or not. Heiress or not, he wanted her. And increasingly, he wanted that little bundle in her arms. His heart ached looking at them together.

No one would doubt they were mother and daughter. Sunlight danced on Jess's red curls, setting them on fire, but the baby wore a little cap to protect her face from the sun, and her ringlets curled out from under it. They were a lighter shade than Jess's, but Elizabeth would grow up to have hair as fiery as her mother's. She'd be a pistol, too, like her mother. Nat's chest tightened as he realized he wanted to be there to see how Elizabeth turned out.

Jess would probably have her on skis before he could turn around. Elizabeth would be hotdogging down the slopes by the time she was seven. And eventually she'd discover makeup and earrings. And boys. The boys would be wild for her.

He imagined her gliding down the stairs dressed for her high-school prom, her date waiting with a corsage and a nervous smile. Who would be there to give that awestruck boy an intimidating stare and ask a few pointed questions about his intentions regarding the lovely Elizabeth?

He would. His heart expanded with hope as he allowed himself to dream of a future that included Jess and this baby he had helped create. His first reaction to hearing of her existence had been born of fear. But the longing he carried with him constantly now was born of love.

Matty walked beside Jess, and she was doing her best to look cheerful, but Nat doubted she felt cheerful at all. If this week accomplished what it was supposed to accomplish, Elizabeth would cease to be a regular resident of the Rocking D.

"Oh my God, we forgot Bruce," Matty said. She turned and raced back inside to search for the sock monkey.

"Ba-ba!" Elizabeth called after her.

"She's getting Bruce for you." Jess hoisted the baby a little higher on her shoulder. Then she glanced up at Nat, and squinted a little in the sunlight. "It's bright out here. I didn't want to wear my sunglasses because Elizabeth would just pull them off."

"Here." Impulsively, Nat took off his Stetson and put it on her head to shade her eyes. It was big on her and she looked adorable in it.

"Oh, I can't take your hat," she said.

"You can have anything of mine you want," he said quietly.

She held his gaze and her throat moved in a convulsive swallow.

"Here's Bruce," Matty called, hurrying out with the sock monkey in one hand.

Elizabeth twisted in Jess's arms and reached out both hands. "Ba-ba!"

"Thanks," Jess said as Elizabeth grabbed the monkey and began gnawing happily on its arm. "We would have been back here in no time if we'd forgotten Bruce."

"I'm glad I remembered." Matty started to reach a hand toward the baby, hesitated and shoved both hands in the pockets of the denim overalls she'd taken to wearing now that her jeans didn't fit. "Okay, now, you're sure you have enough diapers?"

"Sebastian and I loaded in enough boxes of those things to diaper quintuplets for a month," Nat said.

"And my cell phone? Did either of you remember to pick it up off the dining-room table?"

"I put it in my duffel," Jess said.

Matty rocked back on her heels and smiled brightly. "Well, then, I guess that's it. Where's Sebastian?"

"He'll be right out." Nat decided not to mention what Sebastian had gone into the house to get. Matty was nervous enough about letting them take Elizabeth out to the line shack without bringing up a danger that might not even exist anymore.

"I hope that wooden floor doesn't give her splinters when she crawls on it," Matty said. "Do you have some first-aid cream? I never thought of that. How about bandages and stuff like that?"

"Sebastian said everything's in that first-aid kit he keeps in the Bronco." Nat decided it was time to get this show on the road. He opened the vehicle's door. "Jess, why don't you put Elizabeth in her car seat?"

"Sure thing. Maybe you'd better take this back for now." She handed him his Stetson and started to put Elizabeth in the car. Then she paused and glanced over at Matty. "Want to hug her goodbye?"

Matty took a deep breath. "You know, I don't believe I will. I don't want to take a chance on upsetting her." She grimaced. "Or me." She turned toward Nat as if she didn't care to watch Elizabeth being strapped into the padded seat. "Now, if you have the slightest problem, I want you to call. Someone will be here all the time, and one of us can take a run out there in my truck."

"I appreciate that, Matty." This scene was starting to make Nat emotional, too. "I expect we'll have an uneventful week." He expected nothing of the kind. The events of this week would determine his entire future. He didn't know if he, Jess and Elizabeth could form a happy little unit, but this was as close to a trial run as he was going to get.

He was counting on having a crutch to get him through, and that crutch was making love to Jess. Nothing had seemed quite right ever since she'd proclaimed a ban on that activity, and Nat was sure once he could take her to bed again he'd feel more sure of himself in other areas of his life.

"She's in," Jess announced. Then she walked toward Matty. "Can you risk giving me a hug?"

"I can risk it." Matty squeezed Jess tight. "Take care of yourself and that precious little bundle."

"I will." Wiping at her eyes, Jess climbed into the Bronco. "You'd think we were leaving for a year, the way we're carrying on."

"We'll get better at this," Matty said. "We'll have to." She turned to Nat. "Watch out for them," she murmured.

"You bet." He gave Matty a quick hug and walked around the Bronco to the driver's side. Matty had moved back several feet, as if to give herself distance from the pain of watching them drive away. If Sebastian didn't show up soon, people were going to start blubbering, Nat decided. He got in and shoved the key in the ignition. He was about to lay on the horn when Sebastian appeared.

"I'm coming!" he called as he loped down the porch steps carrying a small toolbox.

Nat got out again and went around to open up the back. No way did he want that thing up front.

"Okay, I found you a lock for the clasp," Sebastian said as he tucked the toolbox in among the pile of cardboard boxes, collapsible baby furniture and bags of groceries. He handed Nat a small key. "It's locked now, but I wouldn't leave it that way if I were you." He lowered his voice. "Does Jess know how to handle one?"

"I don't know. I doubt it."

"Maybe you should teach her."

"I'm not sure about that. The noise would be bad for the baby."

"True," Sebastian agreed. "Well, at least you've got it."

"Yeah, thanks." Nat didn't want a gun, but if it would make Sebastian sleep better, maybe that was reason enough.

Jess turned in her seat. "What are you two doing back there?"

"Last-minute stuff," Nat said as he closed up the back again and held out his hand to Sebastian. "I'm going to do everything in my power to make this come out right for you."

Sebastian's grip was firm. "Don't worry about me. Make this come out right for that little kid in there and I'll be happy."

"I'll give it all I've got." With one final squeeze, he released Sebastian's hand, touched the brim of his hat in salute and walked back to the driver's side of the Bronco. In seconds he was in, seat belt fastened, engine switched on. As he put the vehicle in gear he looked up to see Sebastian standing with his arm around Matty.

Please don't let me be the reason for screwing up this good man's life, he prayed as he pulled out of the driveway, tooting the horn once as he headed down the rough dirt road that cut across the Rocking D property and ended at the old line shack on the edge of Sebastian's land. In the rearview mirror he saw Matty and Sebastian still standing there, their arms raised in farewell.

"If I knew nothing else about you," Jess said, her voice

choked with emotion, "I would know you were special because of your friends."

AS THE BRONCO JOLTED over the bumpy road that was little more than a faint track across the countryside, Jessica didn't try to make conversation. Nat had his hands full avoiding rocks and chuckholes, and she wanted to make sure Elizabeth felt safe, so she kept talking to her throughout the ride.

She couldn't see Elizabeth's expression because the car seat faced toward the back, but at least the baby wasn't crying. During one smooth stretch in the road Jessica unlatched her seat belt and leaned over to find out what was going on with her daughter, who hadn't let out a peep so far. Elizabeth looked up at her, eyes wide, as if flabbergasted by the wild trip.

Jessica couldn't help grinning. "Having fun?" she asked.

"Ba-ba!" Elizabeth jiggled in her car seat with every bump in the road and she kept her monkey clutched tight in one fist, but she didn't look remotely ready to cry.

Settling back in her seat, Jessica glanced at Nat. "I think we have a thrill-seeker on our hands."

"There's a scary thought," Nat said as he steered around one large rut and jostled them all anyway when one wheel dipped into another hole in the road.

"At least she's apparently decided to trust us."

"You, not us. The jury's still out on whether she'll tolerate being alone with me. She never has. Come to think of it, she won't be on this trip, either."

"Why not?" Jessica thought this was the very time for that kind of experimentation. "I could take a little walk, so we could test it and see how she does."

"Not this week. This week I'm not letting you out of my sight."

A thrill of awareness arrowed through her stomach. "You mean because the guy still might be out there?"

He didn't take his eyes off the road. "That's right. Besides, it makes a damn fine excuse to keep you close to me." He gripped the wheel tighter as they hit another rocky spot in the road. "Very close."

As heat spiraled through her, she watched those hands control the steering wheel with strength and sureness. How she'd missed his touch. They'd barely begun to enjoy each other again when she'd insisted on ending the physical relationship.

She'd been right to insist on that until he'd had a chance to see Elizabeth and sort out how he felt about her. Unless Jessica was reading him all wrong, he'd made wonderful progress in that regard. Instead of being an obstacle between them, the baby seemed to be pulling them closer together.

And she was ready to be close to this man again. More than ready. Even the bouncing ride seemed to be stirring her up. A week of loving Nat. It had seemed like a long time when the plan had been suggested, but now she wondered if it would be long enough to satisfy the need that she'd built up over the past few days. She didn't want to waste a minute of their time together. She glanced at her watch. Nearly lunchtime. After lunch Elizabeth always took a nap....

"You're pretty quiet over there," Nat said. "Are you having second thoughts?"

She smiled to herself. "Yes."

"What?" He gave her a sharp glance. "So help me, Jess, if you're not planning on making love to me while we're out here, I don't think I can—"

"I'm having reservations about limiting ourselves to one week. Considering how much time I want to spend loving you, I wish we had at least two."

He let out a gusty sigh and shifted in his seat. "Oh, God. We should never have started this discussion."

Immediately she glanced down at the telltale bulge in his jeans, and her pulse began to race. "I probably don't have to ask, but did you bring—"

"Are you kidding? Those little foil packets were the first thing I packed. We have more of them than we do diapers." His jaw clenched. "I want you, Jess. Right here, right now."

The Bronco jolted them all as it hit a large rock in the road.

She was breathing fast, and it had nothing to do with the rough ride. "Here and now isn't what you'd call optimum," she said.

"I'm aware of that."

"How much longer before we get there?"

He glanced at her, his gaze hot enough to melt steel. "An eternity."

CHAPTER SEVENTEEN

JESSICA HAD PREPARED herself for a primitive setting, not that she much cared where she was as long as she could be alone with Nat and Elizabeth. From the outside, the line shack looked about as she'd expected, the exterior weathered to a dull gray and broken up with square windows without curtains. A corrugated tin roof covered with pine needles, leaves and fallen branches topped the structure. The forest debris on the roof almost made it look thatched.

But the shack, humble though it was, sat within a grove of aspens. With their gleaming white trunks fountaining upward to a burst of golden leaves, they were all the decoration the little place needed to make it spectacular.

"It's beautiful," she said as Nat parked the Bronco near the front door.

"Beautiful?" Nat gave her a puzzled glance. "You don't have to pretend it's the Taj Mahal for my sake, Jess. I know you're used to much better."

She stared at him in shock. "Where did that come from?" In their entire relationship he'd never once apologized for their accommodations, and not all of them had been five-star, by any means.

"Well, after all, you are an heiress, and—"

"Nat Grady, have I ever, in all the time you've known me, put any importance in that? In fact, haven't I done my level best to escape that label?"

Elizabeth began to chortle in the back seat as if she wanted to join in the conversation.

"Well, yes," Nat said. "But you can't change the fact that you are connected to Russell P. Franklin."

"As little as possible." She didn't really want to talk about this.

Elizabeth grew louder.

"Are you planning to keep Elizabeth a secret forever?" Nat asked.

It was a fair question if he was considering making a life with her. She looked over at him. "No, I guess not. No matter how I feel about my parents and their power, that wouldn't be right, for Elizabeth or them. I've been thinking about my mother lately," she admitted. "Under better circumstances, I'm sure she'd love the idea of being a granny."

Elizabeth started rocking in the car seat in time to her increasingly demanding babble.

Unsnapping her seat belt, Jessica started to get out of the car so she could tend to the baby. "We should get her inside."

Nat didn't move. "You mean better circumstances, as in a better guy?" he said softly.

She turned to him, saw the naked uncertainty in his eyes and could have kicked herself for her choice of words. Ignoring Elizabeth's agitation for the moment, she reached out and cradled his face in both hands "I have the best guy," she said. "I wasn't talking about you. I was talking about this whole mess with the stalker. I would be proud to tell my parents you're the father of my daughter." *I would be proud to tell them that you were my husband, too.* But she didn't say that. They needed to take care of Elizabeth before they had that kind of discussion.

He covered her hands with his as he gazed into her eyes. "Jess, I never expect to make the kind of money that your father—"

"Nat, shut up," she said gently. Leaning forward, she kissed him. She'd only meant to silence him and stop this ridiculous discussion, but the minute her lips touched his, the need between them exploded.

With a groan he slid his hands around to cup the back of her head and plunged his tongue inside her mouth. In no time they were straining to get to each other over the console between the seats, their breathing labored as their mouths sought deep and deeper access.

"*Da-da!*" Elizabeth yelled at the top of her lungs.

Jessica and Nat drew back from each other immediately, and she was sure her expression of guilt mirrored his. "The baby," they said together.

"My God, Jess." Nat looked down at his hands as if they didn't belong to him, as if he had no idea they'd already unfastened the first button of her blouse. He pulled away as if he'd touched something hot.

She struggled for breath and fastened her blouse. "We'll...have to be more careful."

"I forgot everything. I was ready to—"

"I know." Heart pounding, Jessica got out of the Bronco on shaky legs.

"If you'll take her out of the car seat," he said, "I'll unlock the place and turn on the security system."

"Right." Spurred by remorse, she had Elizabeth out of the car seat in record time. Silly though it might be, she was glad Elizabeth's seat faced backward and the baby hadn't seen that sizzling, highly sexual kiss. As if an eight-month-old would know what was going on.

Yet she wondered how the interior of the cabin was arranged and whether she and Nat would have any privacy whatsoever. She discovered that she craved privacy, considering some of the uninhibited activities she had in mind.

"Sorry to ignore you like that, sweetheart," she crooned breathlessly to the baby. "Mommy got a little involved with...with Daddy." She liked the sound of that. But Mommy and Daddy would have to exercise a little more discipline from now on. Maybe once they'd taken the edge off their hunger, they wouldn't be so ravenous for each other.

As she stepped through the door of the cabin, the first thing she saw was a mason jar full of yellow and white daisies on a wooden table flanked by two chairs. The second thing she saw was a double bed with the covers turned back, snowy pillows plumped, as if someone didn't want to waste any time when an opportunity arose to climb into that bed. The third thing she noticed was the wooden hinged screen positioned at the foot of the bed. Nat had been thinking about privacy, too. Sensuous warmth poured through her.

Glancing in his direction, she found him watching her with a tense expression. She was so touched and aroused by his careful preparations that she wasn't sure she'd be able to speak. But obviously she needed to say something. "The flowers—" She paused to clear her throat. "The flowers are very nice."

"Wish I could say I picked them in the woods, but the time of year's wrong. I had to buy them in town. I realize the vase isn't—"

"Nat, if you say one more word of apology about this sweet little cabin, I'll—well, I'm not sure what I'll do, but you won't like it."

He looked immensely relieved. "Then the place is okay?"

"More than okay. I can't think of anyplace in the world I'd rather be, or any two people I'd rather be with."

"Me neither." He met her gaze and gradually a slow smile appeared as the anxiety in his blue eyes was replaced by a steady flame of eagerness.

Her breath caught at the beauty of this man. And for the next week, he was all hers. Well, hers and Elizabeth's.

As if reminding her of that fact, the baby began to struggle, wanting down.

Jessica loved knowing her daughter was becoming more

mobile. She got a kick out of watching her crawl and could hardly wait until she walked. "If you'll close the door," she said, "I'll put her down and let her explore the room a little."

Nat looked anxious again. "Are you sure it's safe? I didn't think about her crawling around on it until Matty said something about splinters."

Jessica surveyed the wooden floor and decided it looked smooth enough to her. The lack of throw rugs might even be a plus. "She'll be fine." She crouched down in preparation for lowering a wiggling Elizabeth to the floor.

"Wait, is it clean enough? I swept it, but there's no vacuum cleaner out here, so I'm sure I didn't get every little bit. Let me get her playpen. We can put her in there."

She smiled indulgently at him. "Not for a solid week, Nat. She'd go crazy, and so would we. No, she needs to get down. Would you please close the door? Eventually I'll let her explore outside, too, but—"

"Outside?"

Amazed by his scandalized tone, she glanced up. "Sure. Why not?"

"She could pick up anything. Bugs, dirty rocks, *snakes*." He shuddered.

Jessica laughed. "I wouldn't turn her lose and forget about her. I'd follow her every minute and make sure she didn't put anything in her mouth that would make her choke. You can help me follow her every minute if it makes you feel better. She's a good crawler, but I doubt she could outrun us."

"I don't care. The idea of putting that sweet little baby down in the dirt doesn't sit right with me."

She excused his attitude, considering he was so inexperienced. No doubt in a day or so of being around Elizabeth he'd get over it, but he was making her a little nervous. He sounded far too much like her father. She wouldn't tolerate anyone smothering her daughter the way she'd been smothered, even if that person happened to be the sexiest man on the planet.

"Let's start with the cabin, and we'll worry about outside later," she said.

"Okay." Nat walked over and closed the door.

Jess put Elizabeth on the floor, and then sat down beside her in order to take off the baby's cap. "There you go, honey-bunch. Free at last."

Immediately Elizabeth rocked forward onto her hands, and with a cry of glee started off toward the potbelly stove.

"Oh, God," Nat said. "We won't be able to use the stove. She might burn herself."

"Sure we can use the stove. When it's hot, we'll make sure she doesn't get close to it." Jessica kept her eye on Elizabeth as the baby bypassed the stove and went on to the table, where she crawled underneath and sat down, looking pleased with herself.

Jessica chuckled. Elizabeth was obviously mimicking Sebastian and Matty's dogs, who both loved to lie under the dining-room table. "Are you pretending you're a doggy?" she asked.

"Ga!" Elizabeth said, giving Jessica a toothy grin.

"Good girl." Still smiling, Jessica looked up at Nat and was surprised at his frown. "What's wrong?"

"I really didn't expect her to crawl around this place," he said.

"What did you suppose she'd do?"

"I guess I thought we'd carry her, or put her in the playpen, or in that backpack thing that Sebastian uses all the time."

"She's really too old to be confined that way for any long period." Trying to hold on to her patience, Jessica returned her attention to Elizabeth as the baby started crawling toward the bed.

"Then maybe we shouldn't have brought her out here."

Her stomach twisted. "Maybe not, if you're going to be like a mother hen about it."

"I just—Elizabeth, no!" He hurried over and snatched her up. "Give me that!"

Elizabeth started to howl.

Jess was on her feet in an instant. "What? What did she get?"

"Well, it's a long piece of wild grass, but it could have been anything!"

"Give her to me."

He seemed glad to get rid of the baby, and Jessica carried her over to the window. "It's okay, sweetie." She rocked Elizabeth and kissed her wet cheeks. "No problem. Easy does it, little girl. Look! Look out the window! See the birdie? Look at that. A pretty little bird has come to say hello to Elizabeth. Can you say hello?"

"Ba," Elizabeth said, snuffling. Then she took a deep breath and swiveled in Jessica's arms to look at Nat.

Jessica followed the direction of the baby's gaze, and Nat's lost expression ripped at her heart. "She's fine," she said.

He shook his head. "I can't do this, Jess. I'm no good at it."

"Oh, for heaven's sake." Still holding Elizabeth, she walked over to him. She could feel Elizabeth shrink away a little, which was all the more reason to erase the last incident from the baby's memory.

"She hates me," Nat said.

"No, she doesn't. You scared her a little. Talk to her."

"And say what?"

"That she's the prettiest baby in the world. You could give her that piece of grass, too."

"But it's been under the bed!"

"It won't hurt her. Deer eat it all the time."

Nat looked unhappy about it, but he held out the long blade of grass. "Is this what you wanted, Elizabeth?"

"Ga!" She reached for it.

"Tickle her nose with it," Jessica suggested.

"Put it on her face?"

"Yes. Play with her. Remember how much she loved peekaboo. Playing with her is important."

He took a deep breath. "Okay. Hey, Elizabeth, you like this?" He wiggled the tip of the grass against her nose.

The baby laughed with delight.

"You do, huh?" Nat repeated the motion and earned himself another baby giggle. "I like the way she laughs," he said. "It makes her nose sort of wrinkle."

"I know." The tension in Jessica's stomach eased as Nat continued to play the tickling game. Had she thought everything would go smoothly once the three of them were together? If so, she was a foolish woman. She and Nat had never had the basic discussions that future parents needed to have about parenting styles and expectations.

She'd had nine months to read up on the subject of child rearing while she formed her ideas of what kind of mother she wanted to be. Although she didn't want Elizabeth to repeat her own childhood, there had been positives in it, including the certainty that she was loved. Nat had no yardstick for measuring how a loving parent should act.

"It's nearly lunchtime," she said at last. "If you'll get her high chair out of the Bronco and set it up, I'll feed her."

"Okay." He turned away and Elizabeth yelled in protest. He turned back, the beginnings of a smile on his face. "She doesn't want me to leave," he said with some surprise.

"No, she doesn't." Jessica found herself smiling, too. "But she might tolerate it if you give her that grass."

He glanced at the long blade of grass in his hand. "I guess I have to, don't I?"

"Trust me, it won't hurt her. I'll monitor the situation while you're gone."

Reluctantly he handed the grass to Elizabeth, who waved

it and chortled with happiness. When she put it in her mouth, he winced. "I hate that."

"I know. Don't worry, I'll make sure she doesn't choke. She'll be fine."

"She has to be." He looked into her eyes. "Because if anything happened to either of you, my life would be over."

NAT UNLOADED the Bronco and set up the high chair first so Jess could feed the baby. While she was doing that, he brought everything else in and set up the portable crib and the playpen, the one Jess had already informed him they wouldn't be using much.

Now that he thought about it, Elizabeth had crawled around the ranch house quite a bit, but Matty and Sebastian kept the place really clean. And besides, at that point he hadn't assumed the responsibility for what happened to Elizabeth when she was on the floor, because there were always several people around who were ready and willing to do that.

He'd been so hell-bent on getting out here so he could make love to Jess that he hadn't fully realized how the responsibility of the baby would settle on him with the weight of an elephant. When he'd contemplated this week, he'd thought his major worry would be whether Jess's stalker would show up. Now he looked around at the small cabin and saw a million dangers to Elizabeth, none of them having to do with some weirdo on the loose.

Matty had packed sandwiches for their first meal, so once he had the baby furniture up, he took Jess's suggestion to stop for lunch while Elizabeth was still awake. He hadn't missed Jess's meaning when she'd made that suggestion, either. Once that baby went down for her afternoon nap, he and Jess didn't want to waste time with lunch.

How he needed that woman. He couldn't remember feeling this raw and vulnerable in his life, and he ached to take refuge in Jess's arms. But the ache deep inside wasn't only about taking. Now that he understood more of what Jess had been through because of him, he desperately wanted to shower her with all the pleasure he was capable of giving.

He barely tasted his lunch. He was too preoccupied with Jess—the moist invitation of her mouth, the gentle movement of her breasts under her shirt, the snug fit of her jeans when she leaned over to pick up the baby. His groin tightened in response to the flash in her brown eyes and the catch in her voice when she caught him looking.

While she used the portable crib as a changing table and got Elizabeth ready for her nap, he washed up the lunch dishes. He could only see the top of her head above the folding wooden screen he'd set up between the crib and the double bed so they'd have some privacy, and he made a mental note to take the screen away when they didn't actually need it. He hungered for the sight of her.

"I haven't seen anything that looks like an alarm system," she said as she continued to dress the baby for her nap. "Where is it?"

"There's a monitoring screen up in the rafters in each corner of the cabin," he said.

She glanced around. "Wow. I didn't even notice them."

"Seth likes to make his systems unobtrusive," Nat said. "The cameras are on the roof, camouflaged with all those leaves and pine branches. If someone doesn't know a security system exists, they won't try to dismantle it."

"Did Sebastian give you a gun before we left this morning?"

He paused in the act of wiping a dish. "Yes. It's in the green metal box I put on the top shelf. Does it bother you to have it there?"

"It bothers me to have to do any of this. I assume you know how to shoot it?"

"If necessary."

"That's good, I guess."

"I guess."

She murmured something to Elizabeth and began singing to the baby.

He couldn't see her anymore and decided she must be leaning over the crib, trying to soothe Elizabeth to sleep.

She'd accepted the presence of the gun better than he'd thought she would. He remembered the last time he'd held one. It was this same gun, and the guys had been joking around about who was a better shot one summer day at the Rocking D. Sebastian had set up a few beer cans on a fence and everybody had taken some shots except Nat. He hadn't wanted to touch the thing.

Finally, the teasing had become so bad he'd given in. He'd told himself he was over the revulsion he felt at holding a gun, but apparently he hadn't been. He'd nailed the cans—*bing, bing, bing*. It seemed all the hours of practice as a kid had stuck with him. Then he'd put down the gun and walked around to the back of the barn so he could throw up.

His friends had thought he had a case of stomach flu, and he'd let them think that. He had no interest in telling them that when he was thirteen, his father had made him shoot a horse. Sure, the horse had turned mean, but only because his father had regularly beat him the same way he'd beaten Nat. When the animal had kicked Nat and broken his arm, Hank Grady had flown into a rage and forced Nat to shoot that poor horse. Nat hadn't fired a gun since.

Jess was the first person who had made all those bad memories fade. Until he'd left her seventeen months ago, he hadn't appreciated the unique brand of magic she'd brought to his life. Loving her healed him. And God, did he need healing now.

She hadn't reappeared from behind the screen, but he realized that her soft lullaby had ended. Maybe Elizabeth was finally drifting off to sleep. Maybe, at long last, he was going to make love to Jess again.

He stopped working on the dishes and gazed at the screen. The silence was encouraging. Very encouraging. At the thought of what was to come, moisture pooled in his mouth. He swallowed and took a deep breath.

Then her head reappeared above the screen, and she turned toward him with a smile. Oh, such a smile. He'd forgotten how seductive she could be when she put her mind to it.

"She's asleep?" he murmured.

Jess nodded.

Nat tossed down the dish towel. Holding her dark gaze, he started toward the bed, unbuttoning his shirt as he went. Now. Right now.

Then she mouthed the word *wait*.

He stopped and lifted his eyebrows in question. *Wait* wasn't the word he wanted to hear at the moment. *Yes* was more like it.

But she'd turned around again, and he wondered if Elizabeth still had some settling down to do. Okay, he'd wait, even if he was frustrated enough to chew a handful of Boone's horseshoeing nails. Once he started on this program, he wouldn't be able to stop, even if Elizabeth woke up again. So it would be best for all concerned if the baby was fast asleep.

Then Jess turned to look at him again and her cheeks were pink. "Okay," she whispered, and came around the screen.

He nearly lost it.

Her shirt and jeans were gone. In their place was an outfit that belonged in a skin flick. He struggled for breath as she walked toward him. She had fantastic legs. Just looking at her bare legs almost made him climax. This presentation of hers was overkill, but he wasn't complaining. He didn't know where or when she'd come up with the black lace number, but it would live in his fantasies forever.

The sheer, tight material undulated with each step she

took toward him. The top cupped her breasts and pushed them up in a way that made his eyes glaze with lust. A series of ties down the front begged to be undone. He loved it, loved her for going to the trouble of making this an unbelievable moment.

"Gwen and I made a fast trip to Colorado Springs," she said, a trace of shyness in her tone. "Do you like it?"

"Oh, yeah," he said, his voice hoarse. "Very, very much. And after all that effort, I hope you won't be offended when I strip it right off."

CHAPTER EIGHTEEN

NAT REALLY MEANT to undo each of the ties so as not to rip anything on her new outfit, but once he got the first few open and filled his hands with her breasts, his control deserted him. He laid her across the width of the bed without much fanfare or finesse, his mouth hot and seeking against her plump breasts. The first taste of her nipple drove him out of his head.

Dizzy from the wild-strawberry feel of her tight nipple rolling against his tongue, her soft whimpers and the urgent way she clutched his head, he became frantic to have more of her. Ties ripped from their moorings as he yanked the sheer lace down to her knees so he could touch…there, where her waist nipped in and there, where her belly heaved, and God, yes, bury his fingers there, where she was already soaking wet. Gasping, she arched away from the bed.

So that's how it was. With savage joy he stroked her quickly to her first climax. She reached blindly for a pillow, and he had the presence of mind to grab it and hand it to her so she could put it over her mouth and scream into it. Now was not the time to be waking babies. Not when he needed to seek the source of her heat with a tongue that thirsted for the gush of her second climax.

Ah, she was so wild for him that she abandoned her inhibitions and spread her thighs as he slid down, kissing a path from her breasts to her belly, tonguing his way over that sweet terrain to her wellspring of precious, life-giving nectar. He felt energy pour into him as he feasted on her sweetness and she quivered in his arms.

He knew her, knew her secrets, her rhythm, her aching need. He was born for this, to make this woman quake and cry out his name. His name. Nothing he'd ever done in his whole sorry life gave him this sense of rightness. Only loving Jess.

She tensed, her body trembling violently as her hips rose again. As she gulped for breath, she gasped out a plea, wanting more. And he knew that she needed that, too. As much as he had to sink into her to become complete, she couldn't be complete until he had thrust deep and made that ultimate connection.

He didn't bother to undress. There wasn't time. The pressure was too great. He unbuckled his belt, opened his fly and put on the condom. Then he lifted her, moving her higher on the bed so he had room for his knees.

Her head was nearly off the other side, and he cradled it in both hands to steady her. Her silky hair flowed through his fingers. Then, looking into her eyes, he pushed home.

She moaned and wrapped her legs around his. "Tighter," she whispered.

He moved another notch closer to her center and could feel the pulsing begin. "Don't shut me out again," he murmured.

"No." She rose to meet his thrusts.

His breathing grew ragged. "I have to make love to you."

"Yes."

"It's…everything." He plunged into her again and again. And it seemed as if each time he went deeper, and deeper still.

"Yes. Oh, *yes.*"

He held her gaze. "Everything," he gasped, and clenched his jaw against the cry of release that rose from his throat as he exploded within her.

WHETHER BECAUSE of the strange surroundings or the activity from the nearby bed, Elizabeth took a very short nap that day. Jessica borrowed Nat's shirt to have something to put on when she went to get the baby, who sounded as if she might start fussing if nobody paid any attention to her.

Jessica didn't want any more tears from Elizabeth today if they could be avoided. Tears seemed to make Nat think he'd done something wrong, and Jessica wanted him to build on a feeling of success.

"Put something warm on her," Nat called from the other side of the screen. "Let's get out the baby carrier and take a walk."

"You think that'll be okay?"

Nat came around the screen zipping up his pants. "We can set the alarm before we leave, and we won't go far. We'll keep our eyes open. I don't know about you, but I don't want to be pinned down here to the point that we feel like rats in a cage."

"Neither do I. As I'm sure you can imagine." She flashed him a smile and returned to diapering Elizabeth.

"You look good in my shirt."

"I like wearing it," she said. "It has your scent."

"So?"

"It gets me hot. Pheromones, you know."

"I've heard of those little devils. I vote that you just wear my shirt today and keep that pheromone thing going. I'll go grab another shirt."

"All right." She couldn't ever remember wearing anything of his before. It was one more example of how the barriers were coming down between them. Isolating themselves in this little cabin had been a brilliant idea.

He started to walk away, then turned around and came back. "You know, this pheromone business works both ways. I like breathing in your scent, too."

"Oh, yeah?" She finished snapping up Elizabeth's overalls and glanced up with a grin. "Does that mean you'd like to wear that black lace number for the rest of the day?"

"Nah. I don't have the build for it." He moved in close beside her. "I'll have to try something else."

"Such as?"

He put a hand around her waist. "Hold still for a minute. I have an idea."

"I can't imagine what you're up to." She chuckled as she looked into his eyes. She didn't anticipate his next move at all. When he slid his free hand under the shirt and down between her legs, she gasped. "Nat!" She tried to pull away. "This isn't the time for—"

"Hold still," he whispered. "This'll only take a second." And he slipped two fingers inside her.

Secretly thrilled at his audacity, she nevertheless acted shocked. Pretending indignation made the caress even more arousing. "Nat, for heaven's sake. The baby—"

"Has no idea what's going on. Mmm. That should do it." He eased his hand out from between her thighs.

She sighed with disappointment. Not that she really expected him to continue while they were standing here by the crib, but he'd left her throbbing and ready. "Do what?" she asked, her voice unsteady.

He held his damp fingers under her nose. "Pheromones," he said. "My share. This should hold me until the munchkin goes to sleep tonight." And he rubbed his fingers across his upper lip.

She groaned as desire pounded through her. "We'd better get dressed and go on that walk." She was mesmerized by the glow of passion in his eyes. "Now."

"Yep." He cupped her face gently in one hand and brushed a kiss over her lips. "Besides," he murmured, "it seems to me Matty once said that being out in the fresh air helps a kid sleep better. And I want that little girl to sleep like a log tonight." He brushed her lips one last time. "Because I don't plan to sleep at all."

Neither did Jessica. As much as she'd loved the urgency of their lovemaking this afternoon, she wanted a long, lazy session in bed with Nat. She'd like it right now.

But once they'd dressed and stepped out into the crisp afternoon, she decided that if she couldn't be in bed loving Nat, this was a good second choice. Elizabeth rode happily in the carrier strapped to Nat's back as they followed a path paved with golden aspen leaves.

"How's your sixth sense working?" Nat asked.

"I don't think he's here," Jessica said. "Do you suppose that you three men really scared him off when you rode out after him that morning?"

"That would be nice. Sebastian doesn't think so, but the guy's so weird that anything's possible."

Looking up through the shimmering leaves of the aspens to the cornflower sky as she walked hand in hand with Nat, Jessica believed anything was possible. Anything at all.

The crunch of leaves underfoot and the musty scent of the dry forest floor reminded her of another October day two years earlier. "Remember the time I talked you into raking up a pile of autumn leaves and playing in them with me?"

"I remember everything about you, Jess. I've had seventeen months to concentrate on those memories. They're sorted and cataloged, and there's not a cobweb on a single one."

She glanced at him. "What a beautiful thing to say."

He met her gaze. "What a beautiful person to say it to." He smiled and squeezed her hand before turning his attention back to the path. "That last picture you gave me for the collection was a doozy, by the way. I'm sorry about tearing those little ties off. Maybe you can fix them."

"I probably could." Currents of electricity seemed to be running between their joined hands. "You'd like a repeat performance?"

He laughed. "You even have to ask? Except the next

time, you'd better tie those things looser. Or maybe not tie them at all. A man tends to run out of patience when he has an erection stiffer than a tire iron.''

With a comment like that, she felt almost invited to look at the crotch of his jeans, and sure enough, a telltale bulge was beginning to show. "How's your patience right now?" she teased.

"Being tested," he said, not looking at her. "I strongly suggest we talk about something else."

The sweet certainty of being wanted made her laugh with delight, and the sound of her laughter brought on giggles from Elizabeth. If life could get any more perfect than this, Jessica thought, she couldn't imagine how.

In consideration for Nat's comfort, she switched the conversation to her interest in wildcrafting herbs. Since he'd been gone, she'd taken a couple of classes and thought she might even turn the interest into a career. Because Nat was so encouraging, she allowed herself to imagine that he was picturing a future in which he ran a ranch for abandoned children and she roamed the nearby countryside in search of wild herbs.

It wasn't a difficult fantasy to build, considering the hum of sensual excitement between them, no matter what they were discussing. Throughout the afternoon's walk, and during the evening as they prepared supper and fed Elizabeth, every accidental touch sizzled and every deliberate one nearly destroyed their control.

And Jessica discovered an amazing thing. Having the baby around definitely limited their freedom to make love at every opportunity. Frustration levels were at an all-time high for both of them. But she hadn't thought to value that frustration.

During the year she and Nat had been seeing each other, on the weekends they'd spent together, they'd been free to indulge themselves sexually whenever they chose. Looking back on that time, she realized that they'd begun to take their physical relationship for granted.

With Elizabeth on the scene, for the first time they enjoyed the thrill of anticipation. Jessica hadn't understood what a powerful aphrodisiac that could be.

She suspected Nat had figured it out, too, because he didn't put any pressure on her to rush either dinner or Elizabeth's bedtime preparations. He patiently waited until Elizabeth had finished all the finger food on her tray. When she was ready to be changed, he asked to be taught the diapering process, which meant the job took twice as long. Then they both played peekaboo with the baby while taking off her clothes and getting her into her sleeper.

Throughout the activities, Jessica was constantly aware of Nat—his hand reaching for a dish at the same time she did, his hip brushing hers as they stood side by side at the crib, his eyes on her while she worked. She noticed every glance and exactly where it was focused. Sometimes he'd meet her gaze, but often he'd direct his attention elsewhere on her body, with heated results. A burning look could make her mouth tingle, her nipples tighten, her belly quiver.

Fortunately she had the same power. She could stare at his mouth until his breathing quickened and his blue eyes darkened. If her gaze wandered below his belt, she could watch the imprint of his erection become more distinct the longer she concentrated on that area. Once she even drew a soft groan from him.

Until the moment they finally put Elizabeth in her crib for the night, they engaged in a silent, tension-laced duel that was the most exciting foreplay Jessica had ever experienced.

But by the time she laid the baby down on her tummy and began singing her to sleep, Jessica was ready for the waiting to be over. They'd dimmed the lights in the cabin so the baby would sleep—but they'd left one on beside the double bed so they could see each other when they made love.

Nat leaned against the wall, arms folded, watching Jessica rub Elizabeth's back and sing to her. In order to do the various evening chores, he'd rolled the sleeves of his western shirt back over his forearms.

There was something incredibly sexy about a man with his sleeves rolled up, Jessica thought. He looked ready for action. And a little action was exactly what she had in mind.

Of course, in her current frame of mind, every part of Nat, from his ears to his toes, had taken on erotic meaning. Still, she especially liked admiring the strength of his arms. She visually traced the pattern of russet hair and imagined running her tongue along the groove that formed between muscle and bone when he flexed his wrist. Then she stared with lust at the supple length of his fingers as they curved around his biceps. When she finally looked into his eyes, she nearly lost her place in the familiar lullaby. The message in that intense blue gaze was unmistakable.

With a faint smile, he looked over at the sleeping baby. Then his glance returned to Jessica. With blatant intent he allowed it to rove over her body, lingering at all the places he knew how to awaken. She wondered if any part of her would sleep tonight.

Elizabeth gave a little sigh and her body relaxed under Jessica's hand. Jessica muted the lullaby and lightened her touch. All the while, she listened to Elizabeth's breathing to gauge when she was truly asleep. At last she was. Slowly Jessica lifted her hand and stepped back. In the silence, she could hear Nat's indrawn breath.

She looked up and found that he'd pushed himself away from the wall and now stood with his arms at his sides, waiting for her. Heart pounding and body already moistening with need, she held his gaze as she walked toward him.

He took her hand and led her around the screen. As they

stood beside the bed, he was trembling. With great restraint he drew her slowly into his arms and looked deep into her eyes. His erection pressed against her. "I've never wanted you like this," he whispered. "I'm coming apart inside."

"We have to be quiet at first," she murmured. "Just in case."

"I'll try." With shaking hands he cupped her face in both hands, tipped her head back and lowered his mouth to hers. His kiss was furnace-hot and more insistent than she ever remembered. His tongue probed boldly as he slipped his thumbs to the corners of her mouth and nudged her mouth wider.

He kissed her as if he couldn't get close enough, deep enough. She wrapped her arms around his waist and fit his denim-covered erection between her thighs, holding him tight against her. They were both breathing so raggedly that she wondered if their gasps alone would wake the baby.

His hands slipped from her face to the top snap of the shirt she'd borrowed from him. She wore no bra underneath, and she knew that once he began to caress her breasts, she'd lose her mind.

But this time she was determined to give as good as she got. This time she would be in charge. The night was long and she could afford to be generous. As he worked his way down the snaps, she reached for his belt buckle.

Before he finished with the snaps, she'd unfastened his belt. By the time he pushed the shirt over her shoulders, she'd opened the button on his jeans and unzipped his fly. He moaned softly against her mouth.

The prospect of what she planned to do, and how it would no doubt affect him, made her pulse race. Pushing both jeans and underwear down, she discovered that he was, in his words, stiff as a tire iron.

Drawing back from his kiss, she guided him down to sit on the edge of the bed before kneeling in front of him.

"Jess—"

"Shh." She kissed him quickly before shrugging out of the borrowed shirt. The movement jiggled her breasts, but when he reached for them she caught his wrists. "Not yet," she murmured. "Take off your shirt. I'll handle the rest."

Then she tortured him by making him watch her, topless, taking off his boots. She knew the movement of her unfettered breasts excited him. He'd once joked that he wished skiing wasn't so cold a sport, because he'd love to watch her do it topless.

If his harsh breathing was any indication, he was pretty darned excited now. So excited that he'd left the job of taking off his shirt half done. Apparently, after unsnapping it, he'd become so absorbed in watching her that he'd forgotten what he'd been instructed to do.

"Your shirt," she reminded him with a smile. Her skin flushed with anticipation.

She waited until he had it off and then she took a moment to admire his work-sculpted physique. With his well-developed muscles and hair a bit too long to be fashionable, he looked far more like a calendar model than a businessman. She wanted him now, sooner than now.

But instead she took her own sweet time removing his jeans, making sure she brushed her nipples against his thighs, his knees and his calves as she worked. Last of all, she pulled off his socks, leaning down so her breasts tickled the tops of his feet.

When next she glanced at him, each fist was clenched around a section of blanket and his eyes were squeezed shut. As she'd hoped, he was in ecstatic agony. Now for her final gift.

She moved between his legs, nudging his sensitive inner thighs with her breasts. In the process she gave thanks for not being small in that department. For what she had in mind, she needed everything she had.

He opened his eyes to gaze down at her. "You're destroying me," he whispered.

She merely smiled and leaned forward to place a wet kiss on the top of his rigid penis.

He gasped. "Jess, you'd better not—"

"Shh," she said again. "Give me your hands."

Quivering, he held them out, as if he'd become her slave. She cupped them against the sides of her breasts and showed him that if he pressed gently, he would capture the shaft of his penis in that soft, silken valley. As he complied, he groaned and closed his eyes. His fingers began an involuntary kneading motion as he held her breasts snug against his erection.

She moved gently up and down, treating him to slow, tantalizing friction. "Open your eyes," she whispered. "And watch."

When he opened his eyes, they were glazed with pleasure. He looked down as he kept up the sensuous rhythm, and his breath rasped in his throat. "Jess. Oh, Jess, I'm going to—"

"I know." She watched his face, saw the muscles work in his jaw, knew he was close. She increased the tempo.

He made a noise low in his throat.

"I want you to," she murmured. "Come for me, Nat."

He began to quake with reaction.

When she knew he was nearly there, she leaned over and slid her lips over the smooth tip. With a cry held behind clenched teeth, he came. Flushed and triumphant, she swallowed all that he had to give.

NAT WISHED he could write poetry. Then he would write a poem dedicated to Jessica's breasts. After treating him to one of the most fantastic experiences of his life, she'd shucked off the rest of her clothes and they'd crawled under the covers to cuddle.

And it was a world-class cuddle as he nestled his cheek against one of her deserving-of-a-poem breasts and cupped his hand around the other. Besides the benefit of the pillowy warmth supporting his head, he could hear the steady beat of her heart and feel the rise and fall of her chest with each breath. As if all that wasn't enough, she began stroking her fingers through his hair.

Elizabeth was still asleep, and he figured they could talk now without worrying so much about waking her up. Sebastian had lectured him about that before he left. *Once she's fast asleep, you can pretty much enjoy yourselves, so long as you don't start yelling or anything.* Nat remembered Sebastian presenting this advice with total seriousness, and the memory made him smile. He'd wanted to yell during that last episode, but he'd managed to control himself, God knows how.

He sighed happily and snuggled closer. "You just keep piling memories on top of memories, Jess," he said.

"I can't think of a better plan."

"That's because there isn't one." He caught her nipple between his thumb and forefinger and stroked gently, making it hard. "I love watching this happen." He lifted his head and looked into her eyes, seeing the passion flare as he plucked her taut nipple in a slow rhythm. "I love watching you get hot."

"Do you now?"

He smiled. Her voice had taken on that breathy quality that told him exactly what she was thinking about. But he liked to hear her say it. He cupped her breast and swirled his tongue around her nipple to shake up the rhythm of her breathing. It worked. Then he looked into her eyes as he kneaded her breast. "Tell me what you'd like."

She ran a tongue over her lower lip in a way that drove him crazy. "World peace."

"I'm working on that, smarty-pants. Anything else?"

"Come closer and I'll whisper it in your ear, big boy."

He edged up and took that sassy mouth in a kiss that left her gasping. "Anyone who did what you just did to me can say it to my face," he murmured.

And she did. Explicitly. Using good old-fashioned An-
glo-Saxon words to describe exactly what she wanted him
to do to her. His blood roared in his ears and he grew
instantly hard again.

Now his breathing wasn't so steady, either. "I think I
can manage that," he said.

And manage it he did. He loved her hard, repeating the
earthy words she'd used and getting her to say them again
as he drove into her. He loved to watch her mouth when
she spoke that way, knowing she'd never use that language
anywhere else but here, in this bed, with him.

Thanks to her wonderful gift at the start of their evening
together, he had staying power this time. He could exper-
iment with different positions, looking for ways to give her
a climax while holding himself in check. Rolling to his
back, he took her with him and urged her to ride him until
she lost control. Then he took her from behind and brought
her to another explosion.

The room was cool, but they were slick with sweat by
the time he stretched her out on her back and savored his
old-fashioned favorite. The other positions were great for
erotic adventure, and he enjoyed them all. But this one, he
thought as he slid deep inside her and gazed into her eyes,
was for making love.

He laced his fingers through hers in the gesture he
thought of as theirs alone. Palm to palm, bodies joined, eyes
locked. All was right with his world.

Slowly he eased back and thrust forward again. "When
I'm here inside you, I have everything I need," he murmured. "Nothing else matters."

Tears shimmered in her eyes. "I'm glad."

He continued the slow, sensuous rhythm. "But I'm human, and sometimes I forget what's important to me.
Who's important to me. But then I sink into you and I know
all I need to know."

She gazed up at him, her face luminous with happiness.

He cursed himself for ever giving her a moment's doubt. "I love you, Jess. I always have. I always will."

"Oh, Nat." Her words trembled. "I love you, too."

He tightened his grip on her fingers, increasing the pace. "We can't let each other go." He felt her first contraction. This time he would be with her.

"We won't."

"Then hold on to me, Jess." He thrust harder and let himself explode at the moment that she gave a soft cry and arched up against him. "Hold on to me," he said, gasping. Then he covered her mouth with his as they whirled together into the heart of the storm.

CHAPTER NINETEEN

STEVEN PRUITT WAS RUNNING out of money. Harassing Jessica for six months had been the most fun he'd had in his life, giving him more of a buzz than any game of Labyrinth.

Putting her constantly on the defensive had also gone a long way toward healing the wounds from their college days together at good old Columbia U. She'd thought she was too good for him back then, but he'd kept up the pursuit anyway, knowing she was making a big mistake in turning him down. And she'd just begun to thaw when dear daddy had stepped in and offered him a deal to go away.

Some deal. Sure, he'd been able to finish school at Northwestern on Franklin's money, and he'd been given the promised job at a Franklin Publishing newspaper after graduation.

But had Russell P. let him break the story that would have made him internationally famous? Of course not. Steven, believing this was a free country, had protested being muzzled. That's when he'd discovered that this damn country wasn't so free, after all. Russell P. not only had him fired, he had him blackballed. Fortunately, Steven had savings. He'd invested the money he would have spent on dates if he had dates, which he didn't.

But the savings were nearly gone, which meant it was time to stop the kid stuff with Jessica and stick it to Russell P. at last. Therefore he definitely had to take Jessica and the brat from the line shack. He wasn't going to have a better opportunity anytime soon. Unfortunately, in order to make the most of the opportunity, he'd be forced to camp out.

The great outdoors was highly overrated as far as he was concerned. Once he'd figured out where the damn line shack was, he'd tried to come up with a plan that didn't involve staying out in the wilderness, either before or after the snatch, but he'd finally concluded it was the only logical way to make this work.

He'd spent one whole day finding a cave without a bear or snakes already in residence. Then he'd spent another day gathering supplies, stowing them in the cave and setting up camp. The cave was a good two-hour ride from the line shack, with a stream in between that he could use for covering his tracks. Once he had Jessica and the kid, he'd take the route that went across several large areas of solid granite, to be on the safe side.

It was an extremely isolated spot, and he knew people got lost in this kind of country all the time. If not for his photographic memory, he'd probably never be able to find the cave again himself once he'd left it. But remote as the cave was, it was still only a half hour's ride from something very critical to his plan—a telephone wire. Russell P. was only getting one ransom note, and he was getting it the modern way. Steven was going to hook into that telephone line and use his laptop to send the pompous hypocrite an e-mail.

Finally, on a cloudless morning, he was ready to ride to the line shack and stake it out. Jessica only had one man to protect her there, and by the law of averages, the guy wasn't as smart as Steven. Not many people were as smart as Steven. Sooner or later he'd get his opportunity. And then he'd be rich.

JESSICA DID SLEEP, but not until nearly dawn, when she and Nat finally gave in to exhaustion. Cradled spoon fashion in the curve of his body, she slept so soundly that even Elizabeth's babbling didn't penetrate at first. When it finally did, she started to climb out of bed.

Nat restrained her. "I'll go," he murmured in her ear.

Surrounded in the warm glow of their night together and the unspoken promise of forever-afters, she decided maybe he should be the one to go to Elizabeth this morning. He'd never had her all to himself, and if he had any trouble, she'd be right there to help.

She turned in his arms so she could give him a good-morning smile. "Okay," she said. "That would be nice."

He combed her hair out of her eyes. "I can think of something that would be nicer, but I guess we have to act like parents until this afternoon's nap."

She liked the way he'd said *parents*, as if he'd truly accepted that role for himself. "But have you noticed how exciting it is to want to make love and then have to wait?"

"No, really?" He grinned and tweaked her nipple. "Yeah, I'd noticed. That doesn't mean I can't complain a little that nap time is several hours away." He kissed her quickly and got out of bed.

God, he was gorgeous, she thought as he stood there for a minute looking around for his jeans. "They're over on my side," she said, reaching down to the floor for his jeans and briefs. She rolled back over and handed them to him. "We just left them there after—"

"Don't remind me." His penis stirred as he gazed at her breasts. "Or I'll never get these on. In fact, I'd better not look at you lying in that bed." He turned his back and leaned down to step into his briefs.

"Fine. Just moon me and make me suffer." Front or back, he was an arousing sight. She grew moist as she stared at his tight butt and the bounty just visible between his legs.

"You're the one who said she appreciated the advantages of waiting."

"Yeah." She sighed when he pulled up his briefs, obscuring her view. "I'm trying to remember exactly what those advantages were."

"I think you said waiting would make us want each other more, so the lovemaking would be even better." He stepped into his jeans, and when he zipped them the material tightened up beautifully over his behind.

She had to clench her hands to keep from reaching out and giving him a pat. "I guess that's what I said."

He turned around, a shirtless god in snug-fitting jeans. "That's what you said."

"The fact is, I can't imagine wanting you more than I do right now."

He smiled. "We'll test your theory in a few hours, then. Right now, I'm going to change Elizabeth's diaper." Then he walked around the end of the screen.

Heaven, Jessica thought. She was definitely in heaven.

Then Elizabeth started to cry.

"What's wrong?" Jessica called as she fumbled around on the floor for a shirt to put on.

"Hell, I don't know!" Nat sounded frustrated and scared. "I'm doing everything the way you taught me." His voice took on a coaxing note. "Come on, Elizabeth. I just want to take your sleeper off."

The baby's wail only got louder.

"I'll be right there." Jessica climbed out of bed and thrust her arms into the sleeves of the shirt she'd appropriated from Nat the day before. She snapped it hurriedly, not even bothering to fold back the sleeves the way she had yesterday.

The chill in the cabin gave her goose bumps on her bare legs as she charged around the screen, nearly knocking it over.

Nat stood beside the crib, his hands hanging limply at his sides, his shoulders slumped. He looked emotionally demolished. Elizabeth had crawled to the far side of the crib. Her sleeper was half undone and she was screaming at the top of her lungs.

"Hey, Elizabeth," Jessica crooned. "What's the matter, little girl?"

Jessica looked at her and crawled frantically in her direction, still crying.

"She hates me," Nat said dully.

"No, she doesn't." Jessica picked her up and held her close. "There, there, sweetie. It's okay."

"No, it's not okay," Nat said. "How can I be a father to her if I touch her and she starts to scream?"

Jessica rocked the baby and gazed at him over the top of Elizabeth's head. "Don't you remember that she did the same thing to me that first morning I saw her?"

"Yes, but that was because she had no idea who you were at first. She knows me." His eyes were filled with anguish. "I've been around her for days, Jess. I carried her on my back all afternoon yesterday."

"Yes, but she couldn't see your face. And you were always with me. This was the first time you tried to do something with her while you were alone. She might have thought I'd gone off and left her."

He gave the baby a tortured look. "She doesn't like me, I tell you."

"Nat, that's not so. She's not used to you, yet, but—"

"I can't handle this. I'm going to make coffee." He brushed past her.

With a sigh Jessica put Elizabeth back in the crib and began changing her while dishes clanged in the kitchen. "That's your daddy making all that noise," she murmured to Elizabeth, "and I'm afraid you've really hurt his feelings."

The baby sniffed and rubbed at her nose.

"I know you didn't mean to." Jessica grabbed a tissue and wiped Elizabeth's nose. "But it would help matters if you'd be nicer to him next time." Jessica was determined there would be a next time, and soon. She finished dressing Elizabeth and carried her into the kitchen area.

Nat had put on his boots and a shirt. He sat at the table with a mug of coffee in front of him.

Jessica walked to the cupboard and took down a box of crackers they'd brought for Elizabeth. Propping the baby on one hip, she got a cracker out of the box.

Elizabeth crowed happily when Jessica handed her the cracker.

Hoping that meant the baby was over her fit of crying, Jessica set her down on the floor beside the table. "Would you please keep an eye on her while I get dressed?" she asked.

He glanced up at her. "I don't know if that's a good idea."

"It's a fine idea. I'll only be a minute."

His expression was bleak as he stared at her. "It wasn't her crying that was the real problem, Jess." His voice tensed. "It was the way I felt when she cried. I got angry at her for doing it, when I thought she should be used to me by now. I wanted to shake her."

"Well, of course you did." Jessica felt there were land mines ahead and she tried to figure out where they were. "I can understand that."

"No, you *don't* understand. I got *angry*. Don't you see what that means?" His voice rose. "I'm just like my father!"

Elizabeth began to whimper.

"You are not just like your father." She scooped Elizabeth up so she wouldn't start crying again. "You wanted to shake her, but you didn't! That's the whole difference, Nat. All of us get angry at our children from time to time. But we don't beat them within an inch of their lives. And neither will you."

"You don't know that." He shoved back his chair and stood. "You have no idea what would have happened if you hadn't been right here. Who knows what I would have done?''

"I know!" She wanted to cry, herself. They'd been so damn close, and now he was pulling away again.

Elizabeth's whimpers grew louder.

"See?" He pointed to the baby. "She takes one look at me and she's ready to cry again. Smart kid."

"She's starting to cry again because we're arguing. I'm sure she doesn't like that. Now, will you please watch her for a few minutes?"

"No." He pushed back his chair and stood. "I don't trust myself."

"You're kidding, right?"

"No, I'm not kidding." He walked over to the door and grabbed his hat and jacket. Then he punched some buttons on a small box mounted near the door. "I'm going out to do something aggressive like chop wood for the stove. I just turned off the alarm. Turn it back on when I'm out the door."

She watched him go in total amazement. She couldn't believe he'd give up on himself that quick. Not until he was outside splitting logs did she realize that in their preoccupation with each other the day before, he'd neglected to show her how to turn the alarm on and off.

The tiny hairs on the back of her neck rose, as they used to do when she thought her stalker was nearby, watching her. Well, if that wasn't the power of suggestion at work. She didn't know how to set the alarm, so she was freaking herself out. She'd become addicted to having a security alarm on.

Well, she couldn't do anything about the alarm, anyway. Even if she managed to reactivate it, she wouldn't know how to turn it off again when Nat came back in. And he'd be in soon. After he'd split a few logs he'd realize how ridiculous he was being and come back to try again. In the meantime, nobody would try to storm the house if Nat was outside with an ax.

While she was waiting for Nat to come to his senses, she decided she might as well get dressed. She put Elizabeth in the high chair and gave her another cracker to occupy her while she quickly got into her clothes. She glanced out the window once while she was zipping her jeans and saw that Nat had already worked up a sweat and discarded his jacket. He'd be in soon, and they'd talk about this.

They had to talk about this. Too much was riding on the outcome of this week.

NAT SPLIT LOGS as if each swing of the ax struck another blow at the demons within him. He'd never known such agony. He wanted to believe he wouldn't hurt that little baby in a fit of anger, but given his background, how could he be sure? Jessica didn't know. She thought she did, but she'd been sheltered so much during her life that she couldn't conceive of a grown man wanting to hurt a child.

He could imagine it all too well. Over the years, he'd read all the pop psychology articles he could find, and they'd all warned that an abused boy is in danger of abusing when he becomes a man. So he'd decided not to take the chance, to never get married or have a child.

Then Jess had come along. He hadn't counted on a woman like Jess, who made him dream of things he thought he'd given up. But a man couldn't change who he was, and this morning, when Elizabeth had looked at him with horror and begun to cry, anger had boiled up in him. Hot anger, probably the same kind his father had felt right before he went for the belt, or on some days, the rawhide whip he'd bought in Mexico.

And yet...Nat had to remember that he hadn't acted on his anger. He loved Jess more than life itself, and yes, he even loved that red-faced, crying little girl. What if Jess was right and he had overcome the legacy his father had left him? But if he was wrong, he'd be gambling with the lives of two people who meant more to him than anything in world. He didn't really have a right to do that. He—

Behind him a twig crunched. Jess. His heart swelled with love. She'd come out with the baby, ready to ask him to reconsider. And he would try again, because he loved them both so much. After all, they still had nearly a week to work this out. He started to turn at the moment a million stars exploded inside his skull. Then everything went black.

JESSICA SAT in a chair and fed Elizabeth another spoonful of cereal. She wished she knew how to operate the alarm. The funny tingling at the back of her neck wouldn't go away. She told herself it wasn't anything to worry about, and that Nat was outside to stand guard.

She glanced up at the top shelf where the locked metal box held the gun Sebastian had sent along. Nat probably had the key. Even if the box hadn't been locked, she doubted that she'd have climbed on a chair to get it down. Handling a gun would only spook her worse. She didn't even know if it was loaded.

The tingling at the back of her neck was probably because she'd slept at a weird angle and a small nerve in her neck was going into spasm.

Of course. After all the unaccustomed lovemaking followed by sleeping all tucked together as she and Nat had, it was a wonder that both of them weren't full of aches and pains. Gradually she became aware that the sound of Nat splitting logs outside had stopped.

She sighed with relief. Now he'd be coming back in, and they could set the alarm properly and sit down to discuss his relationship with Elizabeth. And maybe he should teach her how to work the alarm. The gun was another matter, though. She wasn't sure she wanted to learn how to use that.

He should be coming in by now, she thought as the seconds ticked by. Handing Elizabeth another cracker, she got up and walked over to the window to see what he was up to.

The door banged open at the same moment that she realized Nat was lying facedown on the ground next to the woodpile. With a cry, she spun around. Before she could move, the man from her nightmares was inside holding a gun to Elizabeth's head. For a moment her brain refused to register the sight.

When it did, her blood turned to ice and she began to shake. She started toward him, ready to kill.

"Don't do anything stupid, or I'll blow this kid away," the man said. "It wouldn't be any big loss to me. I'd still have you."

Did you kill Nat? She couldn't ask because the answer might paralyze her. Elizabeth needed her to stay alert.

Looking curious instead of scared, Elizabeth glanced around at the man, so that the gun was pointed at her face. Then she tried to grab the barrel.

Jessica opened her mouth to scream, but no sound came out.

With a growl, the man knocked Elizabeth's hand away, and she started to cry.

Jessica saw the action through a red haze. Her ears rang as she started forward again.

"Don't!" the man shouted. "I'm warning you, I wouldn't hesitate. I really don't want to fool with the kid, but I figure her granddaddy will pay extra for her."

Jessica barely recognized her own voice. "If you do anything to her, I'll kill you with my bare hands. So help me God, I will."

"The plan is to get money out of your daddy to pay for the two of you. If possible, I'll do that without either of you getting hurt. How it all shakes out is up to you. Now walk over here and pick her up. We're taking off."

"Where?"

"Never mind where. We're leaving."

Jessica forced her mind to move forward. It wanted to go back and replay the picture of Nat lying on the ground outside. But she had to concentrate on keeping her baby alive. "We can't just leave. This is a baby. She needs diapers, and baby food, and clothes."

The man glanced at Elizabeth, who had stopped crying but was looking at him with fear. He sighed. "I suppose we'll have to take a few things. Otherwise the brat will cry all the time." He looked over at Jessica. "I'll give you two minutes to pack up."

"All right." She tried to remember where she'd last seen the cell phone. There it was, over by the sink. "I have to get her diaper bag. It's behind that screen."

"You're not ducking behind a screen so you can pull something. Move the screen and then get the diaper bag. And make it snappy."

Jessica blanked everything from her mind except finding a way to put the cell phone in the diaper bag. After moving the screen, she packed the bag quickly with diapers and clothes, lotion and baby wipes. At the last minute she crammed the sock monkey inside.

Then she turned. "I need to get some food for her." When she was taking jars from the cupboard, she would slip the cell phone in at the same time, using her body to block his view.

"Hurry up."

Focusing on the cell phone brought a stark sense of calm. She didn't look at it as she went into the kitchen area. For a moment her glance flicked over the coffee can. Nat hadn't put the lid back on after he'd scooped out the coffee.

Nat. For a fraction of a second she thought she might lose her grip on sanity.

"Ga!" Elizabeth said.

She wouldn't lose her grip. Elizabeth's life depended on it. Opening the cupboard, she took down several jars of food and some canned milk. She moved fast, all the while creeping closer to the cell phone. In one quick motion she scooped it into the diaper bag.

"What'd you just do there?" the man asked.

"I'm getting food." But there was a quiver in her voice. Damn it.

"Bring that stuff over here."

"Just a couple more things." She reached for something to cover the phone.

"*Now!*"

Elizabeth started to cry again.

Jessica started back toward him, rearranging things as she went. "I don't have everything I need yet," she said. "We should have—"

"Give me that." He grabbed the bag. Holding the gun next to Elizabeth's ear, he turned the diaper bag upside down. Baby-food jars broke as they hit the floor, spraying their multicolored contents over Elizabeth's clothes. And there, in the midst of the mess, lay the cell phone.

"*Food*, huh?" He glanced at Elizabeth. "I should pull the trigger just to teach you a lesson, Miss High-and-Mighty Jessica Franklin."

"It will be your last act," she said. "You don't have enough bullets to stop me from tearing you apart."

"Oh, I think I do. But then I wouldn't have anything to bargain with. And I want your daddy to give me lots and lots of money." He raised his foot and brought his heel down on the cell phone with a sickening crunch. Then he handed Jessica the diaper bag. "Start over."

Elizabeth's crying became more urgent as she spied her sock monkey in the middle of the mess. She strained toward the monkey, which was soaked with mashed carrots.

"What's wrong with her?" the man asked.

"She wants her monkey."

"Then give it to her, and no funny stuff!"

Jessica leaned down and picked up the monkey. Poor

Bruce. His face was covered with orange goo. "I need to clean—"

"Nope. Give it to her like that. We're wasting time."

Jessica handed the gooey monkey to Elizabeth.

The baby grabbed her friend and hugged him to her, which transferred the mess to her. But at least her crying slowed and finally stopped.

"Fill that bag!" the man ordered.

Jessica did, and all the while she worked she tried to think of another plan that wouldn't endanger Elizabeth. She couldn't come up with one.

"You don't recognize me, do you?" the man asked.

"Of course I do." She dumped more jars of baby food in on top of a new supply of diapers and clothes. "You're the same jerk who's been following me for six months."

"That, too. But we knew each other, before. At Columbia. I asked you out a few times."

Her fingers tightened around a jar of apricots and she turned to look at him again. A chill sped down her spine. No wonder he'd looked familiar the few times she'd caught sight of him this summer. She remembered now. He hadn't appealed to her, in spite of his brilliant mind. But she'd felt sorry for him. She'd told her father about him, and had said she might go out with the poor guy, after all.

And then, poof, he'd disappeared.

"Didn't you ever wonder what happened to me?" he asked.

Not for long. But she decided that wouldn't be the best answer. "Of course. What did happen to you?" *What was his name? As crazy as he was, he probably would get crazier if she couldn't remember his name.*

"Your daddy bought me off."

She gasped.

"I didn't think you knew. He paid for me to transfer to Northwestern for my last semester, and he promised me a job with one of his newspapers after graduation, so long as I'd stay far away from you.''

Her brain reeled. She had to wonder how many other potential suitors her father had quietly eliminated in the same way. Men she'd dated had seemed to transfer from Columbia at an alarming rate. But she'd never dreamed...

''So what's my name?''

She knew it was a test. Maybe something starting with an S. Sam? Scott? Damn it, what was his name?

''You don't remember.'' His gray eyes grew hard. ''Well, that will make this little caper all the sweeter. But for the record, the name is Steven Pruitt. I don't think you or your family will ever forget my name after this. Now pick up that kid and let's get out of here.''

CHAPTER TWENTY

THE BACK OF NAT'S HEAD hurt like hell and he tasted dirt in his mouth. Pushing himself to all fours, he fought dizziness as he spit out the dirt. What had happened? Then he knew.

His stomach pitched as he scrambled to his feet. No time to throw up now. No time. Jess. Elizabeth. He half ran, half stumbled toward the open door of the cabin.

"Jess!" he called hoarsely. *"Jess!"* Grasping the door frame for support, he looked in. But he knew what he would find. Nothing.

Spinning away from the door, he looked frantically around. "Jess!" He got no answer but the sighing of the wind through the aspens. He ran around the perimeter of the house, screaming her name. Startled birds flew out of his path, but otherwise there was no sign of life in the small clearing.

Finally he forced himself to think. How had they left? He searched for tire tracks and could find none except those made by the Bronco. But there were hoofprints. Automatically Nat started to follow them, until he glanced up at the sun and realized how much time had gone by. He'd never catch them on foot.

The ranch. He had to contact the ranch. Racing into the house, he searched for the cell phone and finally nearly tripped over it in the muck on the floor by the high chair. Smashed beyond repair. Oh, God.

He had to drive there. Digging in his pocket for the keys, he tore out the door again.

The tires had been slashed.

Nat stared at the ruined tires that he'd missed in his first agitated pass around the cabin. Then he lifted his head and let out a howl of despair.

Slowly the sound of his anguish faded into the forest. But as he stood there with his head exploding in pain, a certainty settled over him that he would find her. He would find her and his baby, and he would kill the man who had dared to take them away. It was as simple as that.

He went back into the cabin, reached to the top shelf for the metal box and unlocked it with the key in his pocket. After checking to make sure the gun was loaded, he pocketed the extra ammunition Sebastian had left in the box. Then he left the cabin. He didn't bother to close the door. There was no longer anything of value inside.

Climbing into the Bronco, he laid the gun on the seat next to him…the seat where Jess had sat when he'd brought her out here. He swallowed another roar of self-loathing. He didn't have time to punish himself now. That would come later. Now he had to drive back to the ranch. He'd ruin the rims on the Bronco, but he didn't care. They could be replaced.

When he arrived, he'd saddle up a horse. Sebastian could call the police if he wanted, but Nat wasn't waiting around for them. However, before he rode out, he had one detail that couldn't be left to someone else. It was his job to call Russell P. Franklin.

JESSICA HAD REMEMBERED the baby carrier before they left, and Pruitt had finally agreed that she could transport Elizabeth in it. She hadn't wanted that monster touching the baby, so she'd propped the carrier against the bed, put Elizabeth inside, and then crouched down and worked her arms through the straps.

Not being used to the weight, she'd been a little unsteady at first, and getting on the horse Pruitt had brought for her was tough, but she knew this would be the best way for Elizabeth to travel in relative safety.

Safety. As if either of them were safe in the company of a wacko like Steven Pruitt. More details about him were coming back to her now. At Columbia she'd thought of him as a typical nerd, the kind of guy whose intelligence had hampered his social skills. She'd been torn between wanting to avoid him and wanting to help him fit in. But apparently there was a little more wrong with Pruitt than a lack of social confidence.

He rode ahead of her, taking her through the forest with a lead rope tied to her horse's bridle. Wearing an L.A. Dodgers baseball cap and pleated pants, he didn't look very natural on the horse. She didn't think he'd ridden much in his life, but then neither had she, and it had all been English, anyway. With Elizabeth on her back she couldn't very well try some fancy maneuver and expect to ride away from him.

He'd tied her hands to the saddle horn, and the diaper bag handles were looped over it, too, so the bag bumped her knees as they moved over uneven, rocky terrain. Elizabeth was quiet in the carrier, probably asleep. Jessica gave thanks for that, but the dead weight made her shoulders ache horribly.

A rest was out of the question. In the first place, Steven probably wouldn't allow her one, and in the second place, Elizabeth might wake up if they stopped. Jessica knew she should be planning their escape, but staying on the horse and enduring the pain in her shoulders took everything she had. She did try to keep track of the route they were taking, but other than the stream they seemed to splash through for miles, the forest took on a sameness that was discouraging.

"So your daddy never mentioned that I was working for one of his papers out in L.A.?" Pruitt asked.

"No."

"Remember that California senator who got kidnapped last year?"

"I guess."

"You *guess?* You must not be keeping up. That was the biggest damn story in the country for weeks. I was on top of it the whole way. Had my share of bylines on *Associated Press* as a result, too."

Jessica didn't respond. Obviously he wanted to brag about himself, but she didn't have to encourage him.

"Then I got a real break," he continued, apparently not needing her participation for his monologue. "When they caught the kidnappers, I got 'em to agree to talk to me, tell me their whole story. I had a series outlined—'Inside the Mind of a Sociopath.' I had all the details of their plan. It was a brilliant piece of journalism. I figured once it ran, somebody would pay me to expand it into a book, or maybe somebody in Hollywood would want the movie rights."

Jessica remembered that Pruitt had always had grandiose ideas. She'd wondered when they'd been acquainted at Columbia if he'd only been attracted to her wealth and connections, but he'd denied that vehemently. She'd naively believed him, but now she could see that's exactly where his interest had been.

"The thing is, my editor checked with your daddy before he ran the series, and Russell P. ordered the piece killed. Not only that, he said since I used the newspaper's time and resources to get that story and write it, he was confiscating everything—my notes, my contacts—everything. He said it would give other sick people a blueprint for doing something like that, and he didn't want to be responsible. What a damn wuss! He coulda raked in a Pulitzer for me and his stinkin' paper."

"My father always has had principles." She realized how proud she felt, saying that. She'd never given her father credit for integrity before. She'd been so busy rebelling against his control that she hadn't stopped to think of his good points. And there were many.

The more she thought about it, the more she became convinced that her father had probably offered more than one man money to stay away from her. If he had, it wasn't a bad test of a guy's character. If the man took the bribe, then he wasn't the one for her. But in Pruitt's case, her father must have been more than a little concerned, to pay for a semester's tuition plus offer the guy a job. Maybe he'd had Pruitt investigated and had uncovered a psychiatric evaluation somewhere.

She had to admit, the conversation was taking her mind off the searing pain in her shoulders. That, more than curiosity, prompted her to ask a question. "So you quit?"

"Hell, no, I didn't quit. I figured right was on my side, so I took my case to anyone with any clout who would listen. I think your daddy was afraid I might get somewhere, because he had me fired. Then he called in all his favors and had me blackballed in the industry. Even though he'd confiscated my notes, I remembered most of the story, and I was prepared to write it for someone else, but I couldn't get a job *delivering* papers, let alone writing for them. Even book publishers didn't want to talk to me. Now, I ask you, does that sound fair?"

"It sounds like my father," Jessica had to admit. When someone within Russell Franklin's organization threatened the empire he'd worked so hard to build, Jessica had no doubt he'd use all the power at his disposal to annihilate that person. She'd also like to think that in this case, her father's contacts in the business agreed with him that Steven Pruitt needed to be stopped.

"Well, he blackballed the wrong guy. I'd just had a crash course in kidnapping, and it didn't take me long to figure out who my target should be."

"How did you find me?"

"You can thank my excellent memory. When we were

at Columbia, you told me that if you could live anywhere in the world, it would be Aspen, Colorado. You'd never been there, but you thought the pictures were beautiful and you were sure you'd like it.''

She vaguely remembered the conversation. Sure enough, she had always been fascinated with Aspen. After meeting Nat there, she'd decided going to Aspen had been her destiny. Oh, God. Nat. An instinct for protecting her child had blocked thoughts of Nat, but now her vision filled with a picture of him lying in the dirt.

Was he…no, he couldn't be…she refused to think the word. She had to believe he'd only been knocked unconscious. Once he woke up, he'd come looking for her.

She should have found some way to leave signs along the way. Damn, why hadn't she thought of that earlier? Maybe it wasn't too late. But what sort of signs? With her hands tied, she couldn't very well drop off bits of clothing.

The diaper bag banged against her knee again. She looked down at it and noticed the tail of Elizabeth's sock monkey sticking out between the overlapping flaps that held the bag closed. She'd crammed Bruce in the diaper bag for safekeeping, despite Elizabeth's protests, because she'd figured if Elizabeth held the monkey while she rode in the carrier, she'd drop him somewhere along the way.

Which would have been a perfect plan.

She needed to keep Pruitt involved in the conversation so he wouldn't suspect she was doing anything covert. "So after all that time, you remembered what I'd said and figured out to look for me in Aspen. That's pretty amazing." Watching to make sure he didn't turn around, she worked the diaper-bag handle up so the monkey's tail was almost within reach.

"Amazing to you, maybe. That's just how I work. I test out pretty high on the charts. I was on scholarship to Columbia, and I probably could have talked Northwestern into giving me one, too, but I liked soaking your daddy."

"I suppose you graduated with honors, then." The ropes cut into her wrist as she strained forward and finally got her fingers around the monkey's tail.

"Could've. But with your old man footing the bill, I decided not to bust my butt. After all, I didn't even have to worry about a job once I got out of college. Why sweat that last semester?"

Her father must have *really* been worried about his guy, Jessica thought. And for good reason, obviously. "Did you like being a reporter?" she asked. Slowly she let the diaper bag drop into its original position, and an orange-stained Bruce popped out through the flaps.

"It was okay. Following you all summer has been better, though. Like espionage or James Bond stuff. I began to wonder if you were having a good time, too. So 'fess up, Jessica. Did I give you a thrill or two?"

Oh, yeah, she'd loved being stalked by a weirded-out nerd like Pruitt. "Sorry, I guess I don't have your sense of adventure." The guy obviously also needed lots and lots of medication.

"You shoulda gone out with me all those years ago, Jessica."

"Maybe so." She had a split second of regret at sacrificing Bruce, but if she didn't find a way to leave a clue for Nat, losing Bruce would be the least of her worries. Keeping an eye on Pruitt, she loosened her grip on the monkey's tail. He slipped down and balanced on the top of the diaper bag.

Saying a quick apology to Elizabeth, Jessica nudged the diaper bag, and Bruce fell to the ground. She was very much afraid that her horse stepped on him. But most important of all, Pruitt seemed to be so wrapped up in his fantasy that he apparently hadn't noticed a thing.

IT WAS LUNCHTIME when Nat banged on the front door of the ranch house. Sebastian opened the door, took one look at him and yelled for Matty.

"He took them," Nat said, breathing hard.

"Oh, God." Sebastian went white.

Matty came rushing to his side and looked from her husband to Nat. "What...oh no. *No.*" She clutched her stomach and began to wobble.

Sebastian and Nat rushed to grab her at once.

"I have her," Sebastian said, supporting her gently. "Come on, Matty. Let's get you on the couch."

"Where are they?" Matty wailed.

"I only know which direction they went. He knocked me out first and took them on horseback."

Sebastian guided Matty down onto the couch and turned back to Nat. "What happened to that goddamn alarm? I thought that was supposed to protect you out there? Where was that fancy alarm system?"

Nat had used the long, grinding stretch of road to the ranch to figure that out. The blame was all his, and he faced Sebastian and delivered the damning explanation. "We had an argument. I went out to chop wood, and I turned it off on the way out. I told her to turn it back on after I was out the door. But she didn't know how. I never showed her how. Oh, God." His throat closed and he turned away. He couldn't break down. He had things to do.

Sebastian's hand closed over Nat's shoulder, and his voice was choked. "We'll get them back. I'll call Travis and Boone. We'll get them back."

Nat dug down and found the strength to meet Sebastian's gaze. "I will. I'll get them back."

Sebastian gave his shoulder a squeeze. "We'll do it together, buddy." Then he turned to Matty. "Are you okay? You're not having pains or anything, are you?"

"No, I'm fine." Matty took a deep breath. "And I want to go with you when you look for them."

266 THAT'S MY BABY!

"No," Sebastian said. "No, Matty. Don't ask that of me, please."

She stood. "I'm not asking, I'm telling! I want to go. I *will* go."

"God, Matty, don't do this."

"But I—"

"Listen to me, you stubborn, can-do woman." He took her by the shoulders. "I know all your abilities, and yes, you could be valuable to us, but I can't risk you, the mother of my child, the person I can't live without. I will be worthless in this search unless I know that you're safe."

She gazed at him, and her throat moved in a swallow. "Okay, I'll stay," she said in a low voice. "But know this, Sebastian. My every instinct is screaming at me to go and find Elizabeth. I am going to stay only out of love for you. And you'd damn well better find that baby."

Sebastian heaved a sigh of relief. "We'll find her. Nat, you and I can saddle the horses while Matty calls Boone and Travis."

Nat glanced at him. "I'll do that, but after Matty calls them, I need to make a call, too."

"If you're thinking of getting the sheriff into this now, I vote we don't waste time with the law. Let's track this guy down before the trail gets old."

"I wasn't thinking of calling the sheriff. I agree with you on that." Nat thought of the promise he'd made to try to preserve Sebastian's privacy. Along with his other sins, he'd have to break that promise. "I want to call her father."

Sebastian regarded him steadily. "Okay."

Nat knew that no man had ever made a greater personal sacrifice for him than Sebastian was doing at this moment.

Sebastian gestured toward the kitchen. "Go do it now. Matty can use my cell phone to call Travis and Boone. I'll meet you in the barn."

Nat gave him a brief nod and started for the kitchen.

"And Nat," Sebastian called after him.

Nat turned.

"Don't worry. The four of us can damn well handle one dude from New York," Sebastian said with the faintest trace of a smile. "No matter how much money he's got."

Nat wasn't thinking of Franklin's money as he reached for his wallet and pulled out the embossed card he'd kept tucked inside ever since he'd paid a visit to Franklin Hall. What he was about to do to Russell Franklin couldn't be softened by all the money in the world.

Nat knew exactly how the man would feel—the helpless panic, the blinding rage, the self-blame. Oh, yes. Nat knew exactly how Russell Franklin would feel. It would undoubtedly be the worst moment of the man's life. But that didn't mean he wouldn't want to know. Nat understood that, too.

Only two rings sounded before Jessica's father picked up. "Russell P. Franklin."

Nat closed his eyes, hating to deliver the blow.

"Hello? Who's there? Jessica?"

"It's Nat Grady."

"Grady! You've found her!"

"Yes, I did. And—"

"Fantastic, son! Hold on and let me call Adele on the other line. She's going to be—"

"There's more." Nat's chest tightened.

"More?" Fear hummed over the wire.

"For the past six months she's been dodging a stalker. This morning he kidnapped her."

This was a deadly silence on the other end. Then Russell's voice roared over the line. "Then what the hell are you doing on the damn phone? Have you called the police? The FBI? Forget that! Tell me where the hell you are! Don't do a damn thing until I get there!"

A cold calmness settled over Nat. "I'm going after her. My friends and I are heading out on horseback from the Rocking D Ranch in just a few minutes. The ranch is near a little town in Colorado called Huerfano. You can stop anywhere in town and get directions out here."

"I've never heard of the place! Probably a bunch of hicks, and sure as the world, you're going to louse this up! Stay put, and I'll—"

"Huerfano's not far from Canon City," Nat said, his tone even. "If you fly into Colorado Springs and rent a car, you can probably get here by tonight. I plan to have her back by then."

"The hell you say! If you so much as move your little finger before I get there, so help me, Grady, you'll wish you'd never heard the name Russell P. Franklin!"

"Sorry, Russell." Nat wasn't even angry at the man. In his shoes, Nat would have issued the same threats. He could completely understand Russell's need for control. He had the same need. "We're going after her. And there's one other thing. The guy didn't get only Jessica. He also took her eight-month-old daughter, Elizabeth."

Russell gasped.

"And yes, in case you're wondering, she's my daughter, too. So now you'll understand why I'm heading out. See you tonight." He hung up the phone. Nothing else they said to each other mattered. Now it was time to go get Jessica.

Matty came into the kitchen. "I got ahold of both Travis and Boone," she said. "Everyone's coming here. The women and little Josh will stay with me while you're gone."

Nat nodded. "Good. I'd better get out to the barn and help Sebastian."

"I'll pack some food for all of you. No telling how long...well, no telling."

"Right." He turned to go out the kitchen door.

"Nat! The back of your head! It's covered with dried blood. Let me—"

"Forget it, Matty."

She grabbed his arm. "You might even have a concussion. Let me look at it."

Gently he pried her fingers away as he gazed down at her. "I don't have time," he said. "By the way, Russell Franklin should arrive here sometime tonight. With luck we'll be back with Jessica and Elizabeth before he gets here."

"Nat, I think you should let me look at your head."

"Thanks anyway, Matty." He leaned down and gave her a quick kiss on the cheek. Then he went out the door.

CHAPTER TWENTY-ONE

"PATTY-CAKE, PATTY-CAKE, baker's man." Jessica sat cross-legged on a blanket with Elizabeth in her lap not far from the mouth of the small cave where Pruitt had set up camp. She'd finally been able to clean the carrot juice off the baby, and so far Elizabeth hadn't seemed to notice that Bruce was missing in action.

For Elizabeth, the forest was obviously a wondrous place filled with birds, squirrels and chipmunks. She was excited, curious, and had no idea that the object held by the man sitting on the far side of the clearing had the power to end her days.

While Jessica played with Elizabeth, she glanced around for potential toys to keep the baby amused. Pruitt had ordered her to keep Elizabeth on the blanket so he didn't have to follow them around and make sure they weren't trying to run off. He lounged on another folded blanket, his back against a tree, and watched them.

The shadows lengthened and the air was turning cooler. Before long it would be dark. Jessica's shoulders still burned from the hours Elizabeth had spent on her back in the carrier. They'd reached the camp about midday, but after a too-brief rest for a little food, Pruitt had ordered Jessica to put Elizabeth back in the carrier and climb on the horse again.

Jessica had thought her arms would come out of their sockets, but she'd done as he'd commanded. Then they'd ridden in a different direction until they'd come to a swath cut through the trees and the first sign of civilization she'd seen so far, a telephone line. Jessica didn't want to think of what had happened next, but the scene was imprinted on her retina as if she'd stared into the sun too long.

At gunpoint, Pruitt had demanded that she transfer the carrier with Elizabeth in it to him. He'd thanked her, in fact, for suggesting they bring the carrier in the first place. Then, with the baby on his back and a laptop computer strapped around his waist, he'd climbed the telephone pole. While Elizabeth crowed in delight at the adventure, Jessica had stood below and prayed as she'd never prayed in her life.

God had answered her prayers, and Pruitt had come back down without falling or dropping Elizabeth out of the carrier. Then he'd returned the baby for the trip back to camp. All the way back, Jessica had been forced to listen to him brag about how he'd tapped into the telephone cable and sent an e-mail ransom note to her father demanding a huge sum of money be wired to his bank account in the Cayman Islands. The following day, Pruitt had said, they'd repeat the maneuver so that he could get her father's reply and confirmation of the money transfer.

Jessica had sent up another prayer, this one asking to be rescued before Pruitt made another journey up that pole with her baby perched precariously on his back. So far, that prayer hadn't been answered. Jessica couldn't remember ever being so tired and sore, except after her hours of labor with Elizabeth.

Pruitt would have to sleep sometime, Jessica thought. Of course he'd tie her up, but surely he wouldn't tie Elizabeth, too? The thought made her stomach clench. She couldn't risk that he'd be inhuman enough to do such a thing. She had to think of a way to disable him before he got sleepy enough to think of tying her and Elizabeth.

"Time for you to earn your keep," Pruitt said. "Get a

can of stew and the camp stove out of that box over there."
He laughed. "Your turn to cook dinner."

She gathered Elizabeth in her arms and stood. That answered her question as to whether or not he planned to build a fire to keep them warm. Apparently he'd figured out that a campfire would make it easier for someone to find them. Jessica decided she'd put a couple of layers of clothing on Elizabeth tonight.

"Oh, and make some coffee while you're at it," he said.

Holding Elizabeth on one hip, she struggled with the camp stove. If only she could figure out a way to poison his food. Or his coffee. *Wait a minute.* As she continued to set up the stove, she wracked her brain trying to remember her notes from her most recent class on herbal remedies. Part of the class had been devoted to the danger of poisonous plants.

But what were those plants? Mistletoe, for sure. But even if she happened to be lucky enough to see some around here, it would be hanging from a branch, probably impossible for her to get without being noticed. But there was another one that grew on the ground. *Foxglove.* And she knew exactly how she'd look for it.

"I'm having a little trouble working while I'm holding Elizabeth," she said.

"Too bad. I sure as hell don't plan to hold her."

"I wouldn't want—I mean—*expect* you to. But if I prop her carrier against a tree and tie it to the trunk, I think it can work like a high chair."

"Go ahead. Just remember, this gun is cocked and pointed at that kid's head."

"Yes." As if she could ever forget. Talking animatedly to Elizabeth, Jessica picked her up and went over to get the carrier and a length of rope Pruitt had left lying on the ground. Looping the rope around her neck, she leaned the carrier against her knees and put Elizabeth inside. "I'm going to find the perfect spot for you," she said, picking it up.

"Ba-ba!" Elizabeth chortled, craning her head around to watch what Jessica was doing.

Jessica walked around the campsite and studied the plants growing there while she pretended to be searching out the perfect tree for securing the carrier. She passed one plant twice, not certain it was the right one. Without the flowers it was harder to tell. Finally she decided it had to be foxglove. And it was growing right behind a tree.

"This is the one," she sang out. "Here we go, Elizabeth." She positioned the rigid back of the carrier against the trunk. Securing the seat to the tree was a tricky maneuver while Elizabeth jiggled around in it. Once, it nearly tipped over. Jessica made a huge production of it as she kept up a monologue about making sure the rope was secure.

Elizabeth twisted and turned, trying to follow Jessica's antics, making the process even more difficult. But Jessica noticed that Pruitt seemed to becoming bored with the extended routine, and finally his attention strayed. That's when she tore a handful of the plant from the ground and stuffed it into her jeans pocket.

"That does it, Elizabeth," she said, dusting off her hands.

The baby seemed perplexed by her new perch, but her feet touched the ground, which she loved. With a grin, she practiced balancing while Jessica moved the camp stove a little closer so she could talk to Elizabeth while she heated the stew.

The foxglove, she'd decided, would go in the basket with the ground coffee. She could disguise it better that way. Cutting off Pruitt's view of the coffeepot with her body, she quickly transferred the mangled foxglove to the bottom of the coffee basket and shoveled ground coffee on top. Then she slapped the lid on and put the coffee on to perk.

She'd evaluated everything Pruitt had allowed her access to, in case any of it would work as a weapon. Apparently he'd thought this through himself, because the cookware was all lightweight and he'd packed only spoons, not knives or forks. Unfortunately, everything she considered, even the flame of the Sterno, might only serve to make him mad, not permanently disable him. The foxglove had to work.

She served him the stew first. Then, heart pounding, she poured him a cup of coffee.

"Hand that to me nice and easy," he said as he reached for it. "I can see the wheels going around, and I'll bet you'd like to toss that hot coffee all over me. But even hot coffee wouldn't stop me from shooting that kid."

"I'm not planning to throw coffee on you," she said. But it worried her that he'd read her expression so well. She tried to make her mind a blank so nothing in her eyes would warn him not to drink the coffee. "As long as you have that gun, I'm not going to take any foolish chances."

"Good. I always figured you for a smart woman."

Here's hoping I'm smart enough. "I'm going to feed Elizabeth now, if that's okay with you."

"By all means, feed the brat. God knows I don't want it squalling." He took a sip of the coffee and grimaced.

Jessica held her breath. If he refused to drink it, that was one thing. If he suspected what she'd done…

"Did anybody ever tell you that you make the worst coffee in the world?" he said. "I can't imagine how you screwed it up this bad."

"I…haven't had much practice." Her heartbeat thrummed in her ears. "I prefer herbal tea."

"Oh, I'll just bet you do, Miss Gotrocks. Probably never had to make coffee for a man in your life, have you, Princess? Cook did all that, didn't she? It's a wonder you figured out how to heat up the stew." He held up the tin cup of coffee. "But I'll drink the damn stuff. I didn't pack much coffee, and I need every bit of caffeine I can get. When this is gone, I'm going to supervise the second pot.''

He didn't suspect! She tried to keep the triumph out of her voice. ''All right.''

He glanced up suspiciously. ''That sounded mighty cooperative. How come you're not telling me to make my own damn coffee?''

She lowered her eyes so he couldn't see her expression. ''Like I said, as long as you have the gun, I'm going to cooperate.''

His eyes narrowed, and his gaze became more calculating. ''Is that right? I'll keep that in mind. It could be a long night.''

Her blood went cold. *Oh, please let that be foxglove I put in his coffee, and please let it be strong.*

''DAMN IT TO HELL.'' Leading his horse, Travis walked around shining his flashlight over the rocky ground. ''I've lost the trail again.''

Nat fought panic. They'd been out here for hours—his three buddies and both the dogs, Fleafarm and Sadie. And now it was getting too dark to see. Somewhere out in this darkness a lunatic had Jess and Elizabeth.

Sebastian sighed and leaned on his saddle horn while he watched Travis continue to search the area for tracks ''I have to say you've done better than I thought you would, hotshot, considering your last performance.''

Travis glanced up at him. ''This is Lizzie we're goin' after, don't forget.''

''Oh, I'm not likely to forget.''

''Maybe if we spread out a little we can pick up the trail,'' Boone suggested.

Nat hated to say what was on his mind, but he figured somebody needed to. He didn't want to be so pigheaded about this search that he put Jess and Elizabeth in even greater danger. "Listen, do you think one of us should go back and call the sheriff's office?"

Sebastian looked around the semicircle of men. "What do you guys think?"

"I'm against it," Travis said. "I think we're gonna pick up that trail again, and if the sheriff's office moves in with a bunch of deputies, and helicopters and god-knows-what, we could have a disaster here."

Boone rubbed the back of his neck. "The way I've always heard it, these kidnappers usually tell you not to bring the cops in on it."

"I've thought of that, too," Nat said. "But I also figure Jess's father is probably at the ranch, or will be pretty soon. If one of us goes back, we can find out if Franklin's received a ransom note yet. And we'll get his opinion on what he thinks we should do. He is Jessica's father. And Elizabeth's grandfather."

"There's some sense to that," Sebastian said slowly. I reckon we all know how we'd feel in his shoes. So, if we decide someone should go back, who goes?"

No one spoke.

"I understand that nobody wants to be the one," Sebastian said. "But—"

"Oh, hell, Sebastian," Boone said. "None of us are going back, and we all damn well know it. Ransom note or no ransom note, that baby is out there, not to mention Jessica, and you know as well as I do we wouldn't trust anybody else to get either one of them back. Not even Jessica's rich daddy."

"Yeah, I do know that," Sebastian said. "But I keep asking myself if we've really been following the right set of hoofprints, or if we've messed up somewhere and we're following the trail of a couple of pleasure riders."

"We're on the right track," Nat said.

Sebastian adjusted the tilt of his hat. "I know you want to believe that, buddy, but—"

"We're on the right track," Nat said again. "I can feel it." And that's what was so frustrating. He could feel Jess and Elizabeth out there ahead of them, somewhere through the dark trees. And yet getting to them was such a slow, painstaking process. He almost felt as if he could find them by letting his instincts take over, but he didn't quite trust himself that much.

"Let's fan out, then." Sebastian glanced around. "Now, where the hell are those dogs? I wonder if we did the right thing, bringing them. They've never been trained to track or hunt, so I don't know what I expected."

A sharp, shrill bark pierced the twilight. Then another.

"Well, great," Travis said. "They've probably scared themselves up a skunk."

"Let's go find out," Sebastian said as he reined his horse in the direction of the sound.

Nat told himself not to get excited by the dogs' reaction. Sebastian was right that they weren't trained for this kind of thing and it might have been pointless to bring them. Fleafarm could drive cattle like nobody's business, but she was no bloodhound. And Sadie, Matty's Great Dane, was a great guard dog, but she didn't know anything about tracking, either.

Nevertheless, Nat kicked his horse into a trot and arrived at the small clearing in the trees where the dogs stood, wagging their tails and looking proud of themselves. Something lay on the ground by their feet.

Nat switched on his flashlight and his stomach churned as the high beam shone on a very grubby-looking sock monkey.

Bruce.

THE PLANT JESSICA HAD PUT into the coffee, whether it was foxglove or not, was having an effect on Pruitt. He'd downed three cups, and Jessica could see that he wasn't feeling good, although he was trying to keep her from finding out. The worse he felt, the sharper his temper. Now every sentence was laced with foul language.

It was nearly dark, and the only light in camp was Pruitt's small flashlight, which he used intermittently. He hadn't asked her to make any more coffee, and she suspected that was because his stomach was cramping and he knew he couldn't hold anything down. She wasn't sure what the effects of the plant were, or if she'd even given him foxglove in the first place. But she'd done something to him, that was for sure.

She'd be thrilled if he'd pass out, but he might only vomit. Even then, however, she might be able to get the gun away from him. She remembered what morning sickness was like. A person would have a hard time holding a gun steady while throwing up.

If that happened, she'd have to move fast. So she'd positioned the blanket on which she sat holding Elizabeth close to the carrier that was still tied to the tree. She had to have a quick place to stash the baby when it was time to grab Pruitt's gun. While pretending to sing a lullaby to Elizabeth, she kept a close eye on Pruitt.

Suddenly he let out a sharp oath and staggered to his feet. "I know what's happened! You bitch! You put something in that coffee, didn't you?"

"Of course not!" Her mouth went dry with fear as she plopped Elizabeth in the carrier and crouched down so she was directly in front of the baby, shielding her. "What could I possibly put in it, anyway? We're out in the middle of nowhere."

"I don't know." He held the gun on her while he clutched his stomach with his other hand. "All I know is I have one hell of a bellyache, and I'd lay money that you did it! Hell, your daddy's probably already transferred my money. I should just shoot you and the kid and be done with it."

She readied herself to spring at him. If he was going to

shoot her anyway, she'd take him with her, somehow. His arm was wavering, so his aim would be off. As long as he didn't kill her instantly, she'd find a way to get the gun away and shoot him before he could aim the weapon at Elizabeth.

"Think I will shoot you." He was nearly doubled over with pain. "I don't know why I thought I had to keep you both around, anyway. Your daddy's going to pay that money. He has to. You're the most important thing in the world to him. That's why I knew that if I kidnapped you, I'd—" He stopped talking. His jaw clenched and his eyes began to water.

"Damn you," he whispered, and dropped to his knees, retching violently. He still held the gun, but it was now hanging loosely from his fingers, the barrel pointed at the ground.

Jessica leaped to her feet, ran to him and grabbed for the gun. Although he was still vomiting, his fingers tightened on it and it went off with a roar, the bullet zinging off the through the trees.

Jessica was frantic to get the weapon. A wild bullet could kill Elizabeth as surely as one aimed in her direction. She wrenched his hand up to her mouth and bit down hard. As her teeth sank through flesh, he screamed and let go of the gun.

She grabbed it, but she wasn't steady as she scrambled away and tried to aim it at him. Before she get her finger around the trigger, he lunged at her and wrested the gun away again.

"That's it!" he screamed, pointing the gun at her. "You're dead, bitch!"

"Drop it, mister!" called a man from the shadows. The high beam of a flashlight focused on Pruitt.

Jessica gasped in relief as she recognized Sebastian's voice.

"Don't try anything. You're surrounded," called another man, and a second flashlight snapped on.

Boone. They had come for her. Oh, thank God.

From a different direction came a third man's voice and a third flashlight beam. "Just drop the gun and put your hands up. We're in no mood for shenanigans."

Travis. But what about Nat? Oh, God, was Nat out there?

Pruitt squinted as he tried to avoid looking into the glare. Then, in one quick move, he grabbed Elizabeth out of the carrier and held the gun to the baby's head.

"No!" Jessica screamed.

Elizabeth began to cry as Pruitt stood and looked around, staring into the darkness. "Any questions, gentlemen?"

A gun blasted. Jessica screamed again and ran at Pruitt, not caring what happened to her. She was just in time to catch Elizabeth as Pruitt's grip on the baby slackened and he went down, a bullet in the middle of his forehead.

Jessica fell to her knees, clutching the crying baby to her as she sobbed. Instantly she was surrounded by Sebastian, Travis and Boone, all trying to comfort her at once.

Eyes streaming with tears, Jessica looked up into their beloved faces. "Which one of you fired that shot?"

"Never mind that now," Sebastian said soothingly, rubbing her shoulders. "All that matters is that you're okay. Elizabeth's okay."

She couldn't look at Pruitt. "Is he—"

"Yeah, he is," Boone said. "He won't be bothering you anymore."

Finally, she had to know the worst. "What about... Nat?" she managed to choke out.

"I'm here." He stepped out of the shadows, Sebastian's .38 hanging loosely from his right hand.

CHAPTER TWENTY-TWO

JESSICA DIDN'T REMEMBER much of the trip back to the ranch. She wondered if she might be in shock, because despite the blanket she clutched around her as they rode, she couldn't stop shivering. Her horse was sandwiched in between Sebastian's and Travis's. Boone came next with Elizabeth in her carrier on his back.

Nat, the man she most needed to see, brought up the rear, leading the horse that carried Steven Pruitt facedown across the saddle. She'd had no idea Nat could shoot a gun with that kind of accuracy, but from what brief comments the other guys had made, she gathered that they'd all known he was a marksman.

She, for one, was profoundly grateful that he was, and would have liked to thank him for saving Elizabeth's life. But Nat didn't seem to want to talk about it. He didn't seem to want to talk to her, period.

But he was alive. Each time she thought of that, she sent up another prayer of gratitude. She could understand that Nat had a lot to deal with right now. Knowing him, he was berating himself because she and Elizabeth had been kidnapped right out from under his nose. And now he had to face the fact that he'd killed a man.

Jessica felt no remorse that Steven Pruitt was dead. She would have killed him herself, given a chance. And yet, she couldn't know exactly what it was like for Nat to realize he was the one who had pulled the trigger. Especially for a man like Nat, who was so against violence.

She and Nat needed to have a long talk. When they got back to the Rocking D, they would find the time to straighten things out between them. Once they'd settled everything with the sheriff's office, she and Nat could take some time alone. They had a lot to discuss.

But as they rode up to the hitching post by the back door and saw the helicopter in the middle of the corral, she began to realize that she and Nat might not have a chance to be alone anytime soon. People came pouring out of the house, and she gazed with disbelief as she recognized that her mother and father were among them.

JESSICA WOKE in the double bed in Elizabeth's room the next morning, and the first thing she heard was Elizabeth babbling happily to herself as she stood holding on to the crib railing and batted at the foam-rubber mobile over her head. Jessica adjusted the pillow under her head so she could look at the baby, her baby.

Slowly the events of the past two days washed over her. The scene once they'd arrived back at the ranch was a blur. She remembered hugging both her parents and crying, and endless questions from everyone, and the arrival of the sheriff's deputies, but finally someone had propelled her back to this bedroom, along with Elizabeth, and they'd both been tucked in like children.

Jessica suspected Matty had done that. She took a deep breath. They'd all made it through. And now she had to find out if she had a future with Nat Grady.

She swung her legs out of bed. "Hi, baby," she said.

Elizabeth bounced happily and grinned at her. "Da-da!"

"Yes, that's what we have to go see about, you and me. Your da-da." She listened for noises from the rest of the house, but it was quiet, although she could smell coffee brewing. Glancing at the clock, she was surprised how early it was. She'd only slept a few short hours. Maybe Matty had set the timer so the coffee had turned on automatically.

Getting Elizabeth dressed was no problem, but putting on her own clothes was painful. The carrier straps had rubbed her shoulders raw and she was stiff from all the unaccustomed riding. But she was alive, and so was her baby. She hugged Elizabeth gratefully as she started down the hall toward the kitchen.

Sebastian and Matty's bedroom door was still closed, and so was Sebastian's office door, where Nat usually slept. Jessica considered sneaking in and waking him up, but she decided against it. When she talked to him, she wanted him to be wide awake.

The last person she expected to see sitting in the kitchen drinking coffee was her father. But there he was, glancing through some ranching magazine he must have found in the living room.

He was unshaven, and his designer shirt and slacks were wrinkled. Jessica didn't think she'd ever seen him like that in her life. Her heart squeezed. He looked...old. She thought about what Steven Pruitt had said. *He'll pay the money. He has to. You're the most important thing in the world to him.*

She paused in the doorway. "Hi, Dad."

He glanced up quickly. "Jessica." Then the most amazing thing happened. Her father got tears in his eyes.

Her throat grew tight and she blinked rapidly, not wanting her own tears to fall. "I guess...I guess I put you through quite a bit, didn't I?"

"Yes." Her father's voice was gruff. He cleared his throat and glanced at Elizabeth. "She looks like you."

"Dad, I—"

He held up a hand. "Before you say anything, I have something to say. I spent a little time talking to...the baby's father this morning, and—"

"Nat? Isn't he asleep in Sebastian's office?"

"No. Your mother's in there. I took the couch. I think Grady slept down at the barn. When I woke up I went out for a walk, wandered down to the barn and found him feeding the horses.''

"Oh." Jessica glanced out the kitchen window toward the barn, as if to catch a glimpse of Nat, but he wasn't in view.

"So, as I was saying, Grady and I had a conversation. He helped me understand how much you've needed... personal freedom over the years. And how little I gave you. How little I was willing to admit that you're a grown woman who can take care of yourself."

She hurried to blame herself before he could. "Some job I did!"

Her father gazed at her. "Some job you did," he said. "You have a beautiful daughter and a fine man who loves you. That's one hell of a job, Jessica."

Her jaw dropped in astonishment. She'd waited all her life to hear those words, and she was speechless. "Thank you," she said at last, fighting tears.

"You're welcome."

She swallowed past the lump in her throat. "Did he—did Nat—tell you he loved me?"

"Yes, he did. But he doesn't think he's good enough for you." He gazed at her fondly. "From my standpoint, that's probably true, because there's not a man out there who *is* good enough for you. But I figure he might be the best of the lot. And I have every confidence you may be able to convince him of that."

Jessica decided she'd never have a better chance than now, before the place started bustling again. She walked over and took Sebastian's sheepskin jacket down from its peg on the wall by the back door.

Then she returned to the table. "Would you hold her for a minute?" she asked.

"Me? I don't know if I should."

She gave him a wobbly smile. "I'm sure you've held a little girl before."

"That was a long time ago."

Jessica settled Elizabeth in his lap. "Well, some things never change," she said brightly. And then, when she saw her father sitting there holding Elizabeth, tears spilled out of her eyes. "Oh, Daddy." She leaned down and wrapped her arms around both of them. "I love you."

His voice was thick. "I love you, too, Jessica."

When she drew back, he blinked and cleared his throat several times.

She wiped at her eyes and put on Sebastian's big coat. "I'm going down to the barn," she said.

"And leave her here?" He sounded both frightened and excited by the prospect.

"Not this time." She scooped Elizabeth up and tucked her inside the coat. "But soon. This time I need her. She's my bargaining chip."

NAT PUT the rubber stopper in the drain of the big metal sink Sebastian had installed on the front wall of the barn. As the water level rose, he rolled back his sleeves. Then he shut off the water, picked up the sock monkey and dunked him in the water. Some of the loose dirt came off and floated to the surface, but the orange stain that decorated the monkey's face and upper part of its body looked permanent.

Matty should be the one doing this job, Nat thought to himself as he scrubbed the orange stain. She probably knew what to use on something like this. For all he knew, he was making things worse. As usual.

He'd really screwed up this time. At least he'd shot the man who had held Elizabeth at gunpoint. He'd never thought he'd be grateful to his father for anything, but he was glad of all those agonizing hours spent in target practice under his father's stern direction. No, he did not for one minute regret firing that gun.

But he regretted the need for it. If he hadn't left Jess and

Elizabeth unprotected, they never would have fallen into the guy's hands in the first place. He would never forgive himself for that.

The barn door opened and Jess, nearly swallowed in Sebastian's coat, came inside. He wasn't ready to see her yet. He didn't have his speech, the one in which he'd convince her she'd be better off without him.

The coat stuck out in front, and when Elizabeth's curly head poked out, he realized she'd brought the baby along with her. Another person he wasn't ready to see. He dropped the monkey down in the water and hoped to hell Elizabeth hadn't noticed it in his hand.

But she had. She let out a squeal and reached toward the sink. "Ba-ba!"

Damn. He glanced pleadingly at Jess. "He's soaking wet," he said. "I was trying to clean him up, and—"

"You were out here washing Bruce?"

"Yeah. I probably should have let Matty do it, but she's still asleep and I was hoping I might get him in some kind of shape before Elizabeth woke up."

The baby started bouncing in Jess's arms and her cries for her monkey became louder.

"I think that's so sweet." Jess came closer.

"Listen, maybe you should take her back up to the house." That would get Jess out of here, too, so he could plan what he wanted to say. It was hard to think of the right words when she was standing there looking so beautiful in the soft light filtering through the high windows of the barn.

"I think it's too late," Jess said as Elizabeth began to fuss and strain in Nat's direction.

He tried to ignore the warmth in Jessica's eyes. She didn't know what was good for her. "Maybe it's not too late. She might forget that she saw him if you distract her. I'll wring him out and hang him on the clothesline for a while, and maybe by noon he'll be ready to go."

Jess gazed up at him, a little smile on her face. "Wring him out now. I don't think she can wait until noon."

"But he'll still be all wet. And God knows what he'll look like after I squeeze most of the water out. Probably like some alien."

"She won't care what he looks like. She needs that monkey, Nat."

He sighed with resignation. "Okay."

Elizabeth made an unholy fuss while he squeezed as much water out of Bruce as he could. Jess tried to jolly her out of being upset, but she was getting crankier by the minute. Man, she was really raising a ruckus. If his father were here, he'd have backhanded that kid so hard...

Nat stopped wringing out the monkey and stared down at his hands. Yes, his father would have slapped the baby by now. But he hadn't even considered such a thing. And he wouldn't, not in a million years. He could imagine what his father would do, and separate that from what he, Nat Grady, would do.

Turning from the sink, the damp monkey in his hands, he stared at Jess, who was so busy trying to keep Elizabeth happy that she didn't even notice he was looking at her. He wasn't like his father! And he'd figured it out twenty-four hours too late.

He groaned in frustration.

Her gaze met his. "What?"

"I'm an idiot, that's what."

She smiled. "Sometimes."

Elizabeth went wild as she spied the bedraggled monkey. "Ba-ba! Ba-ba!"

"Better give it to her." Jess glanced at the monkey. "Maybe he'll look better when he dries."

"Maybe. Here you go, Elizabeth. Here's Bruce." He extended the monkey by the tail.

Elizabeth grabbed him with another squeal and promptly

stuck the tail in her mouth. As she sucked happily, the rest of Bruce hung down and dripped on Jess's shoes.

"She's going to get you wet," Nat said.

Jess looked into his eyes. "As if I care. Now tell me why you think you're an idiot, and I'll see if I agree."

"I'm not like my father, and if I'd only understood that sooner, then none of this—"

"Back up. Did I hear you say you're not like your father?"

"Yeah, but I didn't figure that out in time, and so you got kidnapped by that creep." He took a shaky breath. "You nearly died, you and Elizabeth, because I was such an idiot."

"But we didn't die. You saved us." She made it sound as if he was a hero. "Where did you learn to shoot like that?"

"My father. You know how some kids are forced to practice the piano? I was forced into target practice. Pretty grim, huh?"

"Why did he do that?"

Nat had hated the whole exercise so much that he'd never paid much attention to the reason his father had given. And he had given one. "He said that he wanted me to be able to protect myself. He wanted me to be tough, and he wanted me to know how to handle a gun, in case I ever got in a tight spot." He glanced at her. "I suppose, in his twisted way, he was trying to prepare me for life."

"I think he was." She moved closer, so that now the monkey was dripping on his feet, too. "How long since you've talked to him?"

"Years."

She hesitated, then forged on. "Do you think that maybe…maybe it's time to let go of some of that bitterness? Especially if you now realize you won't turn out like him?"

He edged around the idea of communicating again with

his father. It didn't look like such a terrible concept, the more he considered it. There was a kind of relief built into it. "Maybe. Not for sure, but...maybe."

"After all, that target practice did come in handy."

And there was the rub. "But the only reason I had to use a gun is because I'd screwed up so royally. Don't you see? I make mistakes, costly mistakes, that mean the people I love can get hurt or killed. I can't expect to shoot my way out of every fix I get myself or others into."

"Nat, I—"

"Let me finish." He took another breath. For some reason he was having trouble breathing, but he had to get this next part out. "That's why I want you to forget about me. I want you to put me out of your mind and out of your life." He hadn't expected the pain in his heart to be so sharp. He nearly gasped from the impact.

"No, you don't." She stepped closer, so that the soggy monkey rested against his chest, soaking his shirt. "You don't want me to forget about you."

"I do! How can I expect you to forgive me for risking your life, for risking our baby's life, if I can't even forgive myself?"

"Nat, there's nothing to forgive. I don't blame you."

"You should!"

"Well, I don't." She gazed up at him. "Because I love you. I will always love you. Of course you make mistakes. So do I. We'll continue to do that until we're sharing rocking chairs on the front porch. Even then we'll probably screw something up once in a while. Mistakes are a part of life. And love."

Oh, God, he wanted to believe her. His throat was tight, and he still couldn't seem to breathe easily. "I want only the best for you and Elizabeth."

"Well, that makes things easy. That means we need you." She lifted her face to his.

"I'm not—"

"Oh, yes, you are. Do you remember telling me to hold on to you?"

"I shouldn't have told you that."

"Too late. You told me, and I'm doing it. Nat, I don't come without baggage, either. Don't forget I have a father who's richer than God."

"That's not your fault."

"Exactly. Just as it's not your fault that you ended up with your father. We have a right to try and make a life for ourselves, don't we?"

The ice around his heart began to melt.

She smiled. "I can tell you're thinking about it. That's a start. Do you love me?"

That he didn't have to think about. "More than my life."

"And Elizabeth?"

He glanced down at the little girl wedged between them.

As she continued to suck noisily on Bruce's tail, she gazed up at him with eyes the same shade as his. Then she reached up and patted her hand against his chin.

His throat threatened to close completely as he thought of what had almost happened to her. When that maniac had held a gun to her head, he'd never known such rage...or such fear. "Yes," he said, his voice gruff with emotion. "Yes, I love Elizabeth."

"Then marry us," Jess whispered. "We need you. And you need us."

He met Jess's gaze, and warmth surged through him, pushing away the last of the cold chill that had surrounded him from the moment he'd regained consciousness and found her gone.

"Put your arms around us," Jess urged, her gaze never leaving his.

Slowly, he did. He didn't deserve this, but maybe he could work to deserve it.

"Will you take us to be your lawfully wedded wife, baby and soggy monkey?" Jess asked softly.

With a groan, Nat pulled them in tight, squeezing more water out of the monkey and sending it cascading down on his boots. It was a stretch, but with some adjustments he was able to touch his mouth to Jess's. He brushed his lips over hers, leaned back and smiled down at her, his love, his life. "Yes," he murmured. "I do."

EPILOGUE

A year later at the grand opening of the Happy Trails Children's Ranch.

JESSICA HUNG UP the phone and hurried through the house to the bedroom, casting loving glances along the way at the hardwood floors, the large windows, the rock fireplace. After only a few months, she already felt completely at home in this place she and Nat had found only a few miles from the Rocking D. And today it was dressed for company.

She ignored the slight twinge in her belly. She would *not* go into labor today.

"Nat." She walked into the bedroom where her husband was fastening the snaps on a white western shirt. God, he was gorgeous. They were approaching their first anniversary and he excited her more than he ever had. "That was the governor's office calling to say he's running a little late," she said, "but he and his wife should be here in time for the ribbon-cutting ceremony."

"No problem." Nat fastened the snaps at his wrists. "Travis has already offered to do some magic tricks to entertain the press if we need to buy some time."

She laughed. "It figures Travis would suggest something like that. But we don't have to worry about entertainment. My dad and Sebastian are putting on a show out in the front yard giving contradictory orders to the television crews. It's like a battle between George Lucas and Steven

Spielberg." Another twinge hit her. Probably nothing. "Of course, Boone's trying to mediate."

"I wish him luck on that one." Nat grinned as he tucked his shirttails into a pair of western dress slacks. "That was nice of my dad, to send that big plant and the card, huh?"

"It was. Very nice." She was thrilled that Nat and his father were starting to communicate, and she could tell how much it meant to both of them.

"I'm almost ready." He buckled his hand-tooled belt.

"Good. You can go help Boone keep the peace." She allowed herself a moment to ogle the fit of her husband's slacks, but unfortunately she couldn't linger. As the hostess of this grand-opening event, she had duties. "Well, I'd better see how things are progressing in the kitchen." She started toward the door. "I swear, if Gwen ever wanted to give up the bed-and-breakfast business, she could make a fine living as a caterer. Shelby, Matty and I are in total awe, which is a good thing, because she has us working like galley slaves."

"Jess."

She turned, pleasure zinging through her. Whenever he spoke her name that way, as if pronouncing the most important syllable in the English language, she melted. She met his gaze.

"Come here a sec," he murmured.

"We have no time," she said, even as she walked back to him, pulled by an invisible velvet rope. Darn it, there was another twinge. Actually, she couldn't call them twinges now. It was definitely a contraction.

He reached out and gathered her close. "The day I don't have time to hold my wife in my arms is a sorry day indeed." He glanced down at her round belly. "Are you okay?"

She couldn't go into labor now. She absolutely couldn't. "I'm fabulous."

He looked into her eyes and smiled. "I know that. But

are you sure this whole thing isn't too much for you? I mean, Doc Harrison said it could be any day, and I keep wondering if we should have held off until after the baby came.''

She cupped his face in both hands and willed the contractions to stop. Tomorrow would be fine to have this baby, but not today. ''Are you kidding? We couldn't have postponed a project like this. It's our dream come true, Nat, and we'll be helping so many kids. I can hardly wait until next week when we have our first arrivals, our first little buckaroos, sleeping in those cozy bunkhouses.'' She grinned. ''Just because it feels like I'm twelve months pregnant doesn't mean I can't enjoy this moment.''

He slid both hands down to cup her backside. ''What I want to know is how you can be so pregnant and so sexy at the same time?''

''It's my special talent.'' Another contraction. Shoot! Maybe she'd have to mention it to Nat, just in case.

He caressed her bottom. ''Special talent, huh? In that case, maybe we should have about twenty kids. Because I—''

''Hold on.'' She put a hand over his mouth. ''Do I hear—''

''Babies cryin'!'' Elizabeth raced into the room dragging a sorry-looking sock monkey by the tail. She grabbed Jessica's skirt. ''Come help GammaLu and GammaDell!'' Elizabeth tugged at Jessica's skirt. ''Come on, Mommy!''

Jessica gazed in despair at her daughter, who had looked like such a little angel about twenty minutes ago. ''Elizabeth, what's that on your dress?''

The toddler glanced down at her front, where something green was smeared all over the pink material. When she looked up, her matching pink ribbon hung over her eye. ''I dunno. But babies cryin', Mommy! Come see!''

''Lizbeth!'' Josh yelled, pounding into the room after

her. "Come back in there! GrammaLu and GrammaDell *need* us. It's a regular *rodeo*."

"We'd better go check on things," Nat said.

As Jessica followed Nat down the hall to the bedroom they'd designated as a temporary nursery for the day, Josh and Elizabeth raced ahead of them. Sure enough, babies were crying behind the closed door. And Jessica had another contraction.

Josh flung open the door. "See that? A regular rodeo." He crossed his arms. "That's *girls* for you."

Jessica's mother, Adele, glanced up from her struggle to diaper a screaming Patricia, the three-month-old daughter of Boone and Shelby. Whatever Elizabeth had down her front, Adele had in her hair. It looked like finger paint. And baby spit-up was all over her designer suit. "Oh, thank heaven, Jessica!" she cried above the din. "Can you get Rebecca out of that drawer?"

Jessica started toward Rebecca. Matty and Sebastian's eight-month-old sat in a bottom dresser drawer yelling her head off.

"She climbed in and didn't know how to get out!" Luann shouted by way of explanation as she continued pacing with the squalling four-month-old who belonged to Gwen and Travis. They'd named the baby Luann after her grandmother, but Travis had quickly dubbed her Lulu.

Jessica picked up Rebecca and grabbed a tissue to wipe her nose. Then she turned to Luann. "What's wrong with Lulu?"

Luann grimaced. "She gulped her bottle, like usual, and now she's got enough gas to heat the city of Denver for a month!"

Matty, Shelby and Gwen appeared in the doorway. Matty, with her seven-month-along belly, took up most of the space. She pressed a hand to the small of her back "What's all this noise about?"

Nat stood surveying the room. "The usual," he said with a grin.

Elizabeth waved her hands. "Lizbeth not cryin'," she announced again.

Jessica caught a flash of green on Elizabeth's hands. Uh-oh. Then she glanced down at her linen skirt, the one Elizabeth had been clutching minutes ago. Sure enough, now she had green splotches on her skirt to match the color on the toddler's pink dress. And she had another contraction, this time a hard one.

"Hey, we can hear this racket clear out in the front yard!" Sebastian crowded in behind the women, followed by Boone, Travis and Jessica's father. "What's going on?"

"It's all the girls making noise," Josh said, looking superior.

Jessica glanced over at Nat. "I hate to tell you this, sweetheart, but I think—"

Nat's casual grin disappeared. "It's time?" His voice squeaked.

Jessica nodded.

The group exploded into action. As Nat rushed over to lead her out of the room, Sebastian took Rebecca, Travis scooped up Elizabeth, and Boone picked up Josh. The women followed, with each grandmother carrying a baby.

As they all poured into the living room, someone knocked on the front door.

Jessica's father wrenched it open. "What?" he bellowed.

The television reporter shrank back. "The—the governor and his wife are here, sir. Their limo just pulled up. And I was wondering if—"

"He came in a limo? Great!" Jessica's father turned back to the group surrounding Jessica. "We'll commandeer his limo for the run to the hospital! Come on. Everybody out!"

"But what about the ribbon-cutting ceremony?" Jessica asked as Nat hustled her toward the door.

"It can wait," her father said, beaming at Nat. "Right, son?"

"You bet."

Before Jessica quite realized how it had happened, the governor and his wife were standing on the front porch waving goodbye and all of them were crammed into the stretch limo, crying babies included.

"So," Sebastian shouted above the din as he glanced around at the limo full of people. "What's it gonna be this time, boy or girl?"

Travis, Boone and Nat looked at him, then at each of the screaming babies. The four cowboys grinned. *"Boy!"* they all said together.

Don't miss
an exciting opportunity
to save on the purchase of
Harlequin and Silhouette books!

Buy any two Harlequin or
Silhouette books and save
$10.00 off future Harlequin
and Silhouette purchases

OR

buy any three
Harlequin or Silhouette books
and save **$20.00 off** future
Harlequin and Silhouette purchases.

*Watch for details
coming in October 2000!*

PHQ400

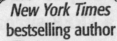

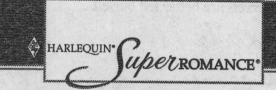